Miss Seeton
Plants Suspicion

*Also by Hamilton Crane
in Large Print:*

Hands Up, Miss Seeton
Miss Seeton by Moonlight
Miss Seeton Cracks the Case
Miss Seeton Goes to Bat
Miss Seeton Paints the Town
Miss Seeton Rocks the Cradle

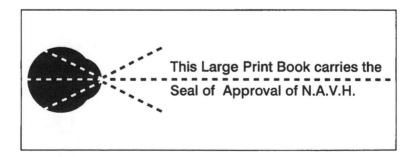

This Large Print Book carries the
Seal of Approval of N.A.V.H.

Miss Seeton Plants Suspicion

&

Hamilton Crane

Thorndike Press • Waterville, Maine

Published in 2002 by arrangement with Curtis Brown Ltd.

Thorndike Press Large Print Mystery Series.

The tree indicium is a trademark of Thorndike Press.

The text of this Large Print edition is unabridged.
Other aspects of the book may vary from the original edition.

Set in 16 pt. Plantin by Minnie B. Raven.

Printed in the United States on permanent paper.

Library of Congress Cataloging-in-Publication Data

Crane, Hamilton.
    Miss Seeton plants suspicion / Hamilton Crane.
      p. cm.
    ISBN 0-7862-4165-9 (lg. print : hc : alk. paper)
    1. Seeton, Miss (Fictitious character) — Fiction.
    2. Women detectives — England — Fiction.   I. Title.
    PR6063.A7648 M568 2002
    823′.914—dc21   2002019945

MISS SEETON
PLANTS SUSPICION

Chapter 1

It was the end of a glorious afternoon in mid-September, an afternoon which keen gardeners the length and breadth of Kent had used to good purpose. Throughout the county, justly famed as the Garden of England, evergreen shrubs, violets, and carnations had been planted; rambler roses and loganberries pruned; grease bands fixed to fruit trees. Maincrop carrots and beetroot had been lifted; the last tomatoes picked; potatoes taken up for storage; vegetable seedlings thinned and pricked out. The air was filled with the snip of secateurs, the snap of shears, the whirr of mowing machines, the song of birds . . . and, at Rytham Hall in the village of Plummergen, the curses of a baronet.

Major-General Sir George Colveden, Bart, KCB, DSO, JP, was not so much a gardener as a farmer. Lady Colveden looked after the Hall's flowerbeds and herbaceous borders; Sir George, with the assistance of his son Nigel, his foreman Len Hosigg, and an assortment of loyal workers, ran the Hall farm — and ran it

7

well. So well, indeed, that his presence was not always absolutely necessary . . .

"We can do without you for a while, Dad — the rest of the day, if you like. For goodness' sake, why not go home and have it out with her, before you die of sunstroke?"

Nigel had come upon his father in the shade of a laden beech tree, loudly complaining that the new straw hat his wife had imposed on him a few weeks ago *still* didn't fit. "No use," he'd barked at his grinning son and heir, "your mother trying to tell me I'll grow into it. May have worked for you children, but —"

"But Julia and I were never such a tough proposition as you. I couldn't agree more." Nigel stared thoughtfully at the top of his father's head. "If you want my honest opinion, I'd say you've proved your point — your bald patch is most impressively red. She'll have to believe you now. Why not, as I said, go home and —"

"Bald?" Sir George blew indignantly through his moustache. "Maybe thinning a bit, m'boy, but surely . . ." Nigel favoured his sire with a quizzical glance, and Sir George subsided, his face turning as scarlet as his sunburned pate. One hat, he muttered, was *not* just like another, no matter what Some People might think . . .

"You could always," suggested Nigel, "tie knots in the corners of your handkerchief instead — if you're scared of having it out with Mother, I mean. Think how convenient —"

"Scared of your mother? Rubbish!" Sir George managed to sound almost convincing as he squared his shoulders and reminded himself that he was a holder of the Distinguished Service Order. "Threw that hat of mine away without a word of warning. Sneak attack. Unsporting — ought to have put m'foot down on the spot." He squinted through the beech leaves towards the richer gold of the slowly sinking sun. "Time to, er, drive into Brettenden, you think?"

Nigel opined that as a grand gesture, an escape to the nearby shopping centre would probably serve little purpose, as everywhere would be long shut by the time his father arrived. It might require, Sir George should bear in mind, a lengthy search before he found another hat of similar . . . similar *character,* said Nigel, to that of the late lamented straw. Though perhaps, if and when he was lucky enough to find a suitable replacement, he should consider buying two, ready for when the next hay bale fell on one of them . . .

9

"Pah!" snorted Sir George, and forthwith set off Hallwards: to Nigel's relief. His father was no more comfortable in hot weather than anyone else, but he refused to give in to discomfort in case it made him feel old. Nigel, whose thick and wavy brown hair showed neither a hint of grey nor a sign of thinning, smiled with all the amused tolerance of the mid-twenties for the late fifties as he watched his father hurry away, and wished he could be a fly on the wall during the coming skirmish — except that on so glorious an afternoon his mother was sure to be in the garden, where walls didn't come into it.

Lady Colveden was not in the garden. True, she had been there since just after lunch, and had worked tirelessly and well for several hours without a break; but she had become conscious of that sort of aching back which only a good cup of tea and some chocolate biscuits can cure, and was administering the last of this cure to herself as her husband stamped into the house and slammed the door behind him.

There came a clatter as the wire letter basket fell to the floor. Sir George's blood, which had been (for all his fine words) cooling rapidly as he approached the house, now froze in his veins. He brushed his moustache with nervous fingers, and greeted his wife with a shamefaced smile as she emerged from the sitting room.

"Hello, George. You're home early. I'm just having a cup of tea. Would you — George!" He tried to shuffle backwards to hide the evidence of his crime, but was too slow. "George, how could you! Martha will be absolutely furious — you know how long it took her to polish away the scratches last time."

"Pah!" said Sir George, as he recalled that Mrs. Bloomer wasn't working at the Hall today. "Parquet? Ought to cover the lot with lino. Wears better. Much less bother."

"Don't be silly, George. It would look hideous, and anyway, who could be trusted to lay it correctly, even if you really wanted it? Which I'm sure you don't, unless you've caught a touch of the — George!" as she observed him clearly for the first time. "You *have* caught a touch of the sun — why on earth didn't you wear your new hat? You look like a — like a boiled lobster, or something equally dreadful."

At least it had taken her mind off the damage done by the wire letter basket to the hall floor. Sir George mopped his forehead warily, and muttered about the desert, and dehydration, and cast hopeful glances in the direction of the kitchen.

"I'll make a fresh pot," promised the wife of his bosom, and she sent him, with an irritated little loving push, to sit down and rest where it was cooler, if he didn't want to explode: lobster, now she came to think about it, wasn't the word for what he most looked like. She didn't want him on her hands with heatstroke when she was so busy now with the garden . . .

Ten minutes later, Lady Colveden entered the sitting room carrying a tea tray — and slightly anxious about her spouse, who would never in normal circumstances have permitted her — or any woman — to bear even so light a burden when an able-bodied man such as himself was within earshot. She found Sir George fiddling with the television set, and concentrating on that to the exclusion of all else.

"George, are you sure you haven't caught a touch of the sun? What *are* you doing?"

"Weather forecast." He shook his head, winced, then brightened as his eyes fell on the tray. "Interested in what it might be like tomorrow . . ."

"I would have thought," retorted her ladyship, pouring tea, "that you'd *know*

12

without needing to be told. Farmer's instincts, and so on. And especially without needing to switch on the television — you know how bad the reception's been since that last thunderstorm."

Sir George, once more twiddling knobs, scowling at the series of black-and-white snowflake lines scrolling their horizontal way up the screen, did not listen. Lady Colveden set his cup on the table with a loud sigh.

"We were lucky the house didn't burn down, with the aerial being hit the way it was — look at how poor Miss Seeton lost her burglar alarm when Sweetbriars was struck by lightning. I suppose if we'd had a colour set instead of black and white, the Hall *would* have burned down . . ."

This was too much for her husband, who proceeded to deliver a lecture on cathode ray tubes which assured his spouse there was no cause for her to feel anxiety over his mental state. Her own, however, began to give her cause for concern, as he continued to twiddle and adjust the old television set to the accompaniment of hisses and crackles which threatened to drive her mad. She poured another cup of tea for the frustrated electrician, collected her own used crockery to take into the kitchen, and

13

spoke of going back to finish weeding the border nearest the drive before calling it a day well spent.

There came a brisk ring at the front door, followed by a rat-tat-tat. Lady Colveden sighed, set down her cup and saucer, then hurried to let the visitor in.

"George, here's the Admiral come to see you. Do switch that thing off and be sociable — I've already explained that I simply must finish my border before supper, so . . ."

Rear Admiral Bernard "Buzzard" Leighton courteously ushered Lady Colveden out of her own front door, bowing with true Naval gallantry. Then, guided by the hisses and crackles from the still-faulty television set, he strode into the sitting room to greet his host and issue the invitation he'd come to deliver.

Sir George rose from his knees to welcome his guest. The Admiral, suddenly realising what he still carried in his left hand, shook his head for his forgetfulness. "Meant to give this to your good lady," he said. "I've been extracting honey, you know. Thought she might like a pot — perfect for toast, or scones for afternoon tea." Above his neat ginger beard, the Buzzard's eyes twinkled. "Should give you both an idea of what to expect if you decide to come in with me next spring. Just pop it down here, shall I?"

Sir George responded with a twinkle of his own. The Admiral, a newcomer to Plummergen, had startled the village by moving into Ararat Cottage with four hives of honeybees, and had managed to fire the major-general with unexpected enthusiasm for this new hobby. Lady Colveden, however, had firmly vetoed a Rytham Hall apiary, and Sir George had been disappointed until Nigel suggested a compromise solution of shared hives, to be kept on the Admiral's property. Sir George, golden visions of next year's honey harvest before his eyes, now accepted the gleaming glass jar with thanks, and placed it on top of the television set, which was still emitting unlovely noises.

The Admiral regarded the troublesome appliance with a frown. "Give the damn thing a good thump," he suggested. "Let it know you won't stand any nonsense — you'd be amazed how often that sort of trick works."

Sir George explained that the fault probably lay in the aerial rather than the set, but that he wanted to be sure before detailing anyone to scramble about on the

15

roof. The Admiral nodded. As bad, he remarked, as dressing the mast at a Naval display — he'd often wondered how the button boy right at the top kept his nerve. For himself, he'd need a couple of stiff drinks inside him before —

"Drinks!" he cried. "Why I came, of course — to let you know I'm hoisting the gin pennant on the fifteenth, Battle of Britain Day. Had some good friends in the Few, God bless 'em," he added gruffly. "Not the sort of chaps we should forget in a hurry, even more than thirty years on." He cleared his throat. "Anyway, there it is. Cordial invitation extended to join me in the wardroom. Sixish." He glanced at his watch, and nodded in a meaningful way.

Sir George was sunburned, weary, and deafened by electrical noises. He was annoyed by the faulty television which emitted them — and he could recognise a hint when one was dropped. "Care for a spot of something?" he enquired, with a genial nod in the direction of the small cupboard which did duty as a sideboard.

"Well," said the Admiral, who had no intention of refusing, "the sun's pretty well over the yardarm, so . . ."

Lady Colveden paused to rub her back

and became conscious that sounds of merriment had been emerging for some time from the window of the sitting room, which in her weeding progress she had steadily been approaching. How fortunate for George that it had been the Buzzard who'd come along just then, and not some less sympathetic soul who wanted to ask about becoming a Justice of the Peace, or to collect for charity or seek advice on some farming matter or other — about which, if she was honest, Nigel probably now knew more than his father. Wye College, on the far side of Ashford, was one of the best places in the country to study agriculture; Nigel had passed out with satisfyingly high marks on the practical side, although his written work had left something to be desired. She smiled.

She jumped, as Nigel's voice suddenly broke into her reverie. "If we have visitors, Mother, why aren't you indoors doing the hostess stunt in your best bib and tucker?" He offered an arm to help pull her to her feet. "If you've been hiding out here since lunch time, I'm prepared to give you absolution for whatever sins you think you've committed, so that you can go inside to join the fun."

"I'm not an old lady, Nigel, thank you all

the same." His mother rose gracefully from her knees and ignored his outstretched arm. "And I'm not doing penance, either — your father's just looking after the Admiral while I finish this border, and then I expect we'll all have a drink together."

"By the sound of it, they've started without you." With his head on one side, Nigel listened to the cheerful bursts of conversation wafting on the evening air from the sitting room, on a background wave of hisses and crackles. "What on earth are they doing in there? It sounds very odd. Hadn't we better go in and restrain them? You know how the Buzzard enjoys his sundowner, and with Dad sitting on his emergency bench again tomorrow, it —"

He broke off, and Lady Colveden uttered a little cry, as a sudden uproar erupted through the window. Shouts, cries, and curses were followed, after a brief pause, by a bellow of masculine laughter which had an ominously resigned note about it. Lady Colveden looked at Nigel, who was grinning. He looked back at her.

"A fine example for a magistrate to set! What's the betting they've broken something in their drunken frenzy, and have decided there's nothing they can do about it, so they aren't going to bother?"

"Nigel, really, you can be very silly sometimes. As if your father would be so . . ." Lady Colveden remembered other instances when the Admiral and the major-general had been drinking together, and fell into a brooding silence.

Nigel was about to say something else when she rallied. "Why, they might be as sober as . . . as judges, for all we know," she told her undutiful son, and set off smartly in the direction of the house to find out whether her optimism had been misplaced.

Things (she decided on first entering the sitting room) could have been a great deal worse. There were the glasses, just as Nigel had suspected; and a bottle, which she was almost sure had been nearly full the last time she'd noticed it, and now wasn't; but a quick look round the room seemed to show nothing broken or torn or over-turned. The two former officers had fallen silent at her appearance, mumbling greet-ings to their boots; but that was (she told herself firmly) no more than typical male unease when surprised in mild folly by a member of the opposite sex. The sitting room was an oasis of calm, apart from the vague buzzing of a very loud bee some-

19

where nearby. Even Nigel stood silent behind her instead of —

Silent. Mercifully, they'd switched off the —

"George!" After which Meg Colveden could say no more, speechless with shock. At her side, a startled Nigel, seeing what his mother had just seen, spluttered. His father shuffled guilty feet and twirled his moustache; the Admiral stroked his beard, and coughed.

"Sorry about, er, all this," he ventured, when it had become clear that nobody else was capable of saying anything. "Trying to, er, fix the television, you know . . ."

At which Nigel could maintain his silence no longer. He let out a sudden guffaw, and rushed from the room. His exit seemed to release the built-up tension, and his mother found speech at last returning: speech she struggled nobly to keep under control.

"George," she said: very, very gently. "I do appreciate the trouble you and Admiral Leighton have gone to, but was it really the only way of fixing the television?" She pointed towards the now-silent set, which had been pulled round to face the light — and out of the back of which a sticky golden stream was slowly trickling. A stream at which Lady Colveden could see bees busily feeding . . .

"Did you," demanded Lady Colveden, "*have* to pour honey into the works?"

Chapter 2

Mrs. Blaine was in the kitchen, chopping young dandelion leaves with a sharp knife. Miss Nuttel, a thoughtful pucker between her brows, was contemplating the small bottle of cold-pressed olive oil which stood on the worktop beside two bulbs of garlic ("Too good for the heart, Eric!") and a sad-looking lemon which would shortly be combined into the salad dressing. The Nuts, as the two ladies who inhabit Lilikot are popularly known in Plummergen, were about to have supper after a busy day, spent half on self-sufficiency and half on scandal: the latter very possibly the more pleasurable half. Erica Nuttel and Norah Blaine ("Bunny" to her friend) are rampant vegetarians and dedicated gossips, whose plate glass–windowed home was chosen originally for its prime position in the village's main street (formally designated, with proud capitals, The Street), overlooking both the bus stop outside Crabbe's Garage and the post office, the village's principal shop, next door.

"Next door," said Miss Nuttel, as the knife completed its rhythmic little solo up and down the scrubbed white wood of the chopping board, and scraped the resultant soggy green mess into a mixing bowl. "The admiral — been thinking, Bunny. Those bees . . ."

Mrs. Blaine shuddered gleefully. "Too dangerous, Eric, as I've said all along — ever since That Man moved in, you know I have. Bees, after all, *sting* — and if anyone's allergic, why, they could be killed!"

Miss Nuttel nodded. "Ballpoint pens," she said grimly. "Emergency tracheotomy — been reading it up, just in case." As Bunny squeaked with horror, Miss Nuttel gulped, and turned pale. "Hope not, though. Can't say I . . . I fancy the idea overmuch," and she sat down heavily on the nearest chair. Miss Nuttel, for all her gruff manner, was unnerved by many things, including the sight — even the concept — of blood.

Bunny clasped plump hands in anguish. "Oh, Eric, too brave of you! We must buy some ballpoint pens *at once* — and I think we should *insist* that the admiral pays for them! If we are *forced* to live so close to his hives —"

Thoughts of expenditure had taken Eric's mind off having to stab her nearest and dearest through an allergy-swollen throat with a hollow plastic tube, and had reminded her of what it was she'd started to say in the first place. With one final gulp, she rose from her chair and strode, a little shakily, towards the kitchen worktop.

"Salad," she said, gesticulating towards the bowl, and the waiting ingredients for the dressing. "Next month, dig up the roots — coffee, you know, dried and roasted. And no caffeine, either. Could even look for wild garlic — but the oil, Bunny." She tapped the mellow green clarity of the small glass bottle with a peremptory finger. "Expensive."

"It's the best quality, Eric, and you know we agreed it would be false economy to lower our standards and risk being contaminated by —"

"Not saying we didn't, Bunny. But the admiral — those bees of his. Been thinking. Won't be buying honey now, will he? Or jam, more than likely."

"We don't buy jam either, Eric." Bunny's blackcurrant eyes narrowed in annoyance that her yearly efforts with the preserving pan seemed to have been so ignored. Miss Nuttel, who knew her friend's temper of old (village wags rightly referred to Mrs. Blaine as Hot Cross Bun, though neither of the Nuts ever realised that nicknames had been bestowed upon them), hurried to make amends before Bunny could throw one of her monumental tantrums: quite apart from the inevitable aftermath of tears and headaches, she was looking forward to their early supper, hungry after their afternoon's brief excursion to the woods.

"Jam's fine, Bunny — splendid. Delicious. Doesn't cost a penny, either, except for the cooking . . . and the sugar. Honey, now — free, with bees. But," loudly, as Mrs. Blaine squeaked again, "can't say I'm too keen, somehow," and she thought queasily of ballpoint pens. "No, no — we'll go on buying sugar. Still, no harm in other ways of economising. Oil, for instance. Been reading it up. *Food for Free*, from the library. Beech nut oil, he says, every three or four years. With a mincer or something — a muslin bag — three ounces of oil for every pound of nuts, Bunny, and it keeps well. Cooking . . . salads . . . beechnut butter . . ."

Miss Nuttel's brisk eloquence eventually convinced Mrs. Blaine that it would at least be worth considering the ideas expressed in the book borrowed from Brettenden Library and studied each day with such intensity by her friend, once the evening's outside work was done. Bunny had been too busy with household tasks to pay particular attention earlier in the week: but now her interest was caught. All through supper she asked questions, and discussed possibilities; and ended up listening to Eric read from *Food for Free* with more interest than she had expected to feel. Mrs. Blaine was not fond of excessive physical labour, and left all the gardening and other heavy work to Miss Nuttel; but the vision of herself and her friend gathering beechmast in an autumn wood, while the sun shone and birdsong filled the air, was an appealing one.

"We'll go the day after tomorrow, if the weather's fine," she said, as Miss Nuttel marked the page with a careful slip of paper. "The bus runs again then, for one thing — and it's not as if there's too much to do in the garden now, is there?"

Miss Nuttel, who secretly felt that there was never any lack of things to do in the garden, was so relieved to have had her suggestion accepted without too much fuss that she merely nodded, and smiled, and spoke of wicker baskets and perhaps a small picnic, if Bunny thought . . .

Miss Nuttel was not the only gardener in Plummergen to feel rather overwhelmed by the size and scope of her horticultural obligations. At the southern end of the village, Miss Emily Dorothea Seeton was coming to the end of a comfortable potter in her small front garden — or what would have been, in more normal circumstances, a comfortable potter. Since the circumstances were not at present normal, Miss Seeton's involvement with her garden was somewhat greater than it had ever been before; and she wasn't entirely sure she knew what she was doing.

When Miss Seeton's godmother and distant cousin, Old Mrs. Bannet, had died and bequeathed to dear Emily her Plummergen cottage, Sweetbriars, and a regrettably small (thought Cousin Flora) sum of money, included in that bequest had been the invaluable services of Stan and Martha Bloomer. Stan, Plummergen born and bred, was a farm worker who had wooed and wed his Martha when she came down from London on one of the annual hop-picking holidays beloved of cockneys through the generations. Martha took to village life with relish, and embarked on a career as general domestic factotum to certain selected households. Rytham Hall was one; Sweetbriars, another. The Colvedens had other people working for them on the

farm and in the garden; Mrs. Bannet —
and after her Miss Seeton — did not. Martha's quick wits soon devised the perfect
solution to this problem. Stan would tend
the chickens, vegetable patch, fruit cage,
and flower beds of Sweetbriars, and would
fully supply from them every want the oc-
cupant of the cottage might express. He
would do this at no charge; but he would
keep for himself any profit he might make
from selling the surplus he was sure, with
his renowned industry, to make. His industry was duly rewarded.

The plan worked well from its inception.
Mrs. Bannet had been unable to do much
around her property for some years before
she died at the age of ninety-eight, and the
Bloomers had taken great pride in man-
aging her household and treating her almost as a member of the family. Miss
Seeton, in her turn, quickly came to rely
on them. Martha had an admirably keen
eye for dust — even keener than that of her
employer, whose former employment as an
art teacher had trained her to notice far
more than the ordinary person: but
Martha Bloomer — where domestic matters were concerned, at any rate — was far
from ordinary.

Stan's services to Miss Seeton were far

more than those of one who could coax hens to lay or trees to fruit. Martha's husband not only knew all about gardening, but was also able (once Miss Seeton had grown accustomed to his strong Kentish accent) to explain its mysteries in simple terms — which is all too seldom the case with experts. Miss Seeton had made the mistake of purchasing (before her first visit, as owner, to the cottage) a gardening manual entitled *Greenfinger Points the Way*. This tome had been recommended to her by a local bookshop proprietor who clearly had no close understanding of his stock, and Miss Seeton spent much of her first year in Plummergen asking Stan to interpret Greenfinger's advice for her. Interpret it, to her complete satisfaction, Stan did; under his kindly tutelage, she grew in confidence year by year; and the knowledge that, should help be urgently required, he could (out of working hours) be found just on the other side of The Street, had increased her confidence still further.

So that when, even for one evening, he wasn't there, her confidence was slightly dented. She couldn't be altogether certain of what she was doing. With a trowel, a dibber, and a one-foot wooden rule, she was trying to plant bulbs along the lines recommended in the Gospel According to Greenfinger (Revised Bloomer Edition) and, to her regret, had reached a point when she realised she'd forgotten what Stan had said about the lilies.

"Such beautiful flowers," lamented Miss Seeton, as she frowned with the effort to remember. "It would be such a pity to make a mistake — yet one cannot help wondering," and she sighed, "if it would be so *very* serious to, well, adopt some sort of compromise." She turned again to Greenfinger's "Second Week in September" section, and sighed softly as she read it for the fourth time. "At least one can be sure that these are not *Lilium candidum*, because those must be planted in July, which would be far too late in any case. But both the other kinds need to be set twelve inches apart, which would hardly cause problems, I fancy — yet would an inch either way up or down really make such a great difference? I suppose, to the lily, it would. Oh, dear — and I had so hoped to finish this bed before supper . . ."

"Good evening, Miss Seeton." The well-known tones hailed her from the front gate. "You look as if you're enjoying yourself — you'll have a grand show there next year."

Miss Seeton smiled with relief on recognising the voice of Miss Molly Treeves, sister to Plummergen's vicar, the Reverend Arthur, and jumped nimbly — silently blessing the inspiration which had made her, so many years ago now, send away for that copy of *Yoga and Younger Every Day* — to her feet to welcome one who knew almost as much about gardens as dear Stan.

"Miss Treeves, how very fortunate. I have been trying so hard to recall what he told me about stem-rooting or not — because it does seem to make a difference, from what the books says, and I would not wish to risk killing them when they are such graceful and attractive flowers. Stan, I mean — about the lilies. As I understand it, they should either be *six* inches or *eight* inches deep. Perhaps you would be kind enough to advise me whether *seven* might be acceptable — though not, I agree, ideal — for both kinds?"

Molly Treeves opened the gate and marched up the short front path to stare down at Miss Seeton's cardboard box of assorted bulbs, saying as she did so: "I gather you haven't spoken to Mr. Jessyp yet, Miss Seeton — though perhaps there has hardly been time."

"Mr. Jessyp?" Miss Seeton looked puzzled. "Why, he can know nothing of my little problem, since I have only in the past few minutes realised that I have forgotten what he said — Stan, that is — and, forgive me, Miss Treeves, but may I say that I feel you are being unduly modest? Mr. Jessyp is a most courteous gentleman as well as an excellent headmaster, and no doubt would do his best to offer advice — but I am sure it could never be of as much help as anything you might tell me, if it would not be ungracious of me to say so about a colleague. He is, you see, unfortunately visiting relations this evening — that is, unfortunately for me, not for him, as it must be a most pleasant experience for them all when they see one another so seldom during the rest of the year. And of course, they are not so much *his* relations as dear Martha's — Stan, I mean. They come every year for the hop-picking. And whether to top-dress them as well, of course, which also seems to depend on if they are, or are not — stem-rooting, that is. The bulbs. I feel sure, however, that you will be able to tell me."

Miss Treeves, deflected from her original gambit by the anxious note in Miss Seeton's voice, gave it as her considered opinion that lily bulbs, whether stem-rooting or not, came to no great harm if planted as close to the surface as five inches, because that was what she always did with hers, resting them (in groups of five, six, or seven rather than singly) on sand and covering them with dried leaves as well as soil. Miss Seeton faintly thanked her, and made a silent resolution to leave the lilies until tomorrow.

Miss Treeves, who knew Miss Seeton of old, realised that the little spinster hadn't understood her reference to Martin Jessyp: no real reason why she should, of course, but it might be a kindness to warn her what might be in store for her, should she choose to accept her assignment — which, knowing Miss Seeton's strong sense of duty and wish to be of service to her adopted home, the vicar's sister was almost certain she would. Molly Treeves was a staunch believer in the community spirit, and considered Miss Seeton an admirable example to one and all.

"Mr. Jessyp," she said, abandoning the topic of the lily bulbs for one of far greater importance, "is having trouble with Miss Maynard again, I'm sorry to say."

"Oh, dear." Miss Seeton shook her head. "Her mother, I suppose — it so often is, poor soul. She had such hopes of the most recent operation, I know, but . . ."

"It's Miss Maynard herself, this time," Miss Treeves said, rather grimly. "It makes a change, of course, as I know it usually *is* her mother or one of those interminable aunts who makes her absent — and it's particularly inconvenient of her to have put her back out right at the start of the school year. Turning her mother in bed, or something of the sort, I gather — a slipped disc, so I heard. That's why I wondered if Mr. Jessyp had spoken to you. I felt sure that if he had, and you'd agreed to take her class for the next few days until she's on her feet again, you'd have been indoors preparing instead of out here. Unless he already has, and you've said no, of course." Molly Treeves uttered a sudden laugh. "Poor Arthur!"

"The dear vicar?" Miss Seeton frowned. "Has he slipped a disc as well? How dreadful — and so awkward, with so many steps in the church tower." Was there any practical assistance one might offer? Or would it be tactless to imply by such an offer that one thought — which of course one would never be so impertinent as to think — the vicar's sister incapable of taking proper care of her brother?

"Goodness, no. Arthur's as fit as he ever

was — or he was when I left him to go to my committee. But he does get so terribly agitated, meeting new people, and if Mr. Jessyp brings in a supply teacher from outside the village, he'll hide in the garden mowing the lawn all week, I expect, in case he has to talk to her. Which is good for the lawn, of course, but only in moderation."

"Oh. Excuse me, Miss Treeves, but — surely not so early in the term, and at such a difficult time? Mr. Jessyp is a most conscientious teacher, I assure you, and a pleasure to work with." Miss Seeton blushed in her struggle to pay due compliment. "Oh, dear — I would never dream of causing him so much anxiety by a refusal that he is obliged to employ a substitute with whom he feels himself unable to converse in a . . . in an unagitated fashion. I must telephone at once, and assure him that there can be no doubt of my agreeing to help out in this . . . this emergency . . ."

But then Miss Seeton fell silent. She frowned. She ignored Miss Treeves's gentle assurance that Mr. Jessyp, as far as she knew, had no inhibitions about strangers . . .

"Unless, of course," said Miss Seeton, "I should be wanted by the police." And she blushed again.

Miss Seeton, the most modest of maiden ladies, is far from being the desperado her previous words might have led anyone not knowing her unique character to suppose. As a teacher of art, she is inspirational and dedicated; as an artist, she is uninspired, conscientious, and dull . . . most of the time. But there is a hidden spark in Miss Seeton's nature: a spark she tries hard to quench, feeling it to be not quite, well, respectable. Any artist, unless a genius — which Miss Seeton sadly knows herself not to be — should, in her opinion, draw or paint nothing except what is there to be seen . . . and it embarrasses her greatly to realise that, try as she may to stop herself doing so, there are occasions when what she sees is completely different from that seen by anyone else. And this completely different view of life has been so useful in the past to the police that Miss Seeton is now retained by Scotland Yard as an art consultant, consulted whenever a case involves anything of the bizarre, the freakish, the exotic: cases which, long after she herself has managed to forget her share in them, will be savoured by those fortunate enough to have shared them with her . . .

If *savoured* and *fortunate* are the right words to use, that is.

Chapter 3

Once the little misunderstanding had been cleared up, Miss Treeves and Miss Seeton chatted together for a few minutes more about the vicar's shyness, and poor Miss Maynard's back, and the possibility that Mr. Jessyp would soon be in touch with Miss Seeton to ask for her help. Miss Treeves then hurried home to the vicarage across the road, while Miss Seeton tidied away her gardening implements and those puzzling lily bulbs about which she would ask Stan tomorrow, or rather would ask dear Martha to ask him to call in when he could spare the time, so that one could ask him — except, of course, that one might not be at home to visitors when he did, if what Miss Treeves had said of poor Miss Maynard's incapacity was true — if, indeed, one would even be at home to ask dear Martha, in the first place.

Miss Seeton's knowledge of anatomy was excellent. She had watched bodies being dissected in a local mortuary during her student days; she had attended umpteen life classes; and she had practised yoga for some seven years now. The back — the spine — so very important for one's basic state of health. The hours spent bending and stooping this afternoon — not a twinge or an ache or a spasm . . . How many times had the purchase of *Yoga and Younger Every Day* paid for itself, over and over again!

And yet one should not become over-confident. It was of course foolish to think of tempting Fate — but it might well do no harm if, rather than waiting until tonight, one just slipped up to the bedroom and ran through a few of the poses most beneficial to that complicated and delicate column of bone which both supported the body and protected the main pathway of the central nervous system. The *Trikonasana* or Triangle Pose, she thought, for the lumbar region in particular; the various *Uttitha Merudandasanas* or Lateral Spine Poses; and the *Baddha Padmasana Shirshasana*, or Headstand in Bound Lotus, which had taken her some time to perfect — if it wasn't conceited of her to use such a term. Miss Seeton, as she trotted upstairs, blushed. Perhaps *master* would be a less, well, exaggerated — a more realistic — term, although even to speak of mastering, when one was the merest beginner — the book spoke of mental planes, of meditation

— the Truth of Self or *Samadhi* which, in its perfect mental stillness, required a lifetime's study to achieve . . .

Miss Seeton slipped off her shoes and skirt, tucked her petticoat inside her bloomers, and unfolded the plaid travelling rug on which she was accustomed, when at home, to perform her exercises. She took *Yoga and Younger Every Day* from the bedside table, and opened it to refresh her memory. Yes, the Triangle first, after a few warm-up postures; then the Laterals; and the Headstand in Bound Lotus when she was thoroughly relaxed. It would be imprudent to cross one's legs one over the other upon one's upper thighs, clasp one's hands behind one's head, and tip oneself upside down into a strictly vertical position without having, as it were, worked one's way up to it. Miss Seeton permitted herself a little smile at the wordplay, then began bending and stretching with enthusiasm. One could certainly feel that it was all doing a great deal of good . . .

Miss Seeton, disturbed by the ringing of her telephone, opened her eyes and blinked as she gazed about her, observing with interest how very different the familiar bedroom appeared when seen from the wrong way up — although, one supposed, to that fly on the ceiling it must be the *right* way up, which only went to prove that viewpoint was merely a matter of what one was accustomed to. What Miss Seeton was accustomed to was a peaceful, uninterrupted period for her yoga practice, followed by a slow uncurling from the final posture and a few minutes' deep abdominal breathing in the *Shavasana,* or Dead Pose. One knew from one's own experience that it was unwise to uncurl too quickly, or to omit the deep breathing — though one could, of course, always curtail it, in an emergency. Which the ringing of a telephone most probably was not. Should the house be on fire, people would be shouting; telegrams would be delivered by a boy on a bicycle who would knock at the door; but anyone who wished to communicate by telephone would either hang on at the other end for a while (which one hoped they wouldn't, as the continuous ringing was intrusive) or try again la—

They were obviously going to try again later. Miss Seeton, flat on the floor, face upwards, arms limp at her side, sighed with relief that the ringing had stopped as suddenly as it had begun, and decided that perhaps she had better not try to achieve detachment this time, so that when whoever-it-was telephoned again, she would be ready to talk to them.

Whoever turned out, ten minutes later — how very foolish of one not to have guessed — to be the headmaster.

"Miss Seeton? Martin Jessyp. I do hope I'm not disturbing you — and I really must apologise for the short notice, but I was wondering . . ."

Miss Seeton assured him that no disturbance was involved and no apology necessary. "How very distressing for poor Miss Maynard," she went on, once Mr. Jessyp had explained full details of his second-in-command's indisposition. Not, after all, a slipped disc, which was, one supposed, a relief — so uncomfortable, one had always feared, having to sleep with a board under one's mattress. "Although even a muscle strain, if neglected, can be serious, I believe. It is very wise of the doctor to prescribe a week's bed rest — and Miss Maynard is an intelligent young woman. I am sure she will appreciate that it is for her own good in the long run — and I do, of course, understand that her absence leaves you in a rather . . . awkward situation." Miss Seeton coughed delicately. "Naturally, I would be only too glad to do anything within my power to assist you.

There is, after all, a great deal to be done as a new scholastic year begins. And so important for the pupils not to undergo any added confusion," added one who, in her time as a teacher in Hampstead, had confused more pupils than the rest of Mrs. Benn's staff put together. "As well as that of leaving their parents for the first time, I mean, although they are, of course, among familiar faces, which is always a help in reassuring them. But if," and she coughed again, "my services as an IdentiKit artist should be required by the police, with luck it will be for only a matter of a few hours — because I am, after all, paid a retaining fee, and in the circumstances . . ."

Mr. Jessyp satisfied Miss Seeton that he would quite understand if she should be called upon by any of her constabulary colleagues to abandon the desk for the drawing block. It had, after all, happened before, had it not? There was to be no question of her neglecting her IdentiKit duties. For the short time they were usually required, he was sure he would be able to manage single-handed at the school: and it was, he reminded her, only for a week. If the fates were kind, the police would have no need to consult Miss

42

Seeton until the next seven days were over . . .

But the fates heard Martin Jessyp's words, and smiled.

Superintendent Brinton was not smiling. He was sitting in his office with a scowl on his face, reading the typewritten pages of a report in a file marked Unsolved. He came to the last page, sighed heavily, and dropped the closed folder on his desk as he turned his attentions to the calendar on the wall beside him. He did a few quick calculations, and emitted a grunt of exasperation.

"Sorry, sir?" At the smaller desk on the far side of the room, underneath the pin-dotted map of the Ashford Police Force area of operations, a young man wearing a vermilion shirt with an over-loud kipper tie looked up from his own paperwork. Detective Constable Foxon, Brinton's sidekick, knew his superior's moods as well as his own, and judged his particular approach at the end of a long day like this ought to be one of modified impertinence, with a hint of enthusiasm. "You said something, sir? Did you want me?"

"I've *never* wanted you, laddie, and especially not when you look as horrible as you do today. My eyes must have been on the blink when I authorised your promotion to the plainclothes branch — plain clothes! That's a laugh!"

Foxon looked pained. He took a lot of trouble with his attire, and prided himself on mixing the fashionable with the practical in equal measure. He could mingle with petty crooks in the pub, or chase a fleeing sneak-thief on foot, with no more than a loosening of his tie. "A suit, sir, is hardly my style," he said gently. "Particularly at my age, you must admit. When I'm, er, more advanced in years, no doubt —"

Brinton's eyes narrowed. "If you don't stop being so damned cheeky, Foxon, you can forget advancing for years — you won't last another minute! I'm not ready to retire yet, and there's no need to carry on as if I'm in my dotage."

"Sir, I promise you I never meant —"

"Shut up, Foxon." Brinton sighed, and scowled at the calendar again. There was a pause. "I'm sorry, lad. Not your fault."

This was serious. Old Brimstone, apologising? No yelling, no chucking things, no blasting him to perdition? Foxon forgot his paperwork, and sat up, peering anxiously into his chief's gloomy face. "Do you —

44

excuse me, sir — do you feel all right? Have you run out of peppermints? Would you like a cup of tea?"

To all these suggestions, the superintendent shook his head, not even bothering to ridicule or condemn them. Foxon was more worried than ever. It couldn't be a hangover — the chief hadn't been drinking at lunchtime, and even if he had, it would have shown before now. Maybe he was feeling ill? Or . . . he'd been muttering over that file for the best part of an hour, not saying a word until now. And when he did, it was much more quietly than he usually spoke his mind . . . and Detective Constable Foxon did some rapid thinking.

"Something's bothering you, sir." He pushed back his chair and came over to perch on a corner of Brinton's desk, all flippancy forgotten. "Mind if I take a look?"

Brinton grunted again, and folded his arms, staring at the ceiling with unseeing eyes, as Foxon reached across to pick up the Unsolved file. When he read what was written on the cover label, he whistled with a long, low breath.

"This one, sir. Yes, of course — I see." In his turn, he gazed at the calendar on the wall, and sighed. "A year ago almost to the

45

day, isn't it? And no nearer catching him now than we were then."

"You needn't remind me." Brinton kicked with a moody foot at the underside of his desk, and tilted his chair back on two legs. "That poor girl . . . It isn't just the horrible mess he made of her, Foxon — which was bad enough, heaven knows. It's the . . . the callous way he treated her afterwards — like a . . . like a common or garden *parcel*, damn him."

"The dignity of death," muttered Foxon, in a sardonic tone. He didn't need to leaf through the documents in the folder to refresh his memory: nobody who'd had any dealings, however remotely, with the murder victim called by the press the Blonde in the Bag was going to forget. She'd been young and pretty, as well as blonde — not that they'd known, at first, she'd been pretty. Not until they'd managed to identify her properly and see a photograph of how she'd looked before whoever had killed her had . . .

Foxon, not normally squeamish, swallowed as he remembered. "A pity we never nobbled him, sir. Not nice, knowing he's still wandering about outside the loony bin with his little pruning knife at the ready when the moon's full, or whatever it was that turned him into such a . . . such a bloody maniac last time. We've been lucky, sir . . ."

Brinton dropped his chair four-square on the ground with a thump. "When they've got minds as warped as our chummie obviously has, I take to 'em even less than normal. Which isn't very much to start with. I'd like to feel his collar, laddie. Before he does it again — because he will, I know. He *enjoyed* what he did to her, Foxon. Every little cut and stab — the pretty patterns he made — the way he wrapped that sack and tied it with string and damned well *labelled* it for the benefit of the poor devil who found her — he loved every fun-filled minute, you could tell he did. And when anyone's had fun, they're not going to miss the chance to have some more when the time's right, are they?" He jabbed a thumb in the direction of the folder, still in Foxon's hand. "When the time's right, laddie. This chummie's a bloody lunatic, all right — and a methodical one, at that. Which is what's making me wonder . . ."

Foxon once more followed his superior's gaze to the calendar. One year ago. A methodical, maniac killer. Twelve months, almost to the day, since an old-age pensioner

47

walking his dog through the woods had come across a black plastic–wrapped parcel, tied with twine, with a plastic-wrapped label written in waterproof ink fixed to the topmost knot. *Send for the police before opening this,* the label advised the old gentleman: whose dog, reaching the parcel before his master, had sniffed and pawed and worried away at a loose fold in the plastic, revealing a hessian strip of an ominously brown-red hue . . .

"You mean, sir — have we been lucky — or has he just not been in the mood for a year?" Foxon tossed the file on top of Brinton's blotter, dropping from the corner of the desk to the visitor's chair. He picked up a pencil, and began doodling on the scratch pad. "September . . . Harvest Moon, sir. If he's a lunatic . . . and the moon shines very bright and full for several days on the trot around now, sir — something to do with the equinox, they said at school, but after so long I don't quite . . ."

Suddenly, Foxon sat up. "School, sir — teachers —"

Brinton recoiled. "Foxon — no! Not one word!"

"But sir —"

"No, Foxon. Not this time. Not Miss

Seeton. And not," the superintendent said, as Foxon began to protest, "because I think you're trying to wind me up the way you generally do — I don't think you are, this time. You really mean it — and so do I. This is — was — a messy business, Foxon, and I know she's handled some pretty hairy cases for us coppers in the past — but nothing like this." His mouth twisted sideways. "Miss Seeton helping us investigate a . . . a sex crime? And such a . . . a *revolting* one, at that. It's not on, Foxon. These artists — they've got imaginations. Miss Seeton lives alone. I don't want her waking up with nightmares for weeks on end, *imagining* he's coming for her next —"

"She wouldn't, sir." Foxon didn't permit even a hint of doubt to enter his voice. "I know she wouldn't — Miss Seeton's not like that. She's one of the best, sir, and she's never, well, shirked her duty since I've known her. And I'm not sure," he added, as Brinton muttered on the other side of the desk, "that she's really got that much of an imagination anyway, sir. Those cockeyed drawings she does — that's not imagination like — well, like science fiction writers or people who make movies. Miss Seeton's more instinct, sir, the way I

49

understand it. I don't honestly believe she's got an imaginative bone in her body."

Foxon was nearer the truth than he knew. Miss Seeton is one of the most literal-minded persons in the world, and the points at which her imagination (if, indeed, she possesses such a faculty) begins or ends, and the results of her indulging in it, have always been moot. Mrs. Benn believed that her school could be thrown into chaos by the mere waving of Miss Seeton's umbrella; Scotland Yard and the other police forces with whom she and her brolly have come into contact over the years see her more as an unwitting catalyst. Unwitting, and innocent . . . and completely unsuited to dealing with savagely-sliced blondes in plastic sacks, and the sordid nature of their demise.

"No, Foxon. Not Miss Seeton," said Brinton again. "And let's hope," he added to himself, "that the fates are kind to us *this* September, and our chummie just keeps quiet . . ."

But the fates were listening to Superintendent Brinton; and they smiled as they listened — and they spun another thread.

Chapter 4

"Ooh, they were great days, dear. Hard work, mind, but such laughs we had, you wouldn't believe — and, of course, if I'd never come down from London hopping year after year, would I ever have met my Stan?"

Martha Bloomer nodded fondly through Miss Seeton's kitchen window to the back garden of Sweetbriars, where Stan could be seen in the distant dusk, busy near the henhouse. The Bloomers had returned sooner than they'd expected from their little excursion to the hop garden where so many of Martha's family and friends were spending their annual working holiday, and had decided to drop in on Miss Seeton for a chat (Martha) and to make up lost time in the garden (Stan). The problem of the lilies duly solved — he'd planted half in clumps and half singly, both halves at their correct respective depths — Stan found plenty of other tasks to occupy him while his loving spouse, having learned that Miss Seeton was once more to take up her old vocation for a few days, gently bullied her employer into making preparations for a prompt start on the morrow.

Miss Seeton, in her own opinion, was well on with her preparations when the Bloomers arrived. She had already taken a sheet of paper from her largest sketching pad, and had drawn on it with thick, black lines intended to be visible from the very back of the classroom; and when the doorbell rang, she was busy sorting out brown paper bags on the dining-room table, wrestling with a roll of sticky tape as she did so.

"The transparent kind," she told Martha, rather breathlessly, struggling to free her fingers from that clear serpentine embrace. "So useful, of course, but — drat — so much more *assertive*, I fear, than ordinary glue, although when time is short, as it is on this occasion, so much faster to dry — except, of course, that it doesn't need to. Bother! Dry, I mean. Because it isn't wet to start with."

Martha couldn't bear to see her Miss Emily so embroiled. "Do let me help, dear, or you'll get yourself in a worse pickle than ever. Got a pair of scissors handy?"

She followed Miss Seeton into the dining room, and beheld with something of a shock the chaos on the table. "If you're sending a parcel," she remarked, snipping neatly at Miss Seeton's left hand, "I'm sure there's a ball of string somewhere in that cupboard under the stairs, not to mention gardening twine in the shed. You know you're never that happy with the sticky. And couldn't you have bought some brown paper from the post office, instead of all this?" She clicked her tongue in disapproval. "Turn my back for five minutes, and look at the mess you make!"

"I'm so sorry, Martha dear, but Mr. Jessyp only told me about poor Miss Maynard after the shops were shut, and it hardly seems right to disturb Mr. Stillman at home, unless it is for a real emergency — sending a telegram, perhaps. He is such an obliging man, and one would hate to take advantage. But . . ." Miss Seeton surveyed the paper-littered surface of the table with a rueful smile. "I should, I realise now, have used weights, to hold each piece in place before I tried to stick it — the kitchen scales, perhaps. And trying to match them all for size was, I suppose, an unnecessary indulgence, as well as slightly awkward — having to close the window, you see, to prevent the draught blowing the bags around, which is another reason for not using glue. In a classroom, it doesn't matter so much, because there is so much more air — but in a small room such as this," said Miss Seeton, in the closest she had ever come to criticism of her home, "glue does tend to, well, *over-power,* sometimes."

Martha chuckled as she snipped the final finger free. "And you don't think the sticky does, do you, dear? Never mind, though — lucky for you we popped in. Many hands make light work, remember . . ."

And now the work was done, and Martha was insisting that Miss Seeton should complete her personal, as opposed to professional, preparations for the morrow. Breakfast things to hand? Thermos rinsed out ready? Kettle filled and waiting? Although that, said Martha with a laugh, was pretty much a habit anyway, wasn't it? You could always tell people who'd lived through the Blitz and had their water supply bombed out. Even after so many years, they always filled the kettle last thing at night, in case they'd nothing in the pipes next morning. Still, it wouldn't — and she lifted the lid — hurt just to check, now would it?

Miss Seeton watched her friend's gyrations with tears in her eyes. Dear Martha — such a treasure. So considerate of one's welfare when really, there could be no real need for her to fuss. Did she suppose one had not fended for oneself very ably through the long — and, one could say it now, perhaps rather lonely — years in London? Of course, one had never felt so much at home in Town as now, in the country — Plummergen, her adopted home . . . so many strangers, and the little flat so . . . so anonymous in that Victorian semi — which must have been a happy place when it was a family home, but divided into so many impersonal households — one couldn't call them homes . . . and now, her dear cottage — and it was pleasant indeed to be, well, cherished — even though one felt one hardly deserved such good fortune . . .

Miss Seeton pulled herself together with a guilty start, and realised that Martha had stopped talking about the War, when she had been a girl in the battered but buoyant East End, and was reminiscing about the postwar days when the first of September each year heralded the invasion (as the locals saw it) of the Cockney hoppers. In early days by special train, latterly in furniture vans or borrowed lorries, they had come to Kent in their hundreds — and they still came.

"Not that I ever fancied walking on

those stilts, mind." Martha chuckled richly as she tried to envisage her younger self strolling ten or more feet above the ground with the studied nonchalance of the regular workers. Hops, grown in clockwise spirals up coir strings in groups of three or four to the wire supports eighteen feet above, required those strings to be attached to the supports — the supports to be regularly checked — the tips of the hop bines cut free when the time came to harvest the crop. "Dear only knows," said Martha, "how they managed before they'd learned *that* trick!"

Miss Seeton murmured of lobbers, and of Mr. Butcher's stringing system. Invented in the nineteenth century, so she recalled having learned when accompanying the children on a school visit to a nearby hop garden, one day last year when it was, for once, Mr. Jessyp who had fallen by the wayside — his wisdom teeth, she believed, and knew from her own experience how uncomfortable that could be — and Miss Maynard had been most pressing in her request that Miss Seeton, although not at that time officially on the school payroll, should join the party. Which Miss Seeton, fully appreciating that fifty Junior Mixed Infants might not be so willing to behave when being supervised by a younger woman on her own, had been happy to do, as well as being interested in the purpose of the excursion, since she knew shamefully little about the produce of her adopted county. "Charles Dickens," she concluded, and quoted with a smile: "Everybody knows Kent — apples, cherries, hops, and women."

"And men, bless 'em," said Martha, nodding again in the direction of her husband, barely visible through the dusk now the kitchen light was on. "Stan, he's a regular wonder, and I don't care who knows it. How he puts up with visiting the family all at once like he does, dear, I'll never know. Such a tiny hut, it is, when you come to think about it — though when the farmer tried to change it one year, oh my word, they didn't half create! — and that corrugated iron roof can really ring when the whole lot of 'em starts yelling at the same time. I'd forgotten," admitted Martha, with a grin, "what they can be like all together, so to speak. But Stan, he never turns a hair, knowing how I do like to see 'em, and with not wanting to pay out on the train fare and neither of us driving, it's as good a way as any to keep in touch when they come hopping every year like they do."

Miss Seeton beamed. "Such a close family," she said, no hint of wistfulness in her voice: why should there be? She had everything and everyone she'd ever really needed, right here in Plummergen. But one could see that a town-bred soul like dear Martha must miss her relatives and friends, even after so many years — how many was it now? — away from them, settled so happily with dear Stan in the country. Martha was not, or so one gathered, a great letter-writer; the telephone she'd had installed was seldom used except for brief local calls, because it was expensive; it must be difficult, mused Miss Seeton, to keep in touch. The yearly hop-picking excursions would be her very best chance of doing so . . .

"There's close — and there's close, Miss Emily, believe me." For the first time, Martha seemed to lose some of her normal bounce. She sounded almost sombre as she added: "And there's family — and family, dear. We've always prided ourselves on staying respectable — my mother, she brought up nine of us and never a hint of bother — but it's different nowadays, what with the telly giving them ideas, and the dole money, and everything so much *faster* than we were ever used to. Motorbikes!"

She sighed, and shook her head. "But here am I, sounding like an old woman: and he's only a second cousin when all's said and done, not what you'd call *close* the way you and Mrs. Bannet were, with her your godmother anyway, and you coming to visit right from a little girl, while I've not clapped eyes on this Barry more than once a year since he was born, and not always then, with him out and about at nights, worrying his mother half to death, him and his so-called friends — making the right contacts, she says he calls it." Martha sniffed.

Then she had to smile. "Well, I'd never have met Stan if I'd stayed in with my mother every night, but . . . he's too much of a one for wandering, is Barry. Can't settle to nothing for long, not a job or a girl or nothing. He's fidgety." Martha, whose inability to keep any part of herself (including her tongue) still for more than ten seconds manifested itself in a quite re-markable appetite for work, frowned in disapproval of even a second cousin's shar-ing the same genetic heritage. "It's not right, upsetting his mum this way, and if I'd seen him today — me and Beryl, we were good friends as girls — oh, I'd have given him such a piece of my mind. But he wasn't there, so I couldn't."

As Martha drew breath in order to sigh again, Miss Seeton managed to slip in a few words. It was in the nature of the young, was it not, to be given to restlessness? Surely no more than a part of growing up. In time, they settled down; but one would not wish them to lose their enquiring spirit too soon. The ability to see with new eyes — from a different perspective, one might say — was very important, as one knew from one's own experience with children. A new perspective might lead to untold benefits: while never thinking of things except in exactly the same way as before . . . well, might not. If everyone, after all, remained content with his or her lot, with no ambition or outside interests, would there ever be any progress? Which was not, surely, altogether a bad thing, as dear Martha must agree. Medical advances — space travel — one might not understand or fully appreciate the benefits, but think how unpleasant it would be if, for example, everyone still lived in caves because nobody had ever felt that twinge of curiosity which would have led to, for instance, proper plumbing —

Martha burst out laughing. "Depends what you mean by proper, dear. They've still got outside lavs at home, so they don't mind the huts not having the flush — but there, you don't want to worry about that," as Miss Seeton gave a little startled cry. Last year's tour of the hop garden hadn't included the hoppers' accommodation. "*They* don't worry about it — if they did, would they keep coming back? There's cousins of mine born here, dear, and their kiddies too, sometimes, by mistake, you might say . . ."

She frowned again, obviously brooding on the restless and hyper-gregarious Barry. Miss Seeton said quickly: "Stan must be finding it very hard to see outside, now the nights are coming on so fast. And until the moon rises above the garden wall . . ."

"Harvest Moon," Martha said at once. "That's what we called it, even in Town, when you were as far from the harvest fields as anyone could be. And that's why we enjoyed the hopping so much every year. You sit under the moon when the light's mostly gone and your work's over, and you have a talk and a laugh and a bit of a picnic, maybe, and then the stars come out and away to bed because it's an early start tomorrow — and, my goodness, if it isn't *you* that's got the early start tomorrow, Miss Emily — and me keeping you here chatting when you did really ought to be making sure you've everything ready. I'll call Stan this minute, and we'll be off and leave you to it."

Saying which, she rapped on the kitchen window and went straight outside without giving Stan time to answer. Miss Seeton peered into the night, watching the brisk figure of her friend marching down the rectangle of golden light on the lawn — watching as two brisk figures, dark against the gold, headed for the door in the garden wall, turned to wave farewell, and vanished — watching as the sky above the wall turned from grey to silver, from silver to brilliant white, as the great round face of the Harvest Moon climbed above the topmost bricks to beam on the world below.

Chapter 5

With the help of textbooks, they had worked their way together through mathematics, geography, and history. Nothing too complex for young minds, this early in the school year: it was enough to know that they were learning to sit still and to pay attention without scuffling, fidgeting, or giggling. And if — as she believed she had — Miss Seeton managed to instill a few facts into those young minds, then she could feel justly proud that she had not lost her touch.

One had to admit, however, that teaching from textbooks subjects with which one was not fully at one's ease could never hold the same attractions as did teaching — maybe even inspiring (Miss Seeton stifled a wistful sigh) — from one's own knowledge and long experience. As the hour for the art lesson approached, Miss Seeton sensed an air of growing excitement in the little classroom: excitement she supposed her pupils to have caught from herself, as she began to look forward to setting small feet for the first time on the road to the appreciation of Art. She smiled on the eager faces turned towards her as she slipped the heavy history book in her desk, and said:

"Now, before we begin our art lesson, you may run about the playground for another five minutes." Long experience had also taught Miss Seeton the wisdom of bowing to superior forces. A sunny afternoon, to youngsters who had seldom before been prevented from frolicking out of doors whenever they wished, was indeed a superior force: but children, she had found, almost always kept their side of the bargain. "While you are letting off steam, I will prepare things here. When I come out to call you back in, I shall expect you to return quietly, without fuss. Do you understand?"

Small heads nodded in silence. Oh, they understood, all right: Miss was going to learn 'em to draw, just like they'd heard from their older brothers and sisters. Never knew just what she'd do, but she always made it fun — so long as you didn't mess with her. Play tricks with Miss Seeton, mind, and she'd most likely play a few tricks of her own — a witch, wasn't she? Everyone knew that. Mother Flax got in a rare taking sometimes, talking about things Miss Seeton'd done — but she wouldn't do them unless she needed to, being careful not to waste her magic — which was powerful stuff. Everyone knew *that,* too. Better not to give her cause to let it loose, just in case . . .

So Miss Seeton's class behaved itself beautifully, without her ever realising that such (uncharacteristic) behaviour was due to her reputation as an enchantress rather than as an educationist — a reputation acquired through a complex system of misunderstandings which had almost split the village as they were argued back and forth. The only persons to remain untouched by argument had been Miss Seeton herself, and the Reverend Arthur Treeves: who, detractors said, never noticed much in any case, and even if he did, wouldn't know what to do about it. Which was, in a way, true: the vicar had long ago lost his faith, trusting now to people's basic good nature and only being truly upset by unkindness, which was the only sin he was prepared to recognise as such — and which, as it upset him so much when he did, he preferred not to notice in the first place.

Miss Seeton, too, might well be seen by some as having a blinkered view of life: although, in her case, it is less a matter of deliberate choice not to notice the unpleasant than a basic inability to accept the truth of whatever she might have seen. She cannot (she always feels) have properly understood: surely there has been some mistake? She will always find good reason not to believe the worst of any situation which everyone else regards with (at the very least) circumspection; and so strongly does she not believe this worst that the nerves of those who know her best are stretched permanently, when she and her umbrella are in full innocent cry, to the very limits.

So the suppressed excitement of the waiting children was translated by Miss Seeton into a vague feeling that her own wishes were making themselves too strongly felt, and that the sooner she worked the burgeoning creative urges out of her system, the better for all concerned. Once she had set the class the little task she had, with Martha's invaluable help, prepared for them last night, she would take out her sketchbook and pencils and . . .

The children came trooping back into the classroom without waiting to be summoned. Those with wristwatches had kept a wary eye on the time, so that Miss wasn't put to any trouble on her pupils' behalf. Keep her in a good mood, and who knew what she might not do?

"Good gracious." Miss Seeton, standing on a chair in front of the easel, turned round in pleased surprise as the thump of cheerful feet announced the return from the playground. "Oh! Oh, dear . . ."

There was a clatter as she dropped the last of the three large bulldog clips with which she was trying to fasten something to the top of the blackboard.

"That's a big envelope you got there, Miss." One of the boys darted forward to retrieve the fallen metal clip, which he handed up to Miss Seeton with a grin. "Take a deal of stamps to post that, won't it?"

"Thank you." Miss Seeton smiled, fixed the final clip, nodded, and jumped neatly down from the chair. "Post it? Oh, no — although . . ." She remembered dear Martha's remark about parcels. "I hardly think it would fit through the mouth of the letter box," she said. "Do you?"

Everyone giggled politely as they hurried back to their places. On each desk was set out a sheet of plain paper and a soft black pencil. "No eraser," said Miss Seeton, as the children exclaimed. "If anyone makes a mistake — why, those can be just as interesting as if they don't, as I hope you will see for yourselves. Because the object of this lesson is to teach you all to see for yourselves — even if you are unable, at first, to make sense of what you see . . ." Which remark (had they been privileged to hear it) would have made Detective Chief Superintendent Delphick of Scotland Yard and his colleagues chuckle. It is from the making sense of what they see of Miss Seeton's instinctive cartoon sketches that they have solved some of their most unusual cases. Once the hidden spark in Miss Seeton's innermost nature is allowed to run riot — that spark which had been, even as she prepared the children's lesson, starting to kindle . . .

"Now, children." Miss Seeton pointed to the large brown envelope-like construction clipped to the blackboard. "What I wish you to do is copy exactly what you see as I slip this cover down the board — and what you will see is a pattern of lines drawn on a sheet of white paper. Copy that pattern as closely as possible on your own sheet of paper — watch where the lines cross, or meet, or curve and move away — see how they lie in relation to the other lines . . . and, after a few moments, I will slip the cover down a little more, and you must add the lines you will next see to those you have already drawn."

There were few questions, easily dealt with. This sounded interesting — sort of like a conjuring trick, only instead of making things vanish, she was going to make them appear. Perhaps they'd see a sort of magic, after all. The children waited, bright-eyed, as Miss Seeton hopped back on her chair, removed the two end clips from the top of the easel, and slid the brown-paper envelope about six inches down the board, then clipped it on either side to stop it slipping further. There were little gasps and exclamations as the "pattern of lines drawn on a sheet of white paper" was revealed; but Miss Seeton, with one look, silenced the whisperers as she said: "You may begin."

And they did.

Miss Seeton smiled on the rows of bent heads and the industriously copying pencils. She walked up and down between the desks, pausing to look, nodding her approval of what she saw, no matter how far from her own vision of the pattern the copyist had strayed. One child, who was squinting quite horribly at the blackboard with her tongue poking through her teeth, was gently urged to swap seats with another, sitting nearer the front; Miss Seeton made a mental note to ask the girl's mother when her daughter last had her eyes tested. She watched, and praised, and walked back to the blackboard to release the brown envelope a further six inches.

"If you think," she warned, "that you recognise what it is you are drawing, please say nothing: it would be a shame to spoil the surprise for everyone else. Just carry on copying the lines *exactly* as you see them . . ."

It was not until the slipping-down exercise had been accomplished twice more that one or two squeals emerged from some of the children. Miss Seeton put her finger to her lips, smiling — the young, so enthusiastic — and the squeals died down, although the squealers bounced and wriggled on their seats as they copied the next pattern of lines. There was a thrilling silence as Miss Seeton finally removed the brown paper completely from the drawing, and some busy copying; then eager voices begged that Miss should tell them what it was they'd been doing: and, with another smile, Miss Seeton instructed everyone to turn their papers round the other way. At the same time, she jumped back on the chair, released the large drawing clipped to the blackboard, reversed it, and clipped it back again.

A murmur filled the room, as those children who hadn't already guessed realised that the pattern of lines they'd been copying, when looked at the right way up, showed the figure of a man on stilts, striding across the paper with a glass of beer in his hand. A vivid sketch, it replaced the rather uninspired dog and cat which Miss Seeton had drawn last night before Martha had talked to her of hop picking and its customs; *local* customs. Miss Seeton had decided to catch the children's attention with something they knew well, to emphasise the point she hoped to make. She twinkled now at her class as she picked up the heavy wooden ruler from its place on the easel pegs, and said:

"Hands up those of you whose picture looks like mine at the top, here," and she laid the ruler on the paper in such a position that the picture was cut in two.

Almost every hand went up. Miss Seeton nodded, pleased. "Now, hands up those who think their second half isn't quite as close to my picture as the first."

The same hands waved at her. Miss Seeton beamed. "And now, hands up those who can tell me anything special about where I've put the ruler?"

Frowns, and mutterings. Finally, a small

voice ventured: "That's where I knew what it was I was drawing, Miss."

"Indeed it is," said Miss Seeton, as a general murmur arose from those who had squealed and bounced. She included the whole class in her next remark. "Can you tell me why your drawings aren't as close to the original from my ruler downwards?" Shaken heads and silence. "No?" And Miss Seeton's smile was kind. "It's because you all stopped seeing the pattern of lines, and you started to see a man on stilts walking upside down — and you told yourselves you couldn't possibly draw men on stilts, because it was much too difficult, when this was your first lesson of the year. Isn't that what you said?"

Wide eyes and open mouths greeted this evidence of Miss Seeton's mind-reading ability. Old Mother Flax had never pulled a stunt like this, had she? Just wait until everyone at home heard how Miss only had to look at you, and she knew what you were thinking!

"And now, I want you to draw the man again, exactly as you see him, the right way up. No," as there came gasps of dismay, "no nonsense, please. You managed perfectly well when you were simply copying lines, didn't you? Until you began to *think* about it, instead of just drawing what you could *see?* Then there is no need," as everyone nodded dumbly, "to be so foolish about copying the same lines again, just as you see them . . ."

Miss Seeton distributed a second round of paper, and waited with interest as the class settled down to a rerun. Would the special insight she'd gained yesterday evening, when she'd seen the world upside down from her yoga headstand, still hold true today? She awaited the results of the children's labours with as much interest as they did . . .

It was a proud class which scurried home at last to display to family and friends its surprisingly recogniseable portrayal of a man on stilts. Like magic, the way she'd got 'em drawing! No doubt of it, she'd cast a spell, all right — and never mind that she *said* it was just teaching 'em to see. How did she think they'd gone on all these years if they couldn't see their way around proper? Must think they were daft! They knew better than that . . .

Miss Seeton, happily oblivious to the effect on Plummergen parenthood of her little experiment, trotted homewards down The Street with her handbag over one arm, the rolled-up drawing under the other, and her umbrella slipped into the middle of the slim brown-paper cylinder to help stop it unrolling. A most satisfactory day: not just the proving of her upside-down theory, but enough to occupy her to stop her fingers twitching in that uncomfortable way they sometimes had when she wanted to draw a sketch, yet didn't really feel she should. It had been dear Mr. Delphick, as she recalled, who once referred to her as a drug-taker with a craving for pencil and paper, not pills. She hadn't quite known what to make of that remark at first. Still, if she was honest with herself — and a gentle-woman ought surely to pride herself on her truthfulness at all times — she believed she *did* know what he meant, but, if one thought about it, it was all rather, well, embarrassing — because one didn't actually know why one was doing it — which made one seem a little foolish, to say the least. "A silly old woman," murmured Miss Seeton as she passed the post office door; and received a furious glare from Mrs. Flax, who had popped in for a tin of creamed rice and a gossip, but there had been nobody there and she'd popped out again.

Still happily oblivious, Miss Seeton continued on her southerly way, vaguely conscious of the tingling in her fingers and promising them she'd let them loose on the sketch pad once she was safely home. Home. A smile curved her lips as she looked along to the end of the road, and saw her dear cottage smiling back at her from where it stood on the corner of that block formed by the division of The Street into two. It narrowed, and ran straight on, bounded on one side by the brick wall of Miss Seeton's back garden; it forked sharply to the right, and ran Rye-wards past (among other places) Rytham Hall, where Sir George and Lady Colveden lived — and dear Nigel, of course . . .

"Hello, Miss Seeton!" She jumped. Out of her private thoughts, Nigel Colveden had manifested himself in person just behind her. She turned, and saw the little red car of which he was so proud, running so much more quietly now that clever Jack Crabbe had done whatever-it-was in the garage, instead of trusting Nigel (who was, after all, more used to the insides of tractors) to fix it for the umpteenth time. Nigel smiled. "Sorry to have startled you, but — would it be silly to offer you a lift home? I was on my way to see you, as a matter of fact."

"That would be very kind, thank you —

and very pleasant, too. Will you stay for tea?" Miss Seeton gesticulated with her brown-paper roll in a manner suggestive of largesse of some sort, probably dietary. The roll began to uncurl, and she snatched at it. "Bother — I should really have found another rubber band after the other broke, but . . ."

With Nigel's assistance, Miss Seeton, the drawing, and her umbrella were loaded into the little MG. He paid particular attention to the umbrella. It was not, of course, the gold-handled model she kept for best, the black silk masterpiece given her by Chief Superintendent Delphick in appreciation of her efforts in the first case on which they'd worked together, but one of the everyday variety. Miss Seeton had a wide selection of umbrellas, and a special rack, with clips, for them in the hallway of her cottage.

"Sweetbriars," said Nigel, swinging the MG round to stop right outside Miss Seeton's garden gate. He opened the door and hurried round to assist his passenger, and her parcel, out of the car and into her house. He watched her put the brolly in its clip, her handbag on the table, her hat on the hall stand. The large brown envelope, still loosely rolled with its cartridge paper enclosure, she carried absently through to the kitchen, Nigel following close behind.

Miss Seeton topped up the kettle, which had been waiting for one, and found an extra cup, plate, and saucer. Nigel, who had asked if he might look at her drawing, was amused when she made him pull it out a few inches at a time, then gloomed over the fact that half the children had guessed what it was and he hadn't. "All depends, I suppose, on how you look at things," he said, with a chuckle. "And, talking of *looking*, Miss Seeton — it seems an awful cheek to ask, but half the fun of going is to have people look at you, and — gosh, this sounds awfully muddled." Miss Seeton, pouring boiling water, nodded in sympathy. Nigel grinned back, and took a deep breath.

"What I meant to say, Miss Seeton, was — that is, I was wondering — please could I borrow your umbrella?"

Chapter 6

Miss Seeton gazed at her young friend in some surprise. One hardly associated farmers, of all people, with umbrellas: weren't they supposed to be, well, hardened to the whims of nature? And so terribly impractical. Tractors, for instance — from the safety point of view, surely it was essential that the driver should keep both hands firmly on the wheel? "Tie it on with string, perhaps," murmured Miss Seeton in some confusion, still clutching the teapot lid.

Nigel was equally confused. "String? Not very festive, is it? I thought, more streamers — and flags, if you didn't mind too much, and if I could persuade Mother to sew them into a sort of cover that wouldn't damage the main fabric. Not your best umbrella, of course, but if you could possibly spare one of the others — I should have asked earlier, I know, but I've been so busy helping to organise the lawnmower race I didn't think — and when I saw you walking down The Street, I remembered I'd meant to drop in before this. We're not really ones for brollies up at the

Hall, you see. My mother has one of those folding ones, and Dad has a singularly battered golfing umbrella, but that would be too big, really — and you'd need far more streamers and flags than I think I could lay my hands on in time."

Miss Seeton came to her senses, and popped the lid on the teapot. She drew a deep breath. "Nigel, I haven't the faintest idea what you're talking about," she said. "Why should anyone want to tie streamers to my umbrella — to any umbrella, if it comes to that? When it rained," she pointed out sternly, "they'd get wet. Which would hardly be practical. Besides, it is my view that the best umbrella to have is the largest one can most comfortably carry — a golfing umbrella, for a strong young man like yourself, would be a far more sensible size than one of my own. Not," she added hastily, in case she'd sounded rude, "that you aren't indeed welcome to borrow an umbrella, if you wish — but I'm rather surprised, that's all, that you should need one."

Nigel clapped a hand to his forehead. "Fool, Colveden! I'm sorry, Miss Seeton, I didn't explain, did I? It's the Young Farmers — we're getting up a party to go into Town on Saturday for the Last Night of the Proms. And, well . . ."

As he shrugged expressively, Miss Seeton's eyes twinkled with a relieved understanding of what he'd been trying to say. "The Last Night of the Proms! Why, Nigel, how exciting for you and your friends. Certainly you may borrow an umbrella, although they are all, I fear, very plain. And with today being Thursday, I do hope there will be time . . ."

"Gosh, thanks, Miss Seeton!" Nigel grinned with pleasure, and waved the airy hand of one who has never in his entire life sewn on so much as a button. "If you'd let me take it back straight away after tea, Mother can start on it at once — I've been in the attic hunting out all the stuff we had for the Coronation, and Martha's promised to look for ribbons and things." Mrs. Bloomer was a celebrated needlewoman as well as a noted domestic and a renowned cook. "It shouldn't take long for Mother to fix it up for me," Nigel assured Miss Seeton, in happy ignorance. Miss Seeton, who was slightly less ignorant about such matters, smiled kindly on his enthusiasm, and said nothing to dampen it.

They had a splendid tea, sitting on Miss Seeton's flagstone patio. Nigel demonstrated, beyond all doubt, that while farmers may indeed be hardened to the whims of nature, they are not hardened against the lure of large quantities of chocolate biscuits. Miss Seeton watched him demolish almost a whole packet as he told her of the Young Farmers' plans for Saturday, then began to expand into a breathless recital of the arrangements he'd been making for the coming Grand Lawn Mower Race, to be held at the Village Playing Field the following Saturday, for the benefit of the Plummergen Pavilion Fund and a favourite charity, in equal proportion. Miss Seeton expressed no little interest in this novel enterprise, and urged him to the consumption (once the chocolate biscuits had all gone) of fruit cake as he told her more. Nigel, only too happy to oblige his hostess, ate two thick slices and confessed himself saved, in the nick of time, from starvation. It was, he explained, an unusually busy time on the farm: they were one man short, since his father — as Miss Seeton of course remembered, a magistrate — was having to take the place every day of a bedridden colleague. Nigel had, however, managed to make the briefest of escapes to see someone about the posters for the Race . . .

"Gosh, yes!" Nigel swallowed his last

crumb, and gazed to the end of Miss Seeton's garden. "I bet Stan Bloomer's clocked up simply hours of practice on your lawn, Miss Seeton. If I talked him into entering, would you let him borrow your mower?" Then he chuckled. "Goodness, I do seem to be horribly on the scrounge this afternoon, don't I? First one of your umbrellas, then your lawn mower —"

Miss Seeton assured him that she didn't mind at all, nor did she consider that one or two friendly requests amounted to scrounging. She was, as surely he realised, only too happy to be of service in any way she could. If Stan wished to use her mowing machine, then naturally he was more than welcome to do so, although she hoped dear Nigel had considered the risk of — so one gathered — crowds of persons running around close together, pushing machines with sharp, rotating blades in front of them. One really could not help thinking that it all sounded rather, well, dangerous.

Nigel nodded. "It would be, if that's what we'd planned — but we're doing it properly, I promise you. I've talked the whole scheme over two or three times on the phone with a jolly helpful chap called Jim Gavin, who's secretary of the, er,

British Lawn Mower Racing Association . . ."

Miss Seeton was long accustomed to Mr. Colveden's aristocratic sense of humour; and she had, though seven years retired from full-time teaching, never forgotten the April Fool tricks her pupils used to play. She raised startled eyebrows as Nigel brought out the final few words, then — the perfect hostess — smiled very politely, saying nothing.

Nigel caught her look, and grinned. "Yes, I know, you think it's just another of my jokes — but it isn't. There's an honest-to-goodness, real-life, full-blown organisation devoted to racing lawn mowers, as true as I'm sitting here — and it's practically on the doorstep! Over in Sussex, anyway, and I'm going over to see him later on this evening, when things have quietened down a bit here, to discuss the details. Apparently, when it all first began it was a crowd of blokes in a pub, chatting about the good old days of car rallies and how the fun had gone out of it as everything got too big and commercial — and, well, one of them said what a pity there wasn't anything else, instead of cars. Somebody suggested combine harvesters, only there aren't enough in the area to give a good day's sport — but pretty well everyone has a lawn of some sort or another, haven't they? And, depending on which size lawn — and mower — you have, there are three classes — if you're running a big competition, that is, but we won't, not when it's only for the village." Nigel paused. He was proud of being a Plummergenite, but there were certain disadvantages to a place with only five hundred inhabitants.

He sighed. "I don't suppose there are enough of the big sit-upon machines to make it worth having a Class Three section, which sounds like the most fun — they even have an all-night race! They fit headlights to the mowers and then charge round the course for twelve hours on the trot, though I know we couldn't run to that — but quite a few people have the towed-seat sort. That's Class Two. And positively dozens have what the BLMRA calls the run-behind models, like yours, the sort you push, except that Jim says a good racer doesn't so much push the machine as get pulled along by it, if it's going well. They're Class One. Even children enter the Class One races — and they run relays, too. And they remove the blades, in case anyone gets hurt — and you keep the grass-box on, to make it safer, in the other classes — and

Jim sent me a copy of the rules, and passed on heaps of tips about safety-straw bales, and old tyres, and so on. And, er, Heather's Red Cross–trained, you know. She thinks we couldn't be more safety-conscious if we tried — oh, yes. Talk about scrounging — I must have a word with the Admiral, too, before I forget."

Miss Seeton blinked. "Admiral Leighton? Do you think, Nigel, that at his age — that is," for she recalled that Sir George was of similar vintage to the Buzzard, and Nigel was fond of his sire, "is it altogether wise to, er . . ."

"Good Lord, I wouldn't dream of asking him to compete! Not unless we had a veterans' class, or something tactful like that." Nigel grinned. "Which wouldn't go down well with Dad and Mr. Stillman and the rest, would it? No, I was thinking I must ask to borrow his Union Jack, to start the races with. You know how he's always making such good use of that flagpole since he had it installed in his front garden. I don't quite know where we'll find a chequered flag for the finish, though. I suppose Mother . . . once she's finished the umbrella, that is . . . if you're sure you don't mind my borrowing it for a couple of days . . ."

And Miss Seeton, quite captivated by the thought of her brolly attending, as one might say, so traditional an occasion as the Last Night of the Proms, jumped up at once from the table and said that Nigel must come through to the hall with her immediately, to choose the most suitable umbrella from the rack.

In the office of Superintendent Brinton, Detective Constable Foxon was putting the final touches to a report. He felt rather pleased with himself, because it would leave his in-tray almost empty: and almost empty was as good as he knew he was ever likely to get. He'd never manage to clear the tray completely, of course. There were always at least four reports waiting to be written up, and very often many more. But when his backlog was reduced to four, Foxon allowed himself a small pat on the back — even though it was a fair bet Old Brimstone would soon pull rank and offload some of his own routine bumf or, worse, sneakily dump it in the tray when he thought Foxon wasn't looking.

But Brinton wasn't in the office right now, and Foxon grinned happily to himself as he copied date, time, and name of witness (in capitals) from his notebook to the last page of the hunt and peck–typed report. Start *and* finish, Brinton always insisted: belt and braces, to be on the safe side when things were quoted in court.

Court wasn't the only place, mused Foxon, where things might be quoted: what was wrong with Ashford Police Station? "Make assurance doubly sure," he said, brooding on belt and braces as he wound paper out of the typewriter with a brisk flourish. They'd done *Macbeth* at school: the Scottish Play, his English master had always been careful to call it. Some theatrical superstition about bad luck — well, Foxon wasn't at school any more, he was a hard-nosed copper with no time for anything except facts. "Macbeth," he announced experimentally to a sparrow which had alighted on the windowsill, "doth murder sleep."

"Don't talk to *me* about murder!" The voice of Superintendent Brinton close behind him set the windowpanes rattling. The sparrow, startled, flapped its wings helplessly as it fell backwards, blown by the blast.

Foxon, who'd been so preoccupied with his typing and its ripping aftermath that he hadn't noticed Brinton's arrival, then turned warily to face his chief. He knew the superintendent's moods as well as his own. "What's wrong, sir?"

"Girl gone missing," said Brinton glumly, and dropped into his chair. "From Brettenden."

Foxon stared. "But — but nobody's said anything to me, sir." He sounded like a young James Forsyte. "You, er, do mean a . . . a grown woman, sir . . . not a schoolkid?"

"Young woman, yes. Name of Myrtle Poppy Juniper Felsted." Brinton, who disapproved of flights of fancy, uttered the rolling floral syllables without comment. "Age, twenty next month." He scowled into Foxon's questioning face. "Blonde," he added heavily.

There was a long pause. Foxon said: "How long's she been missing, sir?"

"Since last night, it seems — no," as Foxon began to say something, "don't. It's not necessarily a crime for a sane and honest adult to do a disappearing act, I know — and it isn't even twenty-four hours, but —"

"But I wasn't going to say that, sir." Foxon seldom interrupted his chief, but on rare occasions would risk it. "What I was going to ask was why nobody notified us before. In the circumstances, I mean."

Brinton's scowl grew even deeper. "How many other people besides us have thought about what happened a year ago? Not even the press, and you know what they're usually like about anniversaries of unsolved crimes — not that it *is* the anniversary, not to the exact day. But — don't tell me this sounds crazy, because I know, but — it's Harvest Moon time, Foxon. Same as twelve months ago . . ."

"Oh." Foxon nodded. "Well then, sir — who reported her gone? And when?"

Brinton grunted. "Boyfriend," he said, as Foxon dragged a fresh sheet of paper towards him and flipped the top off his trusty ballpoint. "He's an Ashford lad — Darren Bannister — two arrs, ee not eye, two enns in Bannister. Seems they had a row a couple of nights ago, so he wasn't surprised not to meet her after work yesterday. They've both got jobs in Brettenden, on the industrial estate. He expected to catch up with her for the big reconciliation scene at lunch-time today, when a whole gang of 'em regularly get together in the pub after they've been paid, to spend their wages on drinks and crisps instead of a decent meat-and-two-veg —" Brinton broke off, remembering that he had more important things to worry about than the eating habits of the younger generation.

"The Arkwright's Arms lot, d'you mean, sir? I know the Brettenden blokes sometimes have to call us in when they've turned a little lively, but by and large they're not a bad crowd. Young," said Foxon, from his lofty late-twenties pinnacle, "and a bit daft, but not like our old friends the Choppers, are they?"

"No, they're not — and this Bannister lad seems a decent sort. Though you can't judge by appearances, of course." Something of the superintendent's normal self gleamed briefly in his eyes. "Anyone looking at you, for example, would think you were a rainbow run riot — and I can't say having your hair pruned a few inches improved your looks . . ." But his heart wasn't in it.

Foxon, too, was not in the mood for repartee. A missing blonde was more important than the pique he customarily affected whenever the superintendent passed comment on his appearance. He said: "So how did Bannister find out she'd done a vanishing act — because she wasn't in the pub?"

"Asked her pals if she was still avoiding him, and they said she hadn't been in to

90

work this morning. Hadn't phoned in sick, either — not that she usually did, being given to what they used to call female complaint in my young day — heaven knows what they call it now — and you don't need a sick note for forty-eight hours, so they just assumed she'd be in on Monday and thought nothing of it. But Darren — the lad's a bit on the slow side — said she'd be wanting her pay packet, and he'd take it round to her lodgings. Some bleak bedsitter place this side of Brettenden, just off the Ashford road. Catches a bus to work whenever she's rowing with Darren — he usually picks her up on his motorbike on the way in — and they squabble most of the time, from what I gather. Modern courtship rituals, I dare say, though you'd know more about that than me."

Foxon had found that lopping his shoulder-length locks to a more conventional length — he'd wondered vaguely about taking his sergeant's exam, and wanted to know how it felt to be sedate and responsible — hadn't ruined his chances with the opposite sex. He smirked; then recalled why they were discussing such matters, and became grave at once. "Go on, sir. So Darren went round to her lodgings?"

"And found she wasn't there — and hadn't been in since the day before, according to the harridan who owns the house and lives on the ground floor keeping an eye on what everyone else does. Ma Coggeshall thought Myrtle had decided to spend the night in Ashford with the boyfriend, so she wasn't surprised the girl didn't come home — disapproved, mind, but not surprised. Not until Darren turned up asking for her. And then he started thinking — I told you he wasn't all that quick in the uptake — and he realised Myrtle'd got no good reason to be off sick — that's modern for you again, laddie, and it makes my hair curl to think of it — but there you are. What with not collecting her pay packet, and no message, and not been seen since the day before, he thought he'd better come along and report it to us.

"And he did." Brinton stared blindly at Foxon, still scribbling the last few notes, his head bent over the paper. "He talked to Mutford on the desk. Mutford got a full description, including the fact she was — *is*, dammit — blonde. And Mutford told him the usual bit about how she was of age, and most likely keeping out of his way after the quarrel, and if he waited she'd come waltzing along to make it up . . . And

I suppose he could always be right, at that.

"But I doubt it, Foxon, I very much doubt it." And the superintendent, with a deep sigh, opened his desk drawer and retrieved last year's Unsolved file for the Blonde in the Bag case — and opened his pocket diary — and brooded.

Chapter 7

"I still don't see," said Lady Colveden crossly, "why you can't decorate your own umbrella, Nigel — I mean, Miss Seeton's. And it was very kind of her to lend it to you, though thank goodness it isn't her best, because I wouldn't have a minute's peace until you'd returned it safely —"

"Oh, I say, be fair, Mother. I never had any intention of asking for the gold one — I told her so, right from the start." Miss Seeton's gold umbrella was renowned throughout the village. Not, as the proud owner was always quick to point out, *solid* gold: that would have been unacceptably heavy, as well as expensive; but not plated, either. It was proper, hallmarked gold — hollow — with a crook handle, and a black silk covering; and it had been the gift of the then Detective Superintendent Delphick of Scotland Yard, a thank-you — even if she could never quite understand why — for what he'd insisted had been her invaluable assistance in the solving of one of his cases, although as far as she was concerned she'd done nothing more than her duty . . .

"Of course I wouldn't want to borrow the gold one," said Nigel, shaking his head for his mother's folly in even thinking such a thing. "But she was jolly decent about letting me choose which one to take, and said she was in no particular hurry to have it back —"

"While you," interposed his mother, "seem to be in a very particular hurry to have the thing decorated. Really, Nigel, sometimes I wonder if you have any sense at all. How long do you suppose it's going to take? Do you suppose it *would* take," she amended hastily, "if I did it, and I really don't see how I can. For one thing, why on earth didn't you tell me about it yesterday, instead of — oh."

Nigel grinned. "If you *will* spend all your time in committee meetings, Mother darling, neglecting your only son in a positively scandalous fashion . . ."

"There's nothing scandalous about the Christmas pantomime," protested his mother. "Besides, if you can go out for the evening, why can't I? And any reasonable person would say that your father neglects you — neglects both of us, if it comes to that — far more than I ever do." She raised her voice in the direction of *The Times*, which Sir George was devouring between slices of breakfast toast. "And I should think it dreadfully unfair of them to call it neglect when all I'm saying is that I don't see how there's time for me to decorate Miss Seeton's umbrella for you by tomorrow. Well, how can there be?"

The Times jerked in Sir George's hands as the baronet emitted a strangled snort of mirth. "Fire screen," he managed to gasp, and *The Times* danced a jig. Nigel began to choke. Lady Colveden turned wide, wondering eyes upon what she could see of her irreverent male companions . . .

And then had the grace to smile. "I always said that was very naughty of you," she told her son. "Once I realised you'd only given it to me for a joke, I mean. But when I think of the hours — days — I must have spent, trying to embroider that wretched thing, I could stab you with a tapestry needle, Nigel, I honestly could."

"Weeks, don't you mean?" Nigel appeared untroubled by her threat. "And why tapestry? I thought it was plain old ordinary sewing — the sort you'll need to decorate the umbrella. Easy as falling off a log!"

"A tapestry needle's longer — I think," she added, "but don't try to bamboozle me, Nigel. I haven't said I'll do it yet —

and I still don't see why I should."

"For the honour and glory of the Colvedens in general," with a wink towards the listening *Times*, "and you in particular," replied Nigel at once. His mother blinked. He nodded. "Imagine how proud you'll be when the television cameras zoom in on your handiwork and it's shown to the whole nation — to the whole world, for all I know. I'll be jolly lucky not to have you charge me for the opportunity for fame and possible fortune — but you won't, will you?"

There was a moment's silence, during which Lady Colveden thought long and hard. At last, she turned to her son with a seraphic smile upon her face. "If I do it — and I haven't said yet I will — then I feel I deserve something by way of a reward. If you can persuade your father to replace the television he and the admiral had such fun demolishing the other evening with a colour set, instead of just another black and white . . ."

"Done," said Nigel, who'd dropped the odd hint himself as the cost of colour television came down while its popularity went up. Sir George, conservative to the core, and thrifty as only a farmer can be, had always retreated behind whichever newspaper he happened to be reading at the time, saying nothing beyond the odd rhetorical question about the need for change when there wasn't any need, especially when they hardly ever watched the bally thing anyway.

"Done," said Nigel, thinking of next year's Test Match, while his mother thought of Wimbledon. "First thing tomorrow morning, we'll take you into Brettenden and buy the best set in town — oh, no, of course, I can't come, I'll be heading for the Royal Albert Hall as soon as I'm awake. It'll be the two of you on your own, then. I hope Dad manages to keep you away from the hat shop without me there to jog his memory."

The Times rustled, but Sir George said nothing: he, too, was thinking of cricket. His wife and son regarded each other with knowing smiles.

"Well, it seems that's settled." Lady Colveden sighed; she was no needlewoman, as her nearest and dearest knew — but, as Nigel had almost said, she was the best they'd got. And the Last Night of the Proms was an occasion into the spirit of which everyone had to enter — couldn't help but enter, as decades of tradition caught even the most hardened in their toils. "But I thought you were going up to Town tonight, not tomorrow morning. What happened to sleeping on the pavement to be sure of your place in the queue? Goodness knows, you've made enough fuss about thermos flasks and air mattresses recently."

"Common sense prevailed." Nigel grinned. "I wondered whether my spine could really stand the strain, and after considerable reflection decided it probably couldn't, with being so long out of training. It's years since I was at boarding school, remember — I'm not as young as I was. If I'd thought about it in time, I suppose I should have asked Miss Seeton if I could borrow her yoga book as well as the brolly, but . . ."

"And the Admiral's flag," interposed his father, putting down his newspaper at last. "And my hunting horn — asked me how to blow Cookhouse, as I recall." He tapped his empty pudding plate with a spoon in the well-known "Come to the cookhouse door, boys" rhythm. "Didn't you mention asking the Buzzard about Sunset, too?"

"No time to learn Sunset," said Nigel. "And the flag's for starting the Lawn Mower Race, not the Proms. What with the brolly and the hunting horn I don't believe I could manage anything else, knowing how crowded it always is — and on further reflection I've decided it doesn't matter if I can't blow proper calls. The odd few tootles as the mood takes me, I think, will suffice — unless, that is, I, er, lend the horn to anyone else who might want to borrow it." Nigel blushed. "Which would really be much more sensible, because then I could take extra care of Miss Seeton's brolly. I'd hate to drop it in all the scrum and have it trodden on when it's —" wide eyes gazed at his mother — "so beautifully adorned. I rather thought I'd open it for twirling in the set pieces — *Rule, Britannia* and so on — and conduct with it closed the rest of the time. As for the sleeping, Heather's organised it so that between the whole crowd of us we've acquired enough ticket stubs for Clive to be able to come, too, if he insists, so if any of the others want to spend the, er, last night before the Last Night on the streets of London, they're welcome, but I won't be joining them."

Suddenly, he was serious. "I know things have been a bit pushed around the place these last few weeks, Dad, what with you and your bench-sitting and me dashing off to concerts every five minutes. I feel I should be here as often as I can, to make the most of the daylight — and especially with the Admiral's gin party this evening. I mean, someone has to be in charge while you carouse — but once Saturday's over," as his father huffed a halfhearted protest, "things will be back to normal, I promise. It's just that when Heather suggested the Proms right at the start of the season, and it all sounded such a lark, well . . ."

Sir George blew through his moustache. "Pretty girl," he remarked. "Only young once, m'boy. Even," with a chuckle, "your spine, eh?"

Nigel blushed; though for what reason, neither of his parents could be sure. He then changed the subject with considerable adroitness. "Talking of the Admiral, Dad — as you're going to his little Battle of Britain knees-up, d'you think you could ask him about the Union Jack? In the ordinary way I wouldn't mind asking myself, of course, but you'd save me no end of time if you could. What with the farm and the Proms and the Lawn Mower Race keeping me so busy . . . I'd love to hear his reminiscences, tell him — but on some other occasion."

A request which Sir George, a realist, knew he could not justifiably refuse.

★ ★ ★

Friday morning also heralded the excursion of Miss Nuttel and Mrs. Blaine to Ashford Forest. They breakfasted on homebaked bread spread with a scraping of vegetarian margarine (Miss Nuttel spoke again of beechnut butter) and restrained dollops of Bunny's strawberry jam, washed down with nettle tea; then Mrs. Blaine did the dishes and left them to drain ("Teatowels, Eric — too unhealthy, harbouring germs!") while Miss Nuttel checked the contents of the haversack she had packed the previous night, and added the picnic she'd just thrown together under Mrs. Blaine's watchful, washing-up eye.

When the bus left for Brettenden, several of their fellow Plummergenites accompanied the Nuts on the first part of their journey, for it was market day. Surprise was expressed that the Lilikot ladies, in response to routine interrogation, admitted (grudgingly) that for once they were not on the lookout for bargains, then refused to give further details. On arrival in Brettenden, instead of leaving the bus station to make for the market, they were observed warily consulting another timetable, checking their watches, and drifting off to join another queue.

"Now, why," demanded Mrs. Flax, "couldn't they just've said straight out they were going to Ashford? Summat odd about it all, if you ask me."

Everyone within earshot nodded. Mrs. Flax, as Plummergen's acknowledged Wise Woman, would have been afforded the courtesy (to her face, at any rate, for safety's sake) of absolute agreement even if she'd suggested something totally outrageous; but there was no need for her audience to prevaricate on this occasion. The behaviour of Miss Nuttel and Mrs. Blaine was, without question, odd. Fishy, others said. Downright queer, now they came to think of it . . .

"What *I'd* like to know," someone said, "is what they'd got in that great shoulder bag as Miss Nuttel was carrying."

Frantic nods, and a chorus of agreement, with Mrs. Flax's voice above all others. "Heavy," she said, "before they'd either of 'em set foot in a shop, so it was — and for why, I ask you?" She did not wait for a reply, but pronounced with the full weight of authority. "You mark my words," said the Wise Woman, "there's Summat Funny going on . . ."

The more dedicated among the shopping snoops even toyed with the idea of

pursuing the Nuts on their Ashford trip —
it was a free country, wasn't it? Anyone
could ride on a bus if they'd the money to
pay for their ticket! — but it wasn't market
day in Ashford, more's the pity. It would
be really annoying to miss out on the
Brettenden bargains for something they'd
be bound to hear all about sooner or later,
the way those Nuts did love to talk . . .

Talking as they, too, loved to do, the
Plummergen crowd moved reluctantly out
of the bus station, leaving Miss Nuttel and
Mrs. Blaine to board the Ashford bus. Neither Nut had been too happy about rous-
ing the curiosity of their fellows, but what
else could they have done? As Miss Nuttel
so succinctly put it:

"Not just saving money not running a
car, Bunny — saving petrol, too. Lead in
the atmosphere — greenhouse effect, as
well. No more than our plain duty to take
the bus."

Mrs. Blaine stifled a sigh. Sometimes —
very, very seldom, but sometimes — she
found herself less fervent an upholder of
their organic, whole-food, back-to-nature
life-style than Miss Nuttel. Not, of course,
that she'd ever dare confess as much to
Eric. Strong-minded and high principled,
that was Eric — too shaming for Mrs.

Blaine even to dream of admitting that the luxury of one's own transport might occasionally be very welcome. To be whisked (Mrs. Blaine had no intention of sitting behind the wheel herself) directly from A to B . . . no queues, no weather, no enforced inhalation of other people's secondhand tobacco fumes . . . Humphrey, brooded Mrs. Blaine as the bus bounced along, had been a smoker. One of the many reasons she'd divorced him — too grim and unhealthy, dog-ends and spent matches and ashtrays and nicotine stains on his fingers . . .

"Bunny." Miss Nuttel jabbed her companion with a bony elbow. "Your teeth. Hear them grinding from here. Bad for the enamel."

"Oh." Mrs. Blaine felt herself turning pink. "I *knew* that nettle tea was a mistake for breakfast — we should have had chamomile, as I said. So much better for the nerves."

But Miss Nuttel was no longer listening: she'd heard too much too often before about her friend's highly strung nature. Her eyes darted from one side of the bus to the other as she surveyed the passing trees of Ashford Forest, trying to make up her mind.

"Here, I think." They were approaching a crossroads: a landmark. Miss Nuttel, tall and thin, reached up with ease from her seat to pull twice on the bell rope, and as Mrs. Blaine began to collect her scattered wits, the bus rattled to a halt. With Eric in the lead, the two Nuts hurried down the aisle, collected the haversack from the luggage rack, grudgingly remembered to thank the driver for stopping — it was the man's job, after all — and climbed down the steps into the middle of nowhere.

When the bus had rumbled on its way, only the rush of an occasional passing car disturbed the birdsong and rustling leaves of Ashford Forest. With the coming of September, there was a hint of gold among the green, a touch more dryness in the underfoot grass and in twigs which snapped more easily when trodden on than they would have done in the lush days of summer. The Nuts, blind to the beauties of nature, trod doggedly on their way towards their goal of such mast-laden beeches as stood more than fifty yards ("Lead poisoning, Bunny — trees breathe too, you know,") from the road.

They went in about a hundred yards, to be on the safe side, and struck up a course parallel to the road, out of sight but still, though barely, within earshot of it. They pushed through undergrowth, and Mrs. Blaine muttered about brambles snagging her stockings and skirt. Miss Nuttel, who was wearing trousers, said that if they didn't want everyone to know what they were doing, they must put up with a little discomfort. Did Bunny really want to risk having the good trees raided by other people — who wouldn't have found them unless shown the way by wiser, more adventurous souls — the instant their backs were turned? They hoped, after all, to return another day, as they'd never manage to carry as much as they wanted on the first trip . . .

"We haven't found *one* tree yet, Eric, good or bad. It's too unfair — you ought to have asked me before stopping the bus." Mrs. Blaine contrived to sound as if she possessed an unerring instinct which would, had it not been thwarted by Miss Nuttel, have taken her straight to groves of beeches whose boughs were breaking under their nuxial burden. As it was, however, she must suffer in silence . . .

Miss Nuttel knew, only too well, that Bunny's sufferings were never silent. They had come upon a glade, formed by the fall of a vast and ancient tree. "Sit down," she said, and swung the haversack from her shoulder. "Have a breather. Bite to eat, perhaps?"

Mrs. Blaine allowed herself to be persuaded, but remarked that the water they'd drawn from their very own well before embarking on this excursion was bound to have been shaken by the judderings of the bus. She thought she could hear the sound of running water, not too far away . . .

Miss Nuttel knew a hint when she heard one. "Back in a jiffy," she said, knowing that a mug in the water was worth two minutes' search — was worth anything to stop a tantrum, with the rest of the day to endure. She fumbled inside the haversack, pulled out two enamel mugs ("Plastic's too artificial, Eric — and a by-product of oil, as well!"), and dumped the bag by Bunny's feet as she strode off streamwards.

A squirrel scuttered along a branch, disturbed by Miss Nuttel's passing. Mrs. Blaine turned to watch it disappear — squirrels, everyone knew, ate nuts. If *she* found a bearing tree when Eric had so patently failed . . .

Sighing, Mrs. Blaine dragged herself to her feet, and set off in the direction taken by the squirrel. She wouldn't bother telling Eric where she'd gone: she'd reappear with a smile of quiet triumph on her face, and —

"Aaaah! Bunny!" The cry came from the place Mrs. Blaine would have expected Miss Nuttel to be — but it wasn't Miss Nuttel who cried. Surely not — that high-pitched, quivering, frantic screech? Mrs. Blaine's heart gave a thump, and she spun round, prepared to sell her honour dearly, ready for whatever ravening masculine monster had invaded this rustic solitude — but not entirely sure she'd do any good if she ran towards that cry — that cry which Eric, surely, had never uttered . . .

It was a trick! He was holding a knife to Eric's throat — forcing her to call — worse, he'd already . . . already . . .

"Bunnnnnyyyyy . . ." And a thump, as the lifeless form fell to the ground. Bunny saw blood spurting, grass red-stained, the gleam of steel as the knife came closer . . .

And Mrs. Blaine, in her turn, rolled up her eyes, threw out her hands, and collapsed in a heap on the forest floor.

Chapter 8

Superintendent Brinton sat at his desk, silent, introspective, staring at the calendar on the wall; his desk was piled high with photographs and scene-of-crime reports and witness statements; his open pocket diary lay beside his blotter. Detective Constable Foxon walked on tiptoe about the office, worrying. He'd never seen Old Brimstone so shattered — and nothing to do with the fact it was another — messy — sort of murder. There'd been enough of those, in the past, and the super had never turned a hair. But this — this second Blonde in the Bag — this had shaken him, all right.

"A lunatic on the loose, Foxon," said Brinton at last. "That's what we've got — and I don't like it one little bit. I don't like the way I knew — I *told* you — it was going to happen, and there was nothing I could do about it . . ."

"Perhaps," ventured Job's Comforter, "it's a copy cat killing, sir. Perhaps he remembered it was a year ago the original blonde was bagged, and —"

"It's chummie again, Foxon — it's got to

110

be." Brinton abandoned his slumped pose and sat upright, glaring. "I'm not going to believe we've *two* loonies on the loose who work to identical patterns — because they *were* identical, Foxon."

"So it seems, sir. The only apparent difference we've found so far is in the place he left her this time, but —"

"*Seems — apparent — so far* — stop splitting hairs, laddie!" There was a flash of Brinton's usual self in the command, but it didn't last. He waved a weary hand at the pile of paperwork on his desk. "What use is your blasted quibbling to young Darren Bannister? His girl carved to ribbons, wrapped up like a parcel, carted off to the woods, and plonked under a bush like rubbish — not to mention having been interfered with beforehand, poor kid . . ."

"I'm sorry, sir. But — maybe Bannister's our man, sir." Foxon offered the suggestion as a man offers meat to a hungry lion. "I mean, statistically it's usually your nearest and dearest, isn't it? And they *had* quarrelled — he said so himself. Suppose it was all a bit more vicious than he let on, and he lost his temper with her, and . . ."

"And carried her out there on the back of his motorbike, riding pillion?" Brinton snorted. Foxon's nonsense, as the superin-

111

tendent saw it, was rapidly restoring him to his old self. "Use your head, laddie. Darren doesn't have a sidecar on that bike, for one thing — and, for another, if we're going to talk about *statistically,* then the one who finds the body's right up there heading the list, isn't he? Or, as we both know only too well, isn't *she.* They. The Nuts." Brinton shuddered. "Potter's tougher than I'd ever dreamed, Foxon — not to have asked for promotion to another district, I mean, with those two practically on his doorstep and him the village bobby. I can understand they were upset and shocked at finding the poor girl — anyone with a spark of humanity in them would be, so I suppose it proves the Nuts *are* human after all — I've sometimes wondered — but how they could have the . . . the consummate gall to say it was anything to do with Miss Seeton . . ."

"It's a thingummy reflex, sir, that's all," said Foxon at once, delighted to see his chief so much improved: and so prepared to give Miss Seeton, for once (though in this case anything else was quite out of the question) the benefit of the doubt. Almost championing her, you could say. "Simple, or conditioned? We did 'em in biology at school — one you learn from experience, one you're born with. Miss Nuttel and Mrs. Blaine were both born suspicious, I'd say, so —"

"Never mind your reflexes, laddie. Those Nuts are both mad, there's no other word for it. Miss Seeton a . . . a razor-killer and a rapist? Stark, staring mad — just like," he added thoughtfully, "our chummie has to be . . ."

"Oh, surely not, sir. I mean — well, they haven't got a car, sir, or even a motorbike. And they couldn't — I mean, they're female, too, sir. I know they're odd, but —"

"They found the body," said Brinton; then sighed, and shook his head. "I'm talking rubbish, Foxon — we both know it. And," he added darkly, "we both know *why*, as well — she does it by remote control, doesn't she? There hasn't been a sniff of her umbrella anywhere in this business, just having her name bandied about by a pair of malicious old biddies — but that's enough to send me off my rocker and start putting up theories no sane man would contemplate for a minute. How she does it, I'll never know . . ."

"The girl, sir," said Foxon, after a pause. "Came from Murreystone originally, didn't she?"

Brinton eyed him sourly. "And Murreystone's only five miles from Plummergen, and deadly rivals — like Miss Seeton and the Nuts, only MissEss probably doesn't know what they think of her, and Murreystone does. Know what Plummergen thinks, I mean — about the other village, not about — good grief! I'm starting to *sound* like the woman now, Foxon! Can you understand why I didn't want her brought in on this case even before it *was* a case? Mrs. Blaine can rabbit on about her blasted nerves all she likes —"

"She certainly did," murmured Foxon, unnoticed.

"— but mine aren't in too healthy a state right now, believe me. *Or* my blood pressure . . ."

Brinton slumped again, the adrenaline draining out of his system and leaving him once more a miserable man. "She came from Murreystone," he said heavily. "And her parents have been notified, and enquiries are in progress, and everything chugging along more or less how it should . . ." With a jaundiced eye, he glared at the pile of paperwork in front of him. "We'll plough through this lot like we're supposed to, and read all last year's stuff again — and again — and then, just maybe, we'll find the lead we've been looking for —

maybe. But somehow, laddie, I don't think so. Something tells me we're not going to enjoy this one little bit . . ."

Brinton's misery was further increased throughout the afternoon, as each completed report was brought in and added to the rest. He and Foxon read, and reread; and each made various suggestions which were either shot down at once by the other, or considered worth a follow-up when circumstances permitted. They did not — as the superintendent had predicted — enjoy themselves one little bit.

In Plummergen's post office, where everyone was enjoying themselves very much indeed, the atmosphere could have been caught and bottled and sold as high explosive. Mrs. Putts, mother of young Emmy who worked behind the grocery counter, herself worked in Brettenden, in the biscuit factory. Coming home at the end of her shift, she had rushed straight off the bus to give her daughter the latest news.

It was sheer coincidence, of course, that the post office was full of shoppers at the very time Mrs. Putts made her announcement. "There's a girl gone missing — one of them Felsteds from Murreystone, lives in Brettenden — and they've arrested her boyfriend along to Ashford!"

Sensation. Mrs. Putts relayed what little else she knew of the matter, together with considerable quantities of what had been invented by other workers on the industrial estate as they queued together for their homeward buses. Young Darren Bannister had quarrelled with his Myrtle the other night — the girl hadn't come in to work for a day or so — when they'd started to wonder why she hadn't phoned in or produced a sick-note, Darren had pretended to be worried about her — had stolen her pay packet and tried to make a run for it — had been spotted by the police and hauled off to chokey . . . This last, courtesy of a shift worker who, like Darren, lived in Ashford, and had recognised his motorbike outside the police station, and had mentioned the fact when he arrived at his factory to find the place seething.

In the middle of all this pleasurable speculation, there came a cry from young Mrs. Newport, standing near the window. "There's a police car outside Lilikot!"

Sensation, followed by stampede. Even Emmy Putts abandoned her official post and scurried to the door — or as near as she could, given the press of older, heavier bodies who'd reached it first. Mr. Still-

man's window display was partly disman-
tled, so that shoppers could see out; Mr.
Stillman's aluminum steps were dragged
from their usual place behind the counter
to be squabbled over by Mrs. Skinner and
Mrs. Henderson, who'd once disagreed
about the church flower rota and had
never been reconciled. Tall persons were
elbowed to the back of the crowd by others
less blessed with inches . . .

And everyone, breathless, watched as
one tall person and one short — one
equine of feature, bony and spare; one
dumpy and querulous, flat of foot — made
their slow and staggering way along
Lilikot's front path; fumbled for their keys;
opened the door; and vanished within,
watched by the driver of the panda and the
eyes of the whole post office.

"Well!" Collective breath was released as
the police car drove off down The Street.
"And where's *he* going now?" Mrs. Flax
pointed a dramatic finger in the direction
of the vanished panda. "Ah, we all know
who lives that end of the village, don't
we?" And she favoured her audience with a
long, portentous look.

"He'll be turning round, that's all," said
young Mrs. Scillicough, sister to Mrs.
Newport. Mrs. Newport had a quartet of

well-behaved offspring; Mrs. Scillicough had triplets whose behaviour was a byword. Mrs. Scillicough had consulted the Wise Woman, and been disappointed; and was inclined to vent her subsequent grievance at every possible opportunity. "That," she said, as the rest of the shoppers thrilled at her challenge to the authority of Mrs. Flax, "was Constable Buckland, that was — him as is a friend to young Foxon, that works over to Ashford along of Superintendent Brinton. And if he's not turning round," she added, as there came no sign of the panda's return past the panting plate glass of the post office, "then he's took the other road. There's more than one way of getting to Ashford from Plummergen, goodness knows." Mrs. Scillicough turned her back on the window, and marched towards the grocery department to await Emmy's return.

Mrs. Flax glowered, then rallied. "Ah, and more than one way of travelling that road than in a police car, as all of us do know." She turned the full force of her personality upon the expectant shop. "There's *the bus* . . ."

Which was enough to send speculation through the metaphorical roof. How could they have forgotten the Nuts had travelled on the Brettenden bus that very morning — travelled with a mysterious load they'd made sure nobody saw them sneaking on the Ashford bus later? And that poor girl gone missing from Brettenden — and the bus going past the very stop she'd have been waiting at . . . Dates, timetables, and common sense were forgotten as gleeful imagination ran riot. Emmy Putts, having reluctantly dragged herself back to the grocery counter in the absence of further activity across the street, clasped rapturous hands in the throes of cutting cheese, and exclaimed:

"*Dope,* that's what it'll have bin in that bag — and then them Nuts *waylaying* the poor girl, and taking advantage of her trusting, innocent nature, and *white slaving* her, sure as eggs!"

"Drink, more like," opined Mrs. Skinner, as the majority digested this theory and found it highly palatable, though a minority of one, in the form of Mrs. Putts, felt a twinge of unease. Had she been (she wondered) right to allow Emmeline to enter the Miss Plummergen contest three summers ago? The blonde wig she'd worn for her coronation seemed to have given the girl . . . *ideas,* mused Mrs. Putts, though her anxious musings were soon drowned out by Mrs. Skinner's next remark. "That shoulder bag of Miss Nuttel's," said Mrs. Skinner, "it looked much heavier nor what I'd reckon dope enough to white slave anyone would need to be. Bottles is glass, and glass is heavy, *and* takes up room. Now, a few gins under a girl's belt, and — well!"

As someone mentioned Mother's Ruin, someone else began to point out that the apparent weight carried by the Nuts could have been large quantities of dope for the express purpose of white slaving any number of young women; but before this delightful theme could be enlarged upon, Mrs. Henderson remarked to nobody in particular, very loudly, that it seemed Some People knew far more about dope than any decent soul did really ought to.

"Drink," retorted Mrs. Skinner, "is easier *by far* than dope for a body to get hold of. Stands to reason, when you can buy it easy as wink if you're over age — which I hope as nobody's daft enough to say the Nuts aren't? There you are, then!" as heads were shaken, and voices murmured of Old Enough To Know Better, with particular reference to Miss Nuttel and Mrs. Blaine —

"*And* Miss Seeton," said Mrs. Flax; with which not even Mrs. Scillicough could disagree.

"Old enough to know better, dear, he really is," said Martha Bloomer, whisking a duster round an already gleaming tabletop in Miss Seeton's dining room. "Says he wants to be a *pop star,* of all the crazy notions. Did you ever hear the like? If there's money in pop music apart from the Beatles, I'm the Queen of Sheba, and my Stan's Mr. Universe. Poor old Beryl. The boy's a trial to her, Miss Emily, and no mistake. Never mind not earning any money to speak of, because of course there's always the dole, if the worst comes to the worst, though honest work is honest work and nobody ought to be ashamed of it — which give him his due he isn't, if you can call it honest work going round places singing and playing that daft guitar — but they won't make their fortunes that way, dear, and what he doesn't give Beryl for his keep — because you have to say that for him, he tries to pay his way — but he never saves a penny of the rest, so Beryl says. Spends it on parts for his motorbike, and drinking, not to mention — well, you know what those clubs can be like, Miss

Emily." Martha frowned. "Not just drink, is it, with these arty types, meaning no disrespect, dear. But there's drugs, too, and that's what Beryl's most afraid of, I know."

Miss Seeton, watching the gyrations of her faithful and energetic servitor, sighed, and nodded. Artists — musicians — poets . . . did genius — *could* genius excuse the taking of drugs in the search for ever greater inspiration? Even if one argued that such a step might not be rather, well, cheating, it was certainly against the law. Was genius above the law? "Indeed not," said Miss Seeton firmly.

Martha quivered. "But she is, Miss Emily, I know for a fact, because she told me so herself. Even when he comes down hopping, away from that lot in Town, he takes off after work on his motorbike and never a word next day about where he's been or what he's done — and that's not right, dear, it really isn't. There's some funny people round these parts, Miss Emily, even if you've not noticed them . . ."

Martha fell silent. She could be fairly sure Miss Seeton had *not* noticed them. Why worry her with things that didn't concern her? "Oh, never mind me, dear, I expect it's just the weather. And he'll grow

out of his nonsense in time, I dare say —
drat!" Waving away the idea of Barry's
nonsense, she had let the duster slip from
her fingers. She bent down, fumbled, and
rose with a red face. "Well, you're decent
enough now, and I'm sorry not to have
done you properly before I went to market
this morning, but what with one thing and
another I've got myself all behind, I don't
mind telling you, dear. Though I won't
make a habit, I promise," as Miss Seeton
assured Mrs. Bloomer that her unexpected
trip to Brettenden had not mattered in the
least. Indeed, she was glad — having spent
the day in school — of some adult company in the evening . . .

"Your supper, dear," cried Martha, remembering. "What's in the fridge did
ought to have been taken out before now,
but if you give it an extra five minutes in
the oven, you'll come to no harm. It's cottage pie, which in this warm weather's a bit
much, I know, but once the sun's gone
down there *is* a bit of a chill in the air, and
apple pie for afters, which won't matter
whether it's hot or cold." She hesitated,
looking into the distance. "They'll be fin-
ishing at the hop garden round about now,
I dare say, and fixing supper at the hut like
we always did — but there you are, dear,

those days are long gone for me, and probably just as well. Pop singers!"

And Martha, with a farewell flick of the duster, cleared her cleaning implements away, instructed Miss Seeton again on the intricacies of her supper preparation, ordered her to be sure to have an early night, and left through the back garden, talking happily of lettuces for Stan.

But as she left, Miss Seeton, waving good-bye through the kitchen window, found her fingers beginning their familiar, urgent dance . . .

Chapter 9

While Miss Seeton, her drawing finished, was boiling the kettle for a cup of tea, drinks of an altogether more festive nature were on offer about four hundred yards to the north of Sweetbriars, halfway up The Street, in Ararat Cottage, home of Rear Admiral Leighton. The Buzzard (Bernard Leighton had brought his Naval nickname with him to Kent) was given to flying the gin pennant — a long, green-and-white triangular flag — from the flagpole in his front garden whenever he found due and proper cause to celebrate: and, as he had spent most of his working life in the Royal Navy, due and proper cause was seldom hard to find.

Today, the fifteenth of September, was Battle of Britain Day. The Senior Service might have mocked the Brylcreem Boys of the Royal Air Force to their faces, but behind their backs they were among the first to admit they'd been a staunch body of men. Winston Churchill, said the Admiral, had, if anything, underestimated the worth and valour of the Few.

"God bless them!" he cried, downing his

third pink gin. His guests echoed the toast: Sir George in whisky-and-water, Colonel Windup in silent whisky-and-whisky, Major Howett in her Horse's Neck (brandy and ginger ale), and the Reverend Arthur Treeves, daringly, in a half-pint of shandy made from equal parts of mild ale and ginger beer.

The vicar wasn't entirely sure how he'd ended up drinking in Ararat Cottage when he'd only gone for a short walk to post a letter; but he'd bumped into the Howitzer (as Major Howett was inevitably known) at the post office door, and she had told him how the Admiral had some time earlier explained that a gin pennant invitation was open to all and any officers who spotted it. Hadn't the Reverend Arthur served in the Home Guard? There he was, then! And Major Howett, who was a great friend of the vicar's sister and no less bossy, swept the Reverend Arthur across The Street and up the path of Ararat Cottage before he could protest that Molly would be expecting him home, and, in any case, he'd only met the Admiral on one or two previous occasions . . .

"Time to get better acquainted, then." Matilda Howett stood no nonsense from the patients in Dr. Knight's nursing home, and she certainly wasn't going to let Arthur Treeves hide away, as Molly had told her he too frequently did, behind the vicarage garden wall. "It's good for you to get out and about, Padre. New horizons — new friends." She did not notice his sudden squirm of embarrassment. "Comrades in arms, the whole crowd — and you'll know everybody else, I'm sure. No need to worry!"

The vicar had been only in part relieved to discover that, apart from the Admiral, those forgathered in Ararat Cottage were already known to him. Sir George Colveden, of course, it was ever a pleasure to meet; but it was rather alarming to encounter Colonel Windup in the flesh. Colonel Windup lived next door to the George and Dragon and spent most of his time there, speaking to nobody except (or so the rumour, which the Reverend Arthur tried to ignore, insisted) to ask for the same again, please. This remark had at least the twin virtues of brevity and clarity: the colonel's other communications tended to be less comprehensible. He spent such times as the pub wasn't open in the writing of cryptic letters which he would unleash upon an unsuspecting public, particularly if it wore (as did the Parochial Church

Council, of which the vicar was *ex officio* a member) an aspect of authority. Colonel Windup was always demanding that Something Should Be Done — but it was never entirely clear about what. Plummergen wits claimed that were it not for the colonel's copious one-way correspondence (for nobody who had once received a letter from him ever troubled to answer a second), Mr. Stillman's takings at the post office would be reduced by half.

"Same again, everyone?" The Admiral was hospitably on his feet, heading for the sideboard. "Come along, Padre, no heel-taps! Major Howett, I'm sure you'll join me. Colveden, Windup — a refill?"

Sir George felt himself weakened by the whirlwind force of the personality behind that ginger beard, and accepted, silently resolving to add more water when the Buzzard was looking the other way. Colonel Windup, never one to refuse a good offer, nodded with pleasure and held out his glass. Muttering about stomach linings, Major Howett began to hand round the platter of sliced pork pie, the only food Admiral Leighton was prepared to tolerate at a party.

"None of your Naafi rubbish, this," remarked the Admiral, as the Howitzer fixed the colonel with a gimlet eye and he meekly took a slice from the plate in front of him. "Remember what we used to say about the blighters?"

Sir George remembered just before the others, and burst out laughing. "My word, yes! No Aim, Ambition, or Flaming Interest — absolutely true, what's more! Early days, anyway. Improved no end once that chap Beale sorted 'em out." His reference to the sterling transformation wrought by Sir William Beale, as its new director and chairman, upon the Navy, Army, and Air Force Institutes organisation in 1940 was greeted with amused approbation by the major and the colonel, though the vicar's Home Guard experience left him blinking at a joke he didn't quite understand. To see his companions in such good spirits, however, more than compensated for this bemusement. He beamed impartially upon the room at large, and failed to notice that the Admiral had mixed him another shandy.

As tongues were loosened, wartime reminiscences came thick and fast. The Buzzard told of a corvette captain so small he'd only been able to see over his bridge rail if he stood on a biscuit tin. "Never bothered him, mind you — nor his crew."

Admiral Leighton chuckled. "They'd have sailed with him if he'd been half the size — believed he brought 'em luck, and there's no doubt he was a damned fine officer. Popular. Had to paint scrambled egg on the peak of his cap when he was promoted, because the men weren't happy with his new brass hat — said it was nowhere near as lucky as the old 'un. Never wore another, right through the war — superstitious lot, sailors." He chuckled again, stroked his beard, then turned politely to the Reverend Arthur.

"You think it's all a load of tommyrot, I suppose, Padre? Good luck, bad luck — hardly your style. The church, I mean," as the vicar blinked again on hearing his opinion sought for the first time in years.

"Good luck?" The Reverend Arthur's wayward memory had been jogged by the Buzzard's words. "Dear me, yes, there were some remarkable examples, remarkable. A fighter pilot, you know, shot down not far from here — who landed, as I recall, precisely in the centre of a minefield. Dear me, they were dark days indeed, with the fear of invasion ever present — dark days." Sighing, he shook a sorrowful head, and drank deeply of his shandy to cheer himself. "Yes, a most fortunate young man —

most. And who can for certain say through what agency or chance he came to be saved?" He sighed again, looking back on happier days when he would have had no doubt that it was by the power of prayer the miracle had been achieved. "Not one of the mines exploded, and the Home Guard extricated him with no loss of life . . ."

"Talking of mines," volunteered Sir George, after a few moments' respectful silence, "something about aerial mines, I remember. Piano wire, parachutes . . . and sheep," he added with a puzzled frown, his voice dropping on the final words as he hastily set down his whisky glass and resolved to ask for plain water next time round.

"Operation Mutton!" cried Major Howett at once, though the Admiral and the Colonel looked as puzzled as the vicar. "Cousin who was an Air Force boffin," she added in explanation, as questioning faces were turned towards her. "Churchill approved — two thousand feet of piano wire, parachute at the top, little bomb at the bottom, drop 'em in front of enemy bombers underneath — but dangerous sport, no matter how careful you tried to be. One poor devil was hit *three times* by his own mines —"

The Admiral emitted a sudden guffaw, then promptly apologised for interrupting Major Howett's narrative. The Howitzer, grimly gracious, intimated that she had nothing more to say on the subject, and the floor was now his. Admiral Leighton stroked his beard and coughed.

"Er, yes — nothing remarkable, really — just, when you said about the chap being hit three times, I couldn't help remembering a couple of signals. Two of our destroyers, out in the Med — heading that way, rather. Leaving port. Which reminds me — port, anyone? Another whisky?" He rose to his feet and headed again for the drinks table, glass in hand, collecting from his guests as he passed. "First chap signalled me something along the lines of *Returning to harbour, have been hit in the stern, probably mine.* Second chap signalled *Referring so-and-so's signal, for mine read me.* Er, yes," he said again, as only a courteous chortle from Sir George and a thin smile from the Major greeted his punchline. Colonel Windup was too busy concentrating on what was being poured into his glass to be polite; the vicar was trying to work out what the point of the story had been.

"Talk about returnin' —" Major Howett

took over — "there was a chap in another cousin's squadron just comin' back from leave when the scramble bell rang. Didn't have time to reach the airfield gate — climbed the fence, hared like a lunatic for the nearest Spitfire, took off, bagged a Dornier bomber, then landed calm as you like and went to report back — no more than twenty minutes before his pass ran out."

This was received with suitable expressions of amusement and amazement from all present: even Colonel Windup could be heard chortling quietly into his whisky. Sir George, without noticing, drained his own scotch and reached for the new and tempting tumbler the Admiral had placed beside him. He sipped, choked, sipped again. "Talking of lunatics," he began, then sipped once more. Everyone waited politely for him to continue.

"Talking of lunatics — that pair next door." Mellowed by whisky, he considered this an entirely reasonable turn of phrase for public consumption — he'd used far stronger epithets in the privacy of his own home. Anyway, dammit, all friends together . . . "Meg tells me no end of rumours flying round about them abducting a girl, and being arrested by the police, or some such bal—derdash," he amended, in deference to the presence of Major Matilda Howett and the Reverend Arthur Treeves. The Reverend Arthur, looking suddenly disturbed, blinked again. Sir George harrumphed, and fingered an uneasy moustache. "Yes, well — hardly the sort of talk we want around the village. Makes people nervous, whether it's true or not. Take it you've noticed nothing . . . out of the ordinary going on, Leighton?"

Before the Admiral could reply, Major Howett nodded a sage head. "Wondered whether you knew about that — didn't care to spoil the party by mentionin' it before. There was talk, you know, while I was in the post office — but then," with a sharp, barking laugh, "there always is. Never known such a crowd for tittle-tattle." As the other men muttered, the Reverend Arthur sighed deeply. Friendly exchanges were one thing — those pleasantries of social intercourse which gave village life such value — but sometimes — true, only sometimes — though regrettably such times, he had to admit, there were — it did seem that, well, perhaps people were rather too hasty to place a less charitable interpretation on events than he would like . . .

"Emmy Putts and her mother," Major Howett was saying, "right in the thick of it this time, eggin' the others on — still, Mrs. Putts works on the same industrial estate as the missin' gel, if she *is* missing, so it might just be true, I suppose. But this nonsense of draggin' poor Miss Seeton into the business the way they did —"

"Pah!" exclaimed Sir George, forgetting himself. "Slanderous blasted females — sorry, Major. Why they've all got their knives stuck into Miss Seeton . . ."

"Couldn't agree with you more, Sir George, and that's what I told the whole silly crowd. May well have been Mrs. Putts who started 'em off, but they're all tarred with the same brush." Major Howett frowned in much the same way as she might be supposed to have chastised the post office gossips. "Even if that precious pair *have* got themselves in a spot of bother — not as if the poor little woman's any particular friend to the ladies in question, is it?"

"Ladies be damned!" exploded Sir George, then recollected himself, and harrumphed with great vigour. "Sorry, Major — Padre — but, I assure you, more than flesh and blood can be expected to stand, hearing them harp on and on about

135

one of the best little souls . . ."

It might have been Sir George's mention of the spiritual which now agitated the Reverend Arthur Treeves. It might have been the general ripening of the language to which he was forced to listen, or the distressing revelations about the character of some of his parishioners; it might even have been that, under the influence of several glasses — how many? Molly would be furious — of shandy, he felt the need for fresh air, or for solitude. Whatever the cause, he suddenly set down his empty glass, and jumped to his feet.

He sat down again, the apologies he'd been on the point of uttering lost in a swirl of echoing voices and a curious hum deep inside the top of his head. His legs felt a little unsteady — hadn't Molly warned him about his blood pressure? He must rise more slowly next time . . .

"I say, Padre, are you all right? You're looking rather green about the gills." Thus spoke the Admiral, concerned for his guest. The Reverend Arthur blinked at him, swallowed, shook his head, and smiled weakly.

Major Howett, regarding the vicar with the eyes of experience, said briskly that a glass of water and a breath of fresh air would soon put him to rights. If Admiral Leighton would allow her to pop along to the kitchen — galley, she begged his pardon . . .

"No, no. It is I," broke in the Reverend Arthur, struggling for a second, more successful, time to his feet, "who should beg pardon. A touch of . . . of the heat, no doubt — and fr-fresh air is a capital sh-suggeshtion." He stood swaying for a few moments, then took a deep breath, and focussed his eyes with some difficulty on the sitting-room door. "Fresh air — and exershize, I think. I think — I think shome time in the garden would not come amish . . ."

And, despite every effort of his friends to dissuade him, the Reverend Arthur Treeves said his farewells and made his way, walking with great deliberation, out of the sitting room of Ararat Cottage and along the front path to the garden gate. He clutched briefly at the gatepost, and took several deep breaths — took several more — and almost at once felt a great deal better. He risked letting go his hold on the post to turn and wave good-bye to the revellers who had remained to enjoy the admiral's hospitality; he noticed the curtains of neighbouring Lilikot twitch, and ventured a little wave in the direction of the watching Miss Nuttel and Mrs. Blaine. Was he not their parish priest, after all? How very distressing for them to have witnessed the abduction of a young woman. One would wish to show them every possible support in coming to terms with their ordeal — although they would, perhaps, not care to be reminded of it directly. The Reverend Arthur brooded on his gender. The presence of a woman like themselves, rather than a man (for it must, he felt, have been a man who had carried out so very shocking a crime), would doubtless be a comfort. He would mention it to Molly as soon as he reached home . . .

"Shocking," he murmured as his waving hand fell to his side, and he began to make his way southwards down The Street. "Comfort. Fresh air — exercise . . ."

And, when he reached home, instead of telling his sister all about it, the vicar vanished into the garden to work off his renewed agitation upon the clerical flower beds and lawn.

Chapter 10

The suspicion aroused in Plummergen by the return of Miss Nuttel and Mrs. Blaine in a police patrol car persisted from the moment the panda was first observed drawing up outside Lilikot to discharge its passengers (its prisoners, as some insisted, though they comfortably managed to ignore the fact that to all intents and purposes the Nuts were still as much at liberty as they had ever been) until one minute past six o'clock that evening.

Six o'clock might be Admiral Leighton's hour for splicing the mainbrace: it was also Plummergen's regular time for tuning in to the television news. When the headlines announced to a horrified audience exactly what terrible discovery had been made that morning in Ashford Forest, suspicion pricked up its ears; and when, after the other headlines, the story was reported in detail, suspicion, at full throttle, careered off immediately in two separate directions. There were those for whom it veered towards certainty: the Nuts, as all with guilty consciences will do, had returned to the scene of the crime, and were attempting to bluff it out for some unspecified reason which would become clear at their trial, once enough evidence had been collected.

On the other hand, there were those for whom the very act of discovery, with its subsequent publicity, rendered the Lilikot ladies now totally above suspicion — though the accents in which their innocence was protested reverberated with resentment. Those who had supposed themselves intimate friends of Miss Nuttel and Mrs. Blaine were aggrieved that no advance warning had been vouchsafed, no hint dropped as to the probable main item of the Six O'Clock News. Tongues wagged, telephone wires hummed around the village as speculation ran riot: the jangle of bells, the shriek of surmise sent husbands hotfoot for the pub in search of refuge.

A great many persons that night dialled the Lilikot number. Not one obtained anything but the engaged tone. Mrs. Blaine, overwrought, had allowed herself to succumb to a headache as severe as that of any pub-bound Plummergen male; Miss Nuttel was consequently conscripted into the brewing of possets, infusions, and herbal teas until she was exhausted. The last thing the Nuts wished to do was talk to anyone until they had recovered from their shocking experience. The newspapers were sure to want to interview them — the star witnesses — tomorrow; photographs would doubtless be taken. Neither Nut intended to present a haggard appearance to the world at large . . . and so the telephone was taken off the hook, the curtains were closed, and Admiral Leighton's next-door neighbours prepared themselves gleefully for their coming public fame.

They had reckoned, however, without Bernard Leighton. It was not until everyone had gone, more than merrily, home after his Battle of Britain Day party that the owner of Ararat Cottage switched on his television for the Nine O'Clock News — to learn, with dismay, that the rumours relayed by Major Howett and General Colveden had been based on truth. Naval gallantry swung at once into action. Was not one of the traditional wardroom toasts *Sweethearts and Wives*? The Buzzard's imagination boggled at the idea of Miss Nuttel or Mrs. Blaine stirring the tender passions in anybody's breast, but they were, nevertheless, ladies. God bless 'em! He'd a fair idea of what was likely to happen tomorrow, if someone didn't do something to stop it. Who better than the chap in the house next door? He'd see to it they weren't plagued by any of those damned pesky Press types who'd splash slander across the front pages without so much as a by-your-blasted-leave, bandying names and upsetting people. No more than an officer's plain duty to protect his — well, he couldn't call them exactly friends, but there they were, two helpless females in for a pretty rough time, if he didn't do something about it . . .

The Admiral duly set his alarm clock, rose at six next morning with no trace of a headache, and broke his fast with a plate of porridge (flavoured with home-produced honey) and two rounds of toast (buttered, more honey). He then collected an assortment of gardening tools from his shed, and took up a dauntless pose at the front of the house, a hoe in his hand, a spade and a pair of newly sharpened shears close by, ready to repel boarders as necessary. Very sensible, keeping their curtains drawn. No risk of telescopic lenses, or prying eyes. The Admiral nodded approval of this most ladylike desire for privacy, and directed his own eyes, gimletlike and gleaming, up and down The Street by turns, on the watch for the start of the anticipated invasion.

Behind those carefully closed curtains,

the Nuts were making their own preparations. "Better leave it off the hook," remarked Miss Nuttel, stifling the warning scream of the uncradled telephone with a third cushion. "Ringing all day, otherwise."

"People from the village," Mrs. Blaine dismissed her intimate friends scornfully, "blocking the line with ridiculous questions, instead of reporters who have a *legitimate interest* in, well, in what happened. Too impertinent, I think." She sniffed as she teased the final curler from her hair, which she had risen early to wash twice in rosemary shampoo. "Far better to make — I mean let — them come to the house. Then they'll be sure of seeing — of talking to us, without any misunderstanding. They'll insist on taking photographs, I suppose." She suppressed a smirk. "Now, you may say I'm wrong, Eric, but I see it as absolutely our duty to give the full facts, no matter how personally repugnant we find the subsequent publicity." Miss Nuttel did not say that she was wrong. Mrs. Blaine's smirk grew more noticeable. "Television, I imagine — certainly the wireless — the press, too, of course. And if it's only the local newspapers, I shall be very disappointed. That a matter of national importance," she added hastily, "has been neglected in this shocking way. Because the Public," pronounced Mrs. Blaine with capitals, "has A Right to Know . . ."

Miss Nuttel agreed, adding that there was, of course, a great difference between legitimate interest and morbid curiosity. On no account should they open their curtains, in case they rendered themselves liable to a . . . a sneak attack. "Candid camera," warned Miss Nuttel darkly, and Mrs. Blaine uttered cries of horror at the thought that anyone might try to snap her before she'd posed to best advantage — before, she said aloud, she'd had time to strengthen herself and to collect her thoughts about that too, too dreadful discovery they had made yesterday in Ashford Forest.

Behind their tightly drawn drapes, the Nuts knew nothing of what was happening outside — or, rather, what was not. Rear Admiral Leighton could have slept until seven o'clock; Mrs. Blaine's hair curlers could have stayed in their battered shoe box. No reporters thronged The Street, no cameras waited to click vigilant shutters when the tip of a Nutty nose should appear on Lilikot's doorstep. The Admiral was not alone in his desire to keep Miss

Nuttel and Mrs. Blaine, literally, out of the picture . . .

"I'll make Traffic put up roadblocks," had insisted an anguished Superintendent Brinton the previous evening, once the panda driver had confirmed that the shaken Nuts were recovering at home from their ordeal. "I'll bribe the Milk Marketing Board to overturn a tanker — I'll let that arsonist out of gaol to burn all the signposts." He clutched at his hair, and groaned. "Reporters! I can't bear 'em! And I'm not having a single one of the blighters within five miles of . . . of . . ."

"Plummergen, sir?" supplied Foxon brightly, as his chief spluttered helplessly to a close. "Or within five miles of a certain retired art teacher of our particular acquain—"

"Shuttup, Foxon!" Brinton slapped a wrathful hand on the topmost file of the tall heap in front of him. "I give Fleet Street ten seconds flat to make the connection — that Forby woman, for one — and then we'll get all those blasted headlines again. *Pandemonium in Plummergen*," he quoted grimly. "*Battling Brolly Finds Blonde in Bag* — and there's no need," as Foxon tried to protest, "to tell me she didn't, laddie. *I* know she didn't, and *you* know — and *they'll* know, in due course — but catch any of 'em passing up the chance to turn it into a better story when even I can see it's crying out for it!"

"Mel Forby's all right, sir," Foxon managed to slip in, as the superintendent paused to mop his brow. "She and her pal Banner — the World Wide Press bloke — they're not the irresponsible type, sir. I mean, the Oracle trusts them, doesn't he? So —"

"Detective Chief Superintendent Delphick," said Brinton repressively, "is a high-ranking officer from Scotland Yard. In the course of his work he no doubt rubs shoulders with all sorts of people he'd run a mile to avoid in real life, given the option. Every one of them is tarred with the same brush, Detective Constable Foxon."

"You mean high-ranking Yarders, sir?" chirped Foxon, uncrushed by Brinton's pointed riding of his highest horse; then ducked as the superintendent snatched an ashtray from the corner of his desk, and hurled it across the room.

Brinton let out one forceful oath, then paused, sighed, and shook his head. "You'll be the death of me yet, laddie. And there've been too many deaths around here recently — two too many." He gestured once more towards the thick pile of reports. I need to be left in peace to think about this little lot, Foxon, and nobody can think peacefully when they know Miss Seeton's on the loose."

"But, sir —"

"Or when," Brinton overrode Foxon's cry, "she might be *let* loose by a load of sensation-seeking nitwits egging her on. I won't have it, laddie. This investigation is going to be carried out in a . . . an orderly fashion, which is about the last thing anyone would ever say when Miss Seeton's anywhere around. I want to be left in peace to catch this maniac before he does it again — twice is twice too often. The girl's family's in a bad way, according to Buckland." PC Buckland had broken the news of their daughter's death to the Felsteds, thoughtfully taking with him WPc Maggie Laver. Mr. and Mrs. Felsted were now being treated for shock. "And no wonder! She wasn't a pretty sight, poor kid. Having to identify her . . ."

Foxon grimaced as Brinton opened his file and stared at the scene-of-crime photographs. The younger man had no wish to refresh his memory — just as the older had no real need. His was an automatic action,

147

a mental kick-start for the *peaceful thinking* session he was about to undertake, using Foxon, his habitual irreverence duly suppressed, as a sounding board. "So let those damned reporters," said Brinton, "try to interview her parents at the hospital — skirmishing with the nursing staff should keep 'em out of our hair for a while. Let 'em talk to the neighbours in Murreystone, or to the boyfriend — or her landlady — or the people she used to work with. But we'll keep 'em away from Plummergen if it's humanly possible, laddie . . ."

And possible, it seemed the next day to a disappointed Plummergen, it proved. The post office remained crowded for most of the morning; the Admiral stayed on duty; the Nuts continued to lurk expectantly indoors: but nobody came. For which Superintendent Brinton, advised regularly as to the state of play by Plummergen's PC Potter, repeatedly thanked his lucky stars, and the skill of his colleagues' ability to lay false trails, as he brooded in peace on his reports.

Such peace, however, was only relative. Late yesterday evening, there had come a sudden series of jaunty rappings on his office door, followed — before he could either invite the rapper in or shout that he

148

was busy — by the turning of the handle; and in walked one whose name he had bandied about not an hour earlier.

"Miss . . . Miss Forby! What the *devil* are you doing here?"

As Foxon looked up from his paperwork to greet her with a grin, Fleet Street's finest shut the door firmly behind her and headed for the superintendent's desk. "Finding out what's really going on," said Amelita Forby, dropping comfortably into Brinton's visitors' chair with a broad smile. "Demon reporter of the *Daily Negative* that I am, I knew there was one hell of a lot more behind tonight's television news than they were letting on — I've made a speciality of Miss S. and her cases over the years, remember."

Brinton choked, turning purple. "I knew it! What did I tell you, Foxon? Give the blighters half a chance, and that woman'll make headlines worldwide!"

Mel shook her head and smiled again, wilfully misunderstanding. "Banner's nowhere near here, Superintendent," she assured him, referring to her close personal friend and professional rival, Thrudd Banner of World Wide Press. "In fact, there's nobody here except me — and I don't plan to be under your feet for long. Promise," she added, suddenly serious.

"You've a nasty mess on your plate this time, Mr. Brinton. I don't envy you having to sort it out. I'll take my hat off to you in a big way when you do, though — starring part in my final report, that's what you'll get, and not a hint from me about Miss S. unless — until — she comes up with the goods as well. Which she's bound to, sooner or later, I'd say . . ."

"Trespass," said Brinton, with a glare. "Obstructing a police officer in the execution of his duty," with a quick hand closing the file in case Mel, whom he knew of old, was trying to read upside down. Mel directed her beautiful eyes to his face, and contrived to look sorrowful at being so misjudged. "Blackmail," added Brinton, "*and* incitement to mutiny," as Foxon snorted with glee in his corner. Sorrow gave way to restrained mirth, followed by firmness.

"Listen," said Mel, as the superintendent found himself torn between the desire to throw something at Foxon or have Foxon throw Mel out. "If you don't know me by now — if you can't trust me, Mr. Brinton, it's a waste of a good few years on the Plummergen Patrol, that's all I can say." She ignored his inevitable groan at her mention of Miss Seeton's home. "I'm not a fool. I know there was no mention of Miss S. on television or the radio, not even by inference. She's a loner, and the reports were clear about *two* women *from a village in Kent* — which is kind of on the vague side for a story as big as this. Deliberately vague. Official obfuscation, at a guess — aha!" in triumph, as despite himself Brinton groaned again. Foxon's snort was louder this time. Mel beamed.

"Pat on the back for inspired guesswork, Forby," she remarked, suiting the action, as far as physically possible, to the words. "A few more guesses, okay?" as Brinton found himself rendered speechless by her sheer audacity. Mel was hard-pressed not to giggle. "Two women," she said again, her eyes never leaving his face. "Could be friends of Miss S. out bird-watching, per-haps — or," as a flicker had shown briefly at her words, "perhaps not so much friends as, well, the opposite. The Nuts? The Nuts!" as the flicker returned in the form of a fiery gleam. "And I can't say I like that pair any more than you do, Superinten-dent."

"I never —" began Brinton; then he broke off, and turned purple again. Foxon chortled out loud, then changed it hastily to a cough. Mel nodded.

"We understand each other, I think. Look, I'm not out to set the hellhound hacks baying for the Brolly's blood any more than you: quite apart from the fact it would mean sharing my scoop with the blighters, I'm too fond of Miss Seeton to do it — and you're too . . . shall we say *wary?*" Foxon in his corner collapsed in a shuddering heap across the desk as Brinton spluttered helplessly. "I can't say I altogether blame you, though. Things tend to . . . liven up when Miss S. might be involved, don't they? After so many years, my reporter's nose starts twitching just as soon as I hear the words *Kent* or *crime* or *mystery* — and I can put two and two together as well as anybody — or," slowly, "one and one. To make two." She nodded, then gazed at the calendar on the wall as she continued:

"I kind of pride myself on being an expert on this part of the world now, Mr. Brinton — and," before he could reply, "on knowing you rather better than the rest of Fleet Street does. Everyone else went scampering off all eager innocence after those lovely clues your people dropped ever-so-carefully, but not yours truly. If I couldn't find the back way into this place after so long, I'd be an idiot. Now, Mel Forby's been called a good few things in her time, but never that. Two . . .

and two, like I said." Mel leaned forward, eyes sparkling, her glance falling now upon the closed files on Brinton's desk, lingering there a little too long for his liking. "We'll strike a bargain, Superintendent. Miss Nuttel and Mrs. Blaine found the blonde, okay, but nobody except us knows that — and far as I'm concerned, that's how it's going to stay. Those two witches give me a pain in the posterior, the things they say about Miss S." — Brinton had the grace to blush, but Mel was too busy talking to take any notice — "and I'm not giving them the chance to say them all over the newspapers, which you can bet your bottom dollar they would, if they could. Only trust me, and I'll get busy and spread a false trail than you could even dream of, to keep my colleagues off the scent. But, in return, I want the full dope on what happens — not the confidential stuff, but the rest — and I want an exclusive, so that when this case is solved, with or without Miss S.'s help, it's my byline that heads the story and the front page of the *Negative* that prints it. Have we got a deal?" And once more her eyes drifted to the calendar on the wall, and she frowned, as if in silent calculation.

"Blackmail," muttered Brinton, but his heart wasn't in it. He knew when he was beaten: hadn't he had dealings with Amelita Forby on previous occasions? And Foxon (though it pained him to admit it) had a point. The Oracle did seem to think very highly of the young woman; said she always played fair. Could be that the right sort of publicity (and, heaven knew, they'd be getting plenty of the wrong sort once other reporters put two and two together the way Mel had done — he supposed they should think themselves lucky she'd been the first) might just help break the dead-lock in this case if orthodox methods failed: *What were you doing a year ago?* stories could jog a witness's memory when routine investigation didn't . . .

"We've got a deal," decided Superintendent Brinton, and Mel rewarded him with her most dazzling smile, while Detective Constable Foxon chuckled into his hand-kerchief. If it had been anyone else, he'd never have believed it — but he'd seen Mel in action before. Old Brimstone was a tougher nut than most, but she'd managed to crack his shell . . .

"Nuts!" exploded the detective constable, laughing all the more; while the reporter and the superintendent regarded first Foxon, and then each other, in a puzzled silence.

Chapter 11

Thus had it come about that Saturday morning found Plummergen waiting in vain for a journalistic invasion. Hopes were raised when it became known that Amelita Forby of the *Daily Negative* had booked a room — her usual, as part-time receptionist/waitress Maureen remarked with a yawn — in the George and Dragon; but Mel's arrival late the previous evening proved, next day, to have heralded a false dawn: the lone Forby swallow did not make a Fleet Street summer. The grapevine soon reported that Mel had hired a self-drive car from Crabbe's Garage — and that she had driven, disappointingly, out of Plummergen soon after breaking her fast without even (the grapevine fermented wildly at this) stopping off first to visit Miss Seeton, long known to be one of her cronies.

Nothing was seen of Mel for the rest of the day. There were a few irritable twitches of the Lilikot curtains, but no firm sighting of the Nuts, whose absence from the scene was sadly missed. Without their inspiration, how was Plummergen to enjoy itself properly as, failing the excitement of media interest, it pondered the behaviour of certain of its citizens? The Buzzard, for one . . .

The Admiral, realising with relief that his chivalrous precautions had been in vain, grew tired of unnecessary gardening, and retreated around the back of Ararat Cottage to inform his bees (as the wise apiarist will always do) of what had occurred, thereafter to dig his vegetable patch until the sun was comfortably over the yardarm and he could splice a welcome mainbrace. The grapevine speculated with enthusiasm as to what had been the purpose of his apparent watching brief, but could reach no satisfactory conclusion, save that there was definitely something odd about his behaviour. Hadn't he exchanged secret signals with Miss Seeton when she'd gone up The Street around eleven o'clock? What more proof did anyone need that the pair of them were up to no good? And with the Nuts, usually so quick to have an answer for everything, in hiding as they were . . .

Miss Seeton had spent a peaceful Saturday going about her normal routine. After washing the breakfast dishes, she dusted the most obvious shelves and a few corners Martha, still worried about her

156

cousin Beryl's boy Barry, seemed to have missed. She penned a letter to her bank manager while drinking a mid-morning coffee, which reminded her that she was running low. Having slipped the letter in the box, she popped into the post office for a jar of rich roasted instant and a packet of chocolate biscuits. Admiral Leighton was hoeing weeds as she emerged into the sunshine, and looked across to wave and smile; Miss Seeton, also smiling, waved back. She greeted other friends and acquaintances as she trotted back home to her own garden, and spoke to still more once she was busy among the flower beds and borders, tidying virtuously.

Such virtue was to receive its due reward. As the hour for afternoon tea approached, Miss Seeton (who had temporarily raised hopes of a Nut-like retreat by vanishing in doors around the middle of the day, only to dash them when she reappeared three-quarters of an hour later after lunch) gathered up fork, trowel, and rubbish bag, and disappeared once more. Behind the high brick wall of the back garden, nobody could see what she was doing (she was, in fact, oiling her tools and putting them away in the shed) and impossible suggestions were made; but, half an hour afterwards, everybody could see her clearly as she came out of the cottage with her umbrella (the gold one!) over her arm and, having locked the door, trotted down the front path. Plummergen held its breath: was she on her way to who-knew-what goings-on at the Admiral's house — perhaps even in London? Miss Seeton, unaware of scrutiny, passed through her gate — Plummergen held its breath — and turned left up Marsh Road in the direction of Rytham Hall. Breath was let out in deep sighs of disappointment. Even on top form, the village was unable to impart sinister connotations to a teatime visit to the home of Sir George and Lady Colveden.

Nigel's mother, her eyes sparkling, met her guest halfway down the drive. "Miss Seeton! I'm so glad you could come." She stifled a giggle, and lowered her voice. "It's in the sitting room, you know, with George desperately trying to pretend he's just checking the aerial's tuned in properly, or whatever you're meant to do. I must warn you, though, he's been checking for an awfully long time — and there isn't even a cricket match on . . . ."

Miss Seeton's eyes sparkled in sympathy as she followed her hostess into the hall and set her umbrella carefully in the stand beside the carved mahogany chest. "Children, of course," murmured Miss Seeton, as electric voices wafted at considerable volume from an open door, "are much the same, until the novelty wears off. With a new toy, I mean — not," in sudden dismay at the possible implications of this casual remark, "that a television set could ever be called a *toy*. And Sir George is certainly — I intended no disrespect, I assure you — far from being in his second childhood. Quite the opposite, in many ways — one might almost say educational. So very many interesting wildlife and nature series, are there not? And far better suited to the greater detail afforded by colour — and one would not be so capable a magistrate if one was. Than black and white, that is. Children — young people — sometimes a little lacking in judgement, perhaps." Her thoughts turned briefly to Martha's second cousin Barry, and his desire to be a pop singer. "Such strong feelings, you see — one could almost say *they* were black and white, as well — and imparting a . . . a bias to one's point of view, which must, of course, in a magistrate be impartial. The point of view," said Miss Seeton earnestly, "is really most important. Most. Which I

159

feel sure he is, reading in the local newspaper some of the cases with which he is obliged to deal — impartial, I mean. Dear Sir George," she paid compliment, "is a man of extremely sound judgement, and fair-minded as well, if I may say so. Entirely without bias. Travel programmes, you know, and art, and historical documentaries — so much clearer than in black and white, though I must confess," with a slight blush, "to a fondness for the older films, which were black and white in any case. It is pleasant to see them again as one saw them first in the cinema, in the comfort of one's own home."

Miss Seeton smiled to herself as memories of her London life came drifting back. Art college first; then teaching, once the sad realisation had been made that one's talent showed few signs of (she blushed again) the genius for which one had hoped — and as one's friends had hoped, for themselves. Some of whom possessed it, and some of whom, sadly, had not. But it had been, nevertheless, a happy time, on the whole, for Emily Dorothea Seeton: youth, ambition, common purpose shared . . . although how much in common she'd really had, even among so many with similar aims and abilities, it had been (she now recalled) a surprise to discover. Rather less than she would, thinking about it, have expected — except, of course, that everyone else had been so much more talented than oneself. But one might have supposed — indeed, one had hoped — to find in so congenial an environment a multitude of kindred spirits — when even in one's own home there had always been the feeling . . . what was the modern phrase which seemed to describe so well the way it had been? Miss Seeton, oblivious to Lady Colveden waiting to usher her into the sitting room, frowned in thought.

She smiled. "On a different wavelength," she said, with a decided nod. Lady Colveden smiled back.

"Don't worry, it will be, once I've had a word with him — or at least at a different setting. Quieter," slipping a casual hand under her friend's elbow and directing her gently televisionwards. Left to herself, she knew, Miss Seeton was perfectly capable of daydreaming (or whatever she'd been doing) by the umbrella stand for hours; and she must, poor thing, be thirsty after her walk.

"We'll go and chivvy George," she said, "and he can show you which buttons to press and so on while I make the tea. I would have liked your opinion of my borders afterwards, but I suppose we'll have to have supper early. Nigel will be furious if he's shown in close-up and we tell him tomorrow morning we missed him while everyone else's parents had a grandstand view. George!" as they entered the sitting room and found it filled with a flickering, multicoloured glow. "Here's Miss Seeton come for tea, and to watch her umbrella being broadcast to the nation . . ."

At the appointed hour, the colour television was switched back on, Lady Colveden having insisted it should be silenced during supper, when nobody was going to be in the room watching it, were they, George? To which her husband responded with a harrumph that he supposed they weren't. Bally contraption could take over your life if you let it . . .

In gleeful anticipation, Lady Colveden and Miss Seeton arranged themselves in comfortable armchairs, with the *Radio Times* between them on a low table, open at the page for Saturday evening. Sir George, bursting with importance, plugged in the television, switched it on, and tuned it to the correct channel. With a low crackle and a rapidly expanding point of light, the screen came to life.

". . . interval," said the invisible announcer, as the camera panned slowly round a sea of distant faces, and the microphones picked up a rhythmic chanting. "Any minute now, the conductor, Sir Stanford Rivers, will put the Promenaders out of their misery — although I really can't remember when I've seen a less miserable crowd than we have here tonight — I should say, he'll put an end to their waiting and respond to these repeated calls for his presence by mounting the podium for the second half of the Last Night of the Proms — the Sir Henry Wood Promenade Concerts. And here," as the camera showed a marble head-and-shoulders bust, "we see Sir Henry himself, complete with laurel wreath. This wreath is given in memory of Sir Henry every year by the Promenaders and, after the Last Night, is laid on his tomb, in the Musicians' Chapel of the Church of the Holy Sepulchre — which, for the benefit of those who have just joined us on the international relay, is near the Old Bailey, of which you may have heard. On behalf of the BBC and the Royal Albert Hall, I'd like to welcome all our overseas listeners. Tonight's concert is being broadcast to more than one hundred million people throughout — ah!"

He fell silent as the rhythmic chanting, now recogniseable as good-humoured singsong yells for "Stan-ford! Stan-ford!" suddenly gave way to an eruption of cheers, whistles, horn blasts (impossible to tell from the camera shot whether Nigel was among the blasters), and bursting balloons as the unmistakeable form of Sir Stanford Rivers, stately, white-haired, a carnation in the buttonhole of his evening dress — a *red* carnation, noted Miss Seeton with pleasure, while Lady Colveden's lovely eyes gleamed — made its unhurried way to the podium. As the conductor stepped up, the roar of the crowd redoubled; the camera, zooming in for a quick shot of Sir Stanford's unique and austere half-smile, stayed focussed on his right hand. Instead of reaching for the waiting baton, the hand was raised in a brief wave of acknowledgement. Louder, more incoherent cheers. The waving hand was lowered. Sir Stanford's distinctive eyebrows arched in surprise at the tumultuous welcome; his noble head bent half an inch in further acknowledgement — and a streamer uncoiled its way from the riotous Promenaders on the floor of the hall to wind itself about Sir Stanford's ramrod shoulders.

The world famous eyebrows arched still

higher. With a frown, the conductor plucked the streamer from his immaculate black piping, regarding it in silence for a moment. He turned to face the seething arena just a few feet below. A hush fell upon the Promenaders as he cleared his throat.

"This," said Sir Stanford, "is nothing less than an insult." The streamer hung limply from the pale, sensitive fingers which could coax, even the sternest critics agreed, rhythm and melody from a comb-and-paper orchestra. "This — for a man of my — not to indulge in ridiculous false modesty — eminence! A paper streamer! I should have thought the very least I could expect would be two!"

He turned just in time towards the grinning orchestra: the subsequent rain of streamers, had it fallen across his face, would have blocked out the slightest view of the sheet music on the stand in front of him, let alone the musicians he was supposed to be conducting. Within seconds, as tootling horns and waving flags accompanied this paper rain, the stark black of the conductor's tailcoat had disappeared beneath a swirling, rustling, ever-growing effervescent cascade of pastel curls.

"Looks just," said Sir George, "like a paper sheep, dammit, been dyed instead of dipped. Feller must be mad."

"This is the third year running," came the announcer's voice, as Sir Stanford raised his baton and the Promenaders at once subsided, "that the Last Night has been conducted by Sir Stanford Rivers. He has chosen to start the second half of this year's concert with Walton's *Facade* Suite . . ."

"Three years running!" snorted Sir George, who would, if given the chance, have loved to play a leading part in the traditional festivities and fun. "Mad — look at him, poor devil! Wonder he can stand up under the weight of it all."

"He'll manage — he always does, doesn't he? Anyway, it looks as if it's more of a hindrance than actually heavy," said Lady Colveden, with a sideways smile for Miss Seeton. Miss Seeton twinkled back at her hostess. They both understood well what emotion had prompted the general's remarks, for they had fond memories of the glee with which Sir George — loudly protesting that he'd only made such an exhibition of himself out of public duty — had taken the star role in the recent Plummergen Cricket Pavilion Fund Auction. In Edwardian evening dress, twirling the waxed moustache he'd deliberately al-

lowed to grow beyond its normal restrained toothbrush length, Sir George,
with Nigel beside him in borrowed overalls
as the holder-upper, had pushed the bid-
ding twice as high as anyone had ever
dreamed it could go . . . and the builders
had begun work the following Monday.

"He seems to be coping admirably," said
Lady Colveden. The movement of the conductor's arms as he led the Fanfare sent
ripples through the festoons of streamers,
which started to slither from his energetic
form to the floor. The camera zoomed in
again, this time towards the black patent-
leather feet which were beginning to disappear in a tumult of paper foam.

"Venus, of course," announced Miss
Seeton, as the Fanfare changed to the
Scotch Rhapsody. "I was wondering, you
see, of whom Sir Stanford reminded me,"
as Sir George and his wife turned politely
to their guest. Sir George looked away
with a choking sound; Lady Colveden
smiled — she couldn't for worlds have
spoken — a question. "Botticelli," Miss
Seeton absently explained, her eyes once
more upon the television screen. Sir
George blinked. Was the little woman
going off her head? Goddesses one
minute, cheese the next: perhaps she'd

been overdoing the sunshine . . .

"Or, rather," said Miss Seeton, "I suppose I should have said *of what*. Anadyomene, you see — rising from the waves."

It was fortunate for the Colvedens' composure that they had no time to find a suitable reply, for the camera, which had swung from Sir Stanford's feet to pan round various members of the BBC Symphony Orchestra, now switched to the main arena, crowded with eager Promenaders. In Rytham Hall, as in homes throughout the country, viewers fell silent with the effort of seeking out well-known faces among the throng.

There was a young man wearing a blue-and-white striped shirt, a scarlet bow tie, and a white top hat crowned with a large pink plastic pig. Two girls had dressed their long hair in a myriad plaits, interlaced with red, white, and blue beads which clattered gently in time to the tango rhythm. A banner with *Proms for Ever!* emblazoned in spangles of patriotic hue waved frantically as those carrying it caught sight of themselves on a nearby monitor.

"No sign of Nigel yet," said Lady Colveden, with a sigh. "Or of any of them, though in such a crowd I doubt if . . ."

A balloon popped; a throat was cleared; the orchestra went into the Yodelling Song. From the Promenaders, not a sound that was not accidental: true audience participation would come later on. Sir Stanford Rivers conducted with his usual brilliance. Feet tapped during the Polka, a few hands clapped in time to the Tarantella — the suite *Facade* finished to a storm of applause, a riot of bugle calls and tootles, the bursting of excited balloons and the waving of red, white and blue flags. Sir Stanford, his celebrated smile as narrow as ever, bowed first to the orchestra, then to the Promenaders, who roared their applause louder still. The camera showed a young man with a toy hedgehog on the end of a bamboo pole decked with ribbons, wildly waving; just out of shot, a multicoloured circle twirled — "Nigel!" Lady Colveden leaped forward in her seat, just as Miss Seeton, her artist's quick eye caught by the sight, gave her own little cry of recognition. "I'm sure that was Nigel with your umbrella — oh! What a pity."

For the cameras had panned away again, back to Sir Stanford on his podium as, turning back to the orchestra, he raised his baton once more. Hysterical cheers from the Promenaders, who knew what was coming; then an excited silence. Even the television announcer said no more than: "Now here's what they've been waiting for — the chance to sing their hearts out . . ."

And the orchestra launched merrily into the first, familiar bars.

Chapter 12

Could there be anyone in the country who did not recognise the music? *Pom, pom, tiddle-iddle-iddle-iddle* — *pom, pom, tiddle-iddle-iddle-iddle* — then a slight rearrangement of notes, the same rhythm; another variation — the whole sequence, repeated . . .

The camera showed the hedgehog again, jigging up and down in time to the *dah-diddle-dah-diddle-dah-dah-dah pom* of the middle section of Elgar's "Pomp and Circumstance." *Dah-diddle-dah-diddle-dah-dah-dah pom Pom Pom Pom Pom Pom Pom Pommm* — a swirl of notes, the lead-in repeated, the glorious tune itself, played unaccompanied by no more than the quiet coughs from six thousand throats, clearing in anticipation.

Sir Stanford, the orchestra, redoubling their efforts in a swirling crescendo of notes. A stab of the baton — *You're on your own* — a quick spin round to face the arena — a toss of the white locks as a streamer fell from above . . .

"Land of Hope and Glory, Mother of

the Free," sang six thousand voices from the television screen. "How shall we extol thee who are born of thee?" Sir George squared his shoulders, a martial light in his eye. "Wider still and wider shall thy bounds be set; God, who made thee mighty, make thee mightier yet." Lady Colveden was humming to herself; Miss Seeton had a smile on her lips. "God, who made thee mighty, make thee mightier yet!"

Uproarious waving of flags as Sir Stanford nodded a curt approval of his ramshackle choir's efforts, then relative quiet as his attention returned to the orchestra. Elgar's musical spell — the composer had boasted that he'd found "a tune that will knock 'em flat, knock 'em flat!" — continued to hold. Miss Seeton sighed.

"A sad dereliction of duty, I fear," she said, above the quieter section of the march. "I remember it all so well."

Neither Sir George nor Lady Colveden knew quite what to say, and so said nothing. The camera swooped past the high-rise hedgehog to zoom in on a young man in the arena conducting the orchestra with a closed umbrella —

"It *is* Nigel!" Excitement filled the sitting room of Rytham Hall. "Oh," cried Lady

Colveden, "why doesn't someone invent a tape recorder for television? He'd be thrilled to be able to watch himself afterwards . . ."

Nobody answered as the final chords and trills led into the reprise of "Land of Hope and Glory." Sir Stanford's baton coaxed yet more sound from the roaring chorus; Nigel with Miss Seeton's umbrella encouraged his friends. A pretty, pink-cheeked girl beside him wore a red, white, and blue blouse. Obviously longing to dance with excitement, she was prevented by the press of bodies. Pinioned by Promenaders, she waved a hunting horn instead.

"Isn't that Heather?" Lady Colveden glanced at her husband, who had coughed. "Yes, it is — and I'm sure that's Linda and Ray behind her, though with those funny hats on it isn't easy to —"

". . . make thee mightier yet!" entreated the voices from the Royal Albert Hall, and the orchestra was almost drowned out in the closing bars as the Promenaders prepared to signal their approval of proceedings so far. The conductor bowed, his head inclined no more than an inch; but it was enough. Streamers fell thick and fast, bugles blew, Nigel in the background opened the umbrella and twirled it with enthusiasm above the heads of his near neighbours.

As the camera at last focussed on other revellers, Miss Seeton said: "I was teaching in London, you know. A small party of us felt so distressed by events — such weak, foolish self-indulgence from one who was supposed to set the highest example — that we visited a variety theatre to cheer ourselves up. The Holborn Empire, as I recall." She sighed, and shook her head. "It was bombed during the war — but when the programme was over, the house manager came on stage and said that, because nobody had any idea what was going to happen, instead of 'God Save the King' we would sing 'Land of Hope and Glory.' I still believe I have never heard it sung with such feeling as during the Abdication . . ."

Her final words were overpowered by resounding applause from the Promenaders. Sir Stanford had succumbed — as Last Night conductors always did — to their wish, and was now instructing the orchestra in their second rendition of "Land of Hope and Glory." "Why, how very interesting, Miss Seeton," said Lady Colveden, when the cheers and shouts had once more died away. "That's a story I've never heard anyone tell before — though I suppose nobody would know about it unless they'd been there, would they? And the chances of meeting one person who'd been in that particular theatre on one particular night — unless, of course, everyone did it every night during the crisis —"

Sir George emitted a snort of disgust as he muttered of dereliction of duty, by Gad. Miss Seeton was absolutely right — chap should have been setting an example rather than chasing off like that after some — harrumph! He begged the ladies' pardon. Forgot himself. Better listen to the music and keep a lookout for Nigel.

Sir George's son and heir did not appear on screen again for some time. Sir Stanford, swayed by the Promenaders' exuberance, agreed, unlike many conductors, to a second encore of Elgar's stirring march before, firmly shaking his head when begged for a third, he brought in the trombones at the start of the ballet music from Holst's *Perfect Fool.* The delight with which the audience received this was evident from the number of camera close-ups that followed. Mascots, banners, crazy costumes, smiling faces: the party atmosphere radiated from everyone to warm the heart of all who watched.

The final notes from the *cor anglais,* and once more the audience leaped up and down, waved, whistled, shouted, and stamped. Sir Stanford bowed again. A balloon loudly burst. A wave of laughter when the conductor pointed his baton sternly in the direction of the noise.

"Ah, yes, now that reminds me." He placed a slim white finger to his lips. "In the piece which follows, some of you may recall that a rather nice little fiddle solo introduces the Sailors' Hornpipe. This year, you know, I should so much like to hear it . . ."

A gale of laughter was followed by cheers, whistles, and then an expectant hush as the trumpets prepared to give tongue. The television voice announced that the fanfare heralded Sir Henry Wood's *Fantasia on British Sea-Songs*, an all-time Prom Concert favourite. "Could do with the Buzzard," remarked Sir George, as the bugle calls rang out. "Tell us what they all were, no doubt of it. Different from the Army."

The rolling sea-rhythms of "The Anchor's Weighed," the euphonium's bouncing jollity in "Saucy Arethusa," the cello's lament for poor Tom Bowling, darling of the crew; a stir among the waiting listeners as the first high notes of the violin sounded "The Sailor's Hornpipe." Despite the earlier warning, hands began to clap in time, feet to stamp. Sir Stanford, spinning round, continued to conduct the orchestra with the baton behind his back, ignoring the gales of laughter which greeted this impressive display. He shook his head at the Promenaders, and gesticulated again for silence. More laughter was drowned out by the frantic shushings which followed his command, and he stared grimly out over the seething arena for a few moments, still conducting, before turning back to the orchestra.

"Never missed a beat," marvelled Sir George. "Clever chap, Rivers — enters into the spirit of the thing remarkably well, considering he always looks so dashed fed-up with life. Good gimmick, I suppose."

"I'm sure it is," said his wife, as Miss Seeton's feet tapped on the floor in sympathy with the youngsters in the body of the hall. "They do seem to like him, don't they?" as the screen showed a banner with *Stanford is Top of the Pops* painted on it.

The flutes and piccolos danced their merry way through the variations on the hornpipe theme, until the moment when the conductor abandoned his orchestra yet again and invited the Promenaders to join in as they chose. He still barely smiled, but his amusement was plain as those who accepted the invitation — almost everyone there — suddenly realised that he had sneakily increased the tempo. The resultant chaos of clapping and stamping had the television announcer beside himself with glee as he explained Sir Stanford's joke for any viewers too tuneless to observe it for themselves.

The hornpipe encore was taken even faster, Sir Stanford having remarked, in an audible aside to the first violin, that a little more rehearsal was required. Nigel, his horrified mother's eyes upon him, in his excitement dropped Miss Seeton's umbrella, and ducked hurriedly out of sight to retrieve it before it should be trodden on.

"Oh!" cried Lady Colveden, as a young man with a red, white, and blue visage was thus revealed. "How very clever of Clive — at least, I *think* that's who it is. Was," she amended, as Nigel reappeared, red-faced from stooping, with his booty, and the young man was once more hidden from view. "A Union Jack. I wonder if they do them for themselves in a mirror, or whether they have to ask anyone else to help?"

"I should imagine," remarked Miss Seeton, as the trombones played the opening bars of "Spanish Ladies," "they would ask somebody else, as one usually does, with stage makeup. At least, that is what happened at school — plays, and pantomimes, and so on. It always struck me as a little odd, for one would have supposed modern girls to be far more used to makeup than their teachers — though possibly the greasepaint is more difficult to apply."

Lady Colveden regarded her guest with interest. "Were you involved in many school plays, Miss Seeton? Or," deceptively casual, "pantomimes?"

"Tableaux, too," said Miss Seeton, in all innocence, with a nod. "It was Mrs. Benn's belief, you see, that self-display of a modest nature, while still at school, would be of assistance to the girls in later life. Helping those who lacked confidence to develop it, that is, and encouraging those who already had it to learn how to moderate the quality to an acceptable level. And those who had insufficient talent for acting would benefit from having learned the habits of cooperation and teamwork — painting scenery, making costumes and props . . ."

"Spanish Ladies" ended; rippling clarinet notes heralded the oboe's song of

"Home, Sweet Home." The camera showed another painted face, this time of a young girl, whose companion had a similar flag pasted round his stovepipe hat. With the rest of the Promenaders, they began to sway and hum in time to the music.

Sir George, unlike Miss Seeton, was very well aware of the direction in which his wife's apparently casual remarks were leading. Rather naughty of Meg — little woman was a guest, after all. At a disadvantage. Hardly fair to bulldoze her into running the Christmas panto before she had time to know what she was doing. Best come to the rescue.

"Ah — not Jack, y'know," he said, as Lady Colveden was congratulating herself on her cunning and preparing to move in for the kill. "The Buzzard told me. So sorry, m'dear." There was a decided twinkle in his eye. Was the apology for having foiled her plan to co-opt Miss Seeton into the Pantomime Committee (it was obvious which side of the family had given Nigel his Galahad instinct) or for having talked apparent nonsense through the middle of "See, the Conquering Hero Comes"? Just how pervasive (Lady Colveden brooded briefly) was the influence of Miss Seeton's idiosyncratic thought processes?

"Asked him if Nigel could borrow it, remember," Sir George continued, as his wife regarded him warily. "Pulled me up sharpish — not a Jack, he said. Not unless it's flown on board ship. Smaller than an ensign," he added, as the conquering hero finally arrived, and the audience broke into loud applause. "Union Flag," explained Sir George vaguely, his eyes turning back to the television screen. "Something to do with a staff-flag, not Jack . . ."

Neither of the ladies knew quite how to respond to this information, and in any case had no time, for down from his podium stepped the stately figure of Sir Stanford Rivers, with a bow for the orchestra and a wave of acknowledgement to the frantic Promenaders as he disappeared in the direction from which he had made his first entrance.

The announcer's voice spoke above the roar which filled the sitting room of Rytham Hall. "And now the conductor has left his post to escort Dame Lavinia Sheering into the hall for that great favourite, 'Rule, Britannia,' in which she will sing the solo verses. And here she comes — yes, just listen to that welcome!" He had almost to shout to make himself heard above the noise. "My goodness! No wonder they're so pleased to see Dame Lavinia tonight," as the camera picked out the two figures of Sir Stanford Rivers, still in evening dress, and the renowned soprano attired in a fashion to lift the spirits of all who saw her.

"Britannia in person!" exclaimed the announcer, as the camera focussed lovingly on Dame Lavinia's white gown with its red and blue ribbons, on the glittering round shield and gleaming trident she carried in either hand, on the shining helmet which crowned her flowing raven locks. "This is certainly the first time I can recall that we've had a Britannia in full costume . . ."

As the conductor's baton was raised to summon the orchestra to attention, the camera moved from Lavinia Sheering's patriotic form to scan the faces of the Promenade audience. Every Union Flag in London, it seemed, was being waved or worn in the Royal Albert Hall as the first bars of Arne's well-known music led into the solo singing of James Thomson's words.

"When Britain fi-i-i-i-irst at Heaven's command," sang Dame Lavinia Sheering, the trident proud in her upraised hand. "Aro-o-o-o-o-o-o-o-ose from out the a-a-a-azure main — Arose, arose, arose from out the azure main!" She tossed her head, and the long black hair rippled on her shoulders. "This was the Charter, the Charter of the Land, And Guardian Angels sang this strain:"

Sir Stanford, spinning round, abandoned the orchestra to its own devices as he conducted the rapturous crowd of Promenaders in the chorus. "Rule, Britannia! Britannia, rule the waves! Britons never, never, never shall be slaves!"

Three more verses followed, during which Nigel and his friends were picked out again, lustily singing. Heather was busily conducting with the hunting horn, Nigel with Miss Seeton's furled umbrella, expending vast amounts of energy. The sitting room of Rytham Hall rang with sudden cries of delight as, while the soprano sang of "manly hearts to guard the fair," Nigel's beaming face was shown in close-up. Sir George blew his nose, and coughed. Lady Colveden, worried about obvious doting, remarked in a deliberate tone that yes, she was sure now that was his friend Clive standing just behind her son, with the flag or jack or whatever it was painted so cleverly on his face . . .

Miss Seeton was neither dishonest, nor deceived. With a sigh of pleasure as the camera moved away at last, she said: "You are right to be so proud of dear Nigel. He has a manly heart indeed — gentlemanly, one might almost say, except, of course, that it would be an impertinence to say it." This, she realised, did not sound quite right. "Because what else could one expect, in the circumstances? With such a happy family life — such a fine example before him — it would be no less than an insult, surely, to suggest even the least surprise . . ."

Miss Seeton floundered to a halt as her hosts both blushed for the compliment; and herself blushed as she wondered whether she had spoken out of turn. The excitement of the evening must excuse her, she thought, as "Rule, Britannia" went into an encore. Her umbrella on television — *colour* television — the stirring songs, the uplifted spirits of all who watched . . .

"Jerusalem" still to come, with its vivid imagery and, as one could not help remembering, always the strange drawings and pictures of Blake in the background of one's mind when one heard the words. Were they indeed a plea for social reform, or had the poet a more physical vision in mind when he wrote of "arrows of desire" and of "clouds unfolding to spears?" One could not study, or teach art for any length of time without realising that truly inspired artists had a rather more unorthodox attitude to certain aspects of life than one would wish for in one's pupils . . .

"Free love," said Miss Seeton, as the second chorus of the encore died away. "Or," as Sir George and Lady Colveden turned startled eyes upon their guest, "education — and the giant compasses, of course. Votes for Women, and Swedenborg — measuring out the world . . ."

And while the Promenaders sang of feet in ancient time walking on mountains with the Lamb of God in England's green and pleasant land, Miss Seeton mused on William Blake's remarkable gifts, and across the faces of Nigel, and Heather, and their Young Farmer friends saw a dark shadow fall, as of dark Satanic mills; and instead of waving bugles and umbrellas, she saw a hundred sleepless swords.

Chapter 13

"Just carry on as if I'm part of the furniture, boys," said Mel Forby, with her most brilliant smile. While most of the nation looked forward to watching the Last Night of the Proms, Brinton and his team pressed on with their investigations into the second Blonde in the Bag murder — the team in question having increased in number by one, albeit unofficial, member. "You just carry on — and," with another smile, "who knows? If I hang around long enough drinking in the atmosphere, I might just come up with some new angle that solves the case for you — and I don't necessarily mean Miss S.," she added, in deference to Brinton's indrawn breath and purpling face. She suppressed a chuckle at Foxon's startled look. "Mind you, I can't deny it would be kind of nice to scoop another Battling Brolly case before the rest of Fleet Street caught on — but even with no Miss Seeton, you could find a woman's instinct comes in handy." She ignored the superintendent's muttered oath. "Didn't I work out the connection with last year's case when nobody else has? Press morgues or no press morgues — not that they won't catch on pretty quickly, I'd say, but right now we're ahead of the pack — which is where I want to stay. And I've been giving it some thought since I first heard the news, you know."

"So," said Brinton heavily, "have we. The police aren't the complete idiots the newspapers make us look, Miss Forby. This heap of files isn't just for show."

"It's a pretty thick heap." Mel gazed at the pile of bulging folders whose contents, she knew, had been Brinton's especial study since the body was discovered. "Impressive. Shows how hard you've been beavering in the archives, all right — only . . . don't take this the wrong way, Mr. Brinton. I'm not for a minute suggesting you're an idiot. But perhaps you've kind of missed seeing the wood for the trees? You're too, well, close to what's happened — maybe if you were one step removed, you could see —"

"I'm a copper, Miss Forby," interrupted Brinton, thumping the pile of reports with an irritated fist. "Are you trying to tell me I'm no good at my job because I'm too . . . too emotionally involved, or some other trick-cyclist claptrap like that? Lacking in judgement? Not professionally detached?

Because if you are, I'd call that a —"

"No, I'm not!" Mel could break into a conversational flow with as much abruptness as Brinton, when she saw the need. "You're doing a grand job — you always do, as everyone knows. But so do I, and everyone knows that, too. I've made this area of Kent my particular pigeon over the past few years, what with Plummergen Pieces and assorted articles on Local Crafts, and Kentish Customs, and History — and," with slow emphasis, "Farming . . ."

Mel's tone made Foxon sit up and Brinton swallow the irate reply he'd been about to unleash. Her shrewd look reminded the detectives that the young reporter wasn't just a pretty face: didn't Scotland Yard's own Oracle think highly of her? "So, Miss Forby," remarked the superintendent, as Mel continued to regard him with that bright-eyed gaze. "What do you think you know about — farming — that all of us seem to have missed?"

Mel smiled, and leaned back in her chair, folding her arms as she shot a triumphant look at her unwilling host. "Hops," she said. "Or rather, hop pickers. If you're looking for someone who was around this place a year ago, who hasn't been in evidence again until now . . ."

Foxon uttered a muffled exclamation; Brinton simply stared. Mel, pleased with the effect she'd created, added thoughtfully: "You know, it could just be worth checking on the coppers' grapevine if anybody else has had the same sort of thing happen on their patch during the last twelve months, and hushed it up for some strange reason." Then she grinned. "Still, if I'm right about the hop-picking connection, Scotland Yard are the logical ones to investigate other Blondes in Bags — and as far as I know they haven't had any. There's not very much that goes on around Town I don't hear about, one way or another . . ."

Brinton found his voice at last. "Foxon, get me Detective Chief Superintendent Delphick on the blower, will you?" He nodded his astonished thanks to Mel. "Could be I've misjudged you, Miss Forby. If the Yard *have* got anything like this on their books and haven't told us . . ."

As Foxon asked for an outside line, Mel sighed. "Remember, it's a pretty long shot, Mr. Brinton — though it's certainly worth a try. But you know the Oracle, and how he always plays fair. Would he really sit on a story like this, when he could never be sure I wouldn't be after him to spill the beans at the very first hint of a scoop? I'd have his guts for garters if he tried to pull a stunt like —"

At Brinton's sudden gesture, she stopped speaking, looking on with interest as he picked up the telephone from his desk in response to Foxon's signal. "Oracle? Chris Brinton here . . . Yes, up to my eyes. You must have heard our latest . . . Yes, poor kid. A regular nasty mess — which is why I'm calling. It's what you might call a pretty long shot." He winked at Mel. "Suggested, I might tell you, by a friend of yours who waltzed in here without so much as a by-your-leave and made herself very much at home — and who'd like to be remembered to you, I dare say," as Mel made a face. "Guessed it in one!" Brinton grinned, holding out the receiver so that Mel could hear the burst of tinny laughter echoing down the line. She blew a cheerful kiss towards the telephone, and smothered a giggle as the superintendent looked shocked. He became serious all at once. "Now, listen, Oracle, our mutual friend Miss Forby harbours deep suspicions of you and your pals in the Smoke . . . Yes, I know, but she could just have a point, so I thought it was worth checking . . ."

Five minutes later, Mel was apologizing for having wasted police time, hoping Mr.

Brinton wouldn't back out of the bargain they'd made because she'd guessed wrong. She'd said all along, she reminded him, that it was unlikely —

"But you're right, it had to be checked," Brinton told her cheerfully, "so no real harm done. And it doesn't mean that you were wrong the whole way through — why *shouldn't* our chummie be one of these hop pickers? Maybe he only goes doolally when he's off his own territory, so to speak."

Foxon cleared his throat. "Could be there's something in the air, sir, that makes him go peculiar. When you think how many, well, odd types there are within a fifteen-mile radius of here —"

"Shuttup, Foxon!" Brinton, with a new trail to pursue, was almost his old self again. "I've warned you before about winding me up with talk of a certain re-tired art teacher and her assorted friends . . . and enemies," he found himself add-ing, as he mused on the oddness of the Nuts as well as on his blood pressure.

"Sorry, sir," chirped Foxon, who had ig-nored the rebuke as he rummaged through his own files. "If Mel — Miss Forby," as Brinton shot him a blistering look, "is right, and chummie *is* one of the hopping lot, then with the description those three

191

witnesses gave we might be able to pull him in for questioning, at least."

"*If* she's right," said Brinton. "And if the witnesses were right, too. From the statements, I admit it *sounds* as if it was the girl they saw — but when these youngsters are all dressed up, their mothers couldn't necessarily be sure it was them, in a crowd. And as for the bloke they think she was with . . ." He retrieved his copies of the witness statements from the files, hesitated, glanced at Mel — who favoured him with her most wide-eyed, entreating gaze — and read aloud:

"Twentyish, jeans, wavy brown hair, athletic build . . . Middle to late twenties, tallish, light brown hair . . . About twenty-five, thick brown hair, slim build, casual dress . . . Could be almost anyone, dammit." He glared again at Foxon. "Could even be you, if it comes to that — depending on what they mean by *casual* dress, heaven help us all." He switched the glare from Foxon to Mel, who was stifling a snigger as she recalled her days as the *Daily Negative*'s fashion reporter. Foxon, she knew, prided himself on his appearance and sense of style: she rather admired them herself, although he had a long way, in her prejudiced eyes, to go to equal the manifold charms of Thrudd Banner.

Brinton scowled down at the witness statements, and Foxon brooded in his corner. Mel stared at the ceiling for a few thoughtful moments, waiting.

"It would be," said Brinton at last, "entirely against regulations for you to accompany us on official business, Miss Forby, whether or not the expedition might have been partly due to your own suggestion." Mel smiled sweetly at him as she continued to wait. He sighed. "You've hired a car, I suppose?"

"From Crabbe's Garage," agreed Amelita Forby at once, in her most dulcet tones. "You may know the place, Mr. Brinton — it's in Plummergen, where I'm staying for a few days."

The superintendent shuddered. Foxon, moving out of his superior's sight, shook a warning head in Mel's direction. She ignored him as she went on: "I'd thought, you know, of writing another article in my *Kent: County of Contrasts* series for the *Negative*. Contrasting modern farming methods with the old ways — seeing what's lasted through the generations, and what's given way to new technology. I thought," she said pointedly, "of starting with the hop industry — show how Kent is different from

Worcestershire. Everyone knows Kent," she assured him brightly. "Apples, cherries — hops . . . and women. Some more than others, of course . . ."

"Blackmail," groaned Brinton, shuddering again.

"Ten out of ten," said Mel, with another smile. "Amelita Forby can read a map and drive a car as well as any newshound in the country — and, right now, she's the only newshound in this particular corner of the country, remember. The others — including Banner, the Boy Wonder — have gone chasing off after red herrings . . . though I don't imagine it would take them long to work out how they'd been fooled, if anyone happened to drop the right sort of hints . . ."

Foxon, who knew Mel rather better than did Brinton, gave a choking cry at the very idea of her letting a scoop escape her for the sake of thwarting the police by allowing others to share it; but Brinton was by now so rattled that the risk of her carrying out her threat struck him as all too likely. He rolled his eyes, and clutched at his hair.

"The Oracle, lord knows why, says you're to be trusted," he said, in tones of deepest despair. "I'm damned if I'm taking you as a passenger, though — and I'm damned if you're going to be allowed to sit in on any interviews we might have with any suspects. But . . ."

"But there must be a dozen or more hop gardens within a five-mile radius of here," said Mel. "And who's to say I wouldn't find the right one before you did?" She shook her head, and frowned. "Guess it would just be put down to good old coincidence if the *Negative* splashed an exclusive interview with a selection of murder suspects all over the front page before the police had even arrived . . ."

Brinton, with one final groan, pushed back his chair and rose to his feet. "Miss Forby, I think I hate you almost as much as I hate Foxon — but it seems I'm stuck with the pair of you. And if the Oracle's got it wrong about trusting you, I'll . . . I'll . . ."

"He hasn't," Mel assured him, rising in turn from her chair. "One hundred and one per cent, that's Amelita Forby, and no kidding. So carry on, Superintendent — me and my reporter's notebook, we're right behind you!"

Hops have been farmed in Kent for hundreds of years. The quaint variety of their names is music to the ears of ale lovers: Brambling Cross, Wye Saxon, Fuggle, Janus, Golding, Bullion, and Early Bird — whose tendency to suffer from the dreaded verticillium wilt can send shivers down the spines of dedicated drinkers. Each spring, the long-established roots send up new shoots which are trained to a high framework of overhead wires from which, in summer, the strange flowers known as cones hang down. The air in a hop garden, sheltered as it is from the wind, is lush and heavy; a rich green light filters through the interlacing of hop bines above the workers' heads.

The greatest number of workers is needed in the picking season, which traditionally begins on the first of September. Before then, only skilled labour (walking on stilts is no easy task) is used to "string" the growing hops up their coir ropes to the high wire frames; to earth-up the mounds known as hills on which the vines grow; to mulch between the rows of hills with the unique mix of mattress flocking and chopped rags on which the hops thrive — and, as they thrive, to prune them back within their cage to a manageable shape.

With the coming of September comes

also the great crowd of unskilled workers who descend upon the hop gardens from London's East End. A farm worker will act as foreman to his gang of ten or a dozen Cockneys, first freeing for them the hop bines from the poles with a long rod, then watching as they strip the fruit from the vines by hand, and collect it in wicker baskets. For each bushel picked, a worker is given a token, carved wood or pressed metal: some plain, with no more than the farmer's initials or the number of bushels counted; some decorated with monograms, or with quaint emblems or scenes of country life. It is a life which has changed very little over the last hundred years . . .

"All the locals," Brinton told Mel, as they walked from his office to the police station car park, "look down on the hoppers, by and large — call 'em troublemakers and gyppos, and worse — though on the whole they're no great bother unless they've had a drop too much. And they're usually so tired after the day's work they haven't the energy to go down the pub, so most of 'em drink what they've brought with 'em, or what they can scrounge from the farmer, which means we don't have a lot to do with 'em, thank the lord, in an official capacity. They keep themselves to themselves, and we let 'em sort out their own problems unless it's anything serious — and until now," with a sigh, "I can't remember the last time there was anything serious."

"I could be wrong," said Mel, not sounding as if she believed it. Brinton sighed again, and shook his head. Now she'd made the suggestion, he was three-quarters of the way to accepting it. It made sense, after all . . .

Foxon, driving, dawdled politely until Mel had retrieved her hire car and fallen into place behind him, then gunned the engine and headed for the first of a depressingly long list of local hop gardens. Mel, her camera discreetly out of sight with her notebook, tried to look like someone who had every right to accompany the two detectives as they made their enquiries at each farm in turn, hovering just within earshot and paying close attention.

After six or seven such visits, she could have asked the questions herself — and returned the answers, too. The hoppers, it seemed, were a close-knit crowd. Not one of them had been out of sight of his comrades for more than a few minutes at the relevant times: teamwork was the order of the day. And, once the day's work was done, the teams had congregated outside their huts to enjoy a convivial supper and gossip before turning in for a well-earned night's rest — rest of a kind which could hardly be called private. Brinton heard jocular remarks about so-and-so's snores, someone else's restless waterworks, someone else's habit of talking in his sleep . . .

"I suppose," he said, as Foxon drew a despondent line under another list of names, "someone could be lying — trying to protect one of their own. It's only human nature."

Mel raised her eyebrows. "For a crime as revolting as this? No, don't answer. I can guess."

Brinton snorted. "You can't have been on the crime beat very long, Miss Forby, if you haven't realised the lengths to which some people — usually your doting wives and mothers — are prepared to go, to make excuses for their menfolk. Pretty damned feeble excuses most of them are, mind you, and they aren't the best of actors, so we tend to see through 'em without much difficulty. But I can't say I've felt that old tingle in my bones with any of the people we've talked to this afternoon, more's the pity — and then, even if the families're willing to cover up, I don't imagine any of the locals would be. She came from Murreystone, remember."

"Which is how many miles further along this road?" mused Mel, consulting the map she had now drawn from her handbag. "Not that close — but close enough to count as a local, if my guess is right. So the nearer we get with each farm, the more likely it is we'll be hearing the truth, from the full-time workers if not from the hoppers. How many more do you plan to see today?"

Brinton eyed her with interest. "Bored, Miss Forby, or just exhausted? Police work's never as interesting or glamorous as the likes of you journalists make out, and as for the people who write detective stories — well! The simple truth of it is, even in a murder case there's hours and hours of plain, plodding routine to be got through before we solve the case — if," he said, sighing, "we ever do."

Mel and Foxon looked at each other. In a snatched and private moment, the young detective had explained Brinton's reluctance to involve Miss Seeton in the current investigation. Mel had been prepared to concede that the superintendent had a point — but not much of one, she added privately. She agreed with Foxon that Miss Seeton was the last person on earth to imagine crazed knifemen pursuing her through her dreams. Although it was Mel's intention to follow Brinton on his hop-garden tour until a likely suspect presented himself, she hoped to spare a few convenient minutes to visit Sweetbriars, so close to her hotel; for Miss Seeton, she was sure, would be hurt if she found out that her friend Mel had been in Plummergen without calling on her. And if, during that call, the subject of Drawing should happen to come up in conversation — why, Mel would, of course, like a good guest, follow her hostess's lead . . . But Brinton had not yet decided to call it a day, and Amelita Forby wasn't going to be the first to give in now.

"Neither bored," said Mel, very firmly, "nor exhausted, Mr. Brinton." Once more she consulted her map. "So, where do we go next? They all look much of a muchness, to me . . ."

Indeed they did. It was not until next morning that one in particular was to etch itself permanently into the young reporter's mind: the Cana Hop Garden.

Chapter 14

With all the excitement of Saturday evening, Miss Seeton was a little surprised to find herself waking some thirty minutes before her customary hour next day. It was a day which promised well for outdoor pursuits: no clouds were in the sky, a breeze rustled the leaves of nearby trees. It would, Miss Seeton mused, be an ungrateful waste to spend too long indoors, away from this glorious sunshine, this fresh September air — air even more than usually invigorating, when one was already partway to invigoration by having arranged oneself in the *Mahamudra* . . . Miss Seeton, in her bedroom, on her tartan travelling rug, sat with her left knee bent, the heel tucked against her crotch, and with her spine curving forward so that her outstretched hands could clasp her right foot, her head could rest on her right knee — a pose which required considerable contracting of muscles and holding of breath, but for which *Yoga and Younger Every Day* promised so very much . . . And with, one was so pleased — Miss Seeton released her pent-up breath, relaxed, and reversed the pose to favour her left leg — such honesty. One almost felt no need for breakfast. It would, however, be unwise to go fasting to church — Miss Seeton allowed herself to relax again, and breathed deeply — for there was, as one knew, despite the brilliant sunshine sometimes a chill in the air so early in the morning at this time of year . . .

Early. Perhaps, if she omitted one or two of the less vital exercises, she could attend the early service rather than her more usual eleven o'clock, which would leave the rest of the day delightfully free. One could then, with a clear conscience, enjoy oneself in the eradication of weeds, the planting of yet more bulbs — Stan was there to be consulted should further problems arise — and the gentle pruning of shrubs. Perhaps, (if one's conscience permitted the indulgence) a picnic lunch under the apple tree, instead of a more formal meal indoors? With the approach of the equinox, the gradual shortening of the day became more obvious; and, with that shortening, came the as-gradual cooling of the air. One would display no more than common sense, Miss Seeton told herself as she lay in the *Shavasana* or Dead Pose and practised her rhythmic breathing, if one made the very most of such good weather as remained before winter finally arrived . . .

Autumn. One's favourite season, when leaf-fall and the dying back of the last summer flowers revealed more clearly the stark and graceful forms of nature in bare branches and lightened stems blowing freely in the wind — or, as it was today, breeze, which made gently swirling patterns of the first few drifting leaves as they danced their way down to the waiting earth . . .

All through early service, Miss Seeton daydreamed guiltily of her own waiting earth. Having duly worshipped, she smiled a greeting to her various acquaintances among the congregation, shook hands politely with the Reverend Arthur Treeves as he stood outside the porch to bid farewell and godspeed to his parishioners, and hurried home to change into gardening clothes before anything might occur to distract her from her purpose. It would have cheered her, perhaps, to know that the thoughts of the vicar had been as wayward as her own during the hymns and prayers. The Reverend Arthur was as enthusiastic a gardener as Miss Seeton, and almost as knowledgeable as Stan Bloomer: and, in his enthusiasm, had been of the same wistful opinion as his parishioner that the day was indeed remarkably fine.

As the church bells summoned Plummergen to morning prayer, Miss Seeton was once more to be found upon her knees. This time, however, she was busy with trowel and fork rather than handbag and hymnbook, grubbing happily in the well-tilled soil in her walled, sheltered garden. At the bottom of the garden, chickens pecked and squawked and sunned themselves behind the wire; wild birds sang in wind-tossed trees, their whistling a counterpoint to the pealing of the bells. Miss Seeton, lost in thoughts of ground elder and sucker shoots, let the sounds of Sunday drift about her, and smiled to herself, humming an off-key anthem.

"Oh!" As the peal fell silent, just before the clock struck eleven, the tramp of footsteps became audible above the avian chirrups and Miss Seeton's tuneless humming. A visitor, thought Miss Seeton, rising effortlessly from her knees to see who it might be coming round the side of the cottage — a visitor who knew her well enough to guess that she would be found in the back, rather than the front, garden on a

Sunday. She removed her gloves, turned, and smiled as she recognised her guest.

"Nigel! Why, this is a most unexpected visit — though welcome, of course," hastily, for fear he should feel insulted. "It is just, you see, that after so late a night, one would have supposed you all — yourself and your Young Farmer friends — to be sleeping it off. That is — oh, dear. The late night, I mean." Miss Seeton turned pink. "It would be the greatest impertinence, naturally, even to suggest that any of you had been . . . well, intoxicated."

"Only with the atmosphere," he told her, with a grin. "Talk about a night to remember — gosh, you've absolutely no idea — and as for your umbrella, it was pretty much the hit of the evening!" Nigel, who had been carrying the borrowed brolly carefully over one arm, now unfurled it and favoured its owner with a brisk twirl to express his high spirits. "Thanks awfully, Miss Seeton, for lending me this. Heather — er, everyone said it was one of the best there, and the parents tell me it made a first-class show on the box." He sighed, and twirled the umbrella again, brooding on the ribbons and bunting his mother had stitched with such care, and which she had that morning insisted her son was well able, last train home or no last train, to remove unaided before returning Miss Seeton's property in person. "Gosh, how I wish I'd been able to see it as well as be there — but of course you can't be in two places at once, can you? And it was an unforgettable experience — tiring, though," he added, stifling a yawn as he furled the umbrella prior to handing it back to its rightful owner.

"Oh, dear — Nigel, this is dreadful," exclaimed Miss Seeton, as she took the umbrella from his hand, and clicked her tongue.

Mr. Colveden blinked. "I'm awfully sorry — I thought I'd snipped all the loose stitches off," he began. "And Mother was certain she didn't tear the —"

"Oh, no," cried Miss Seeton, blushing again as she realised how her innocent remark had given so wrong an impression. "No, indeed, Lady Colveden will have taken the greatest care, I feel sure — and in any case, as we agreed when you first asked to borrow it, this is merely one of my second-best umbrellas, and what are they between friends? A few loose stitches, that is, though I cannot see," as she opened the brolly for herself, and gave it an experimental twirl, "that there are in fact any.

But for you to have woken up so early, I mean," as she closed and furled the umbrella yet again. "After coming home on the last train as your mother told me you had planned to do — and," venturing a twinkle, "having to drive your friend Heather home . . ."

Nigel grinned, and blushed in his turn before assuring Miss Seeton that farmers were used to rising with the lark, particularly in a good cause, which he couldn't help but feel the return of someone else's borrowed belongings would be considered by anyone. "Though mind you," he added, with another yawn, "late nights and early mornings mean a chap's system takes time to wake up properly. If anyone happened to be making a cup of coffee, for instance . . ."

They sat under the apple tree, and Miss Seeton offered chocolate biscuits. Nigel did not refuse the offer. Picnicking, he remarked, cheerfully munching, had been of necessity in recent weeks rather fashionable among the Young Farmers; not that, even in a good cause, he was a slavish follower of fashion — but, now it was all safely over, he'd be interested to see (in a minor sort of way) what he'd been missing by way of fun. He helped himself to a second biscuit, and absently rubbed the base of his spine.

Miss Seeton looked puzzled. "I would have thought," she ventured, "from what I have observed, that you would be far too busy for picnics at this time of year. Farmers, I mean. And from what dear Stan has told me," hastily, in case her knowledgeable guest should take offence at her apparent assumption of an expertise she most emphatically did not possess. "Stubble burning, I understand, and ploughing —"

"And taking the ewes to market," Nigel broke in rapidly, "and buying new lambs — and trying to argue a decent price for our cereal crop — not to mention clearing the ground of weeds — and drilling — oh, yes, farmers aren't short of work at this time of year, believe me. But then, is it ever any different?" He chuckled as he answered his own question. "No, it jolly well isn't, so we have to squeeze time out to enjoy ourselves whenever the chance presents itself."

"*Carpe diem,*" murmured Miss Seeton, as she pushed across the plate of biscuits so that her young friend could help himself to those on the farther side. Nigel, whose knowledge of Latin was limited to the occasional botanical name, decided it was safer to ignore her remark. He grinned, and rubbed his spine again.

"I don't mind a spot of hard work now and then, but I do object when it's my bed that's hard! My ghastly experience at boarding school left me with a taste for interior springing and decent pillows I doubt if I'll ever lose — and pavements in Town, even one night at a time and with an inflatable mattress, don't particularly appeal, strange to say." He pulled a rueful face. "Lucky not everyone felt the same way as me, or we'd never have collected enough points for Clive to be able to come with us — although," half to himself, "it might not have been such a bad thing if he hadn't. Still, I was the one who drove her home . . ."

"Pointes?" Miss Seeton brightened. "Why, I understood them to be only Promenade *Concerts,* Nigel. I had no idea there had been a ballet as well. What an interesting departure from custom. No doubt it was shown during the first half of the programme, while we were eating supper. Which ballet was it?"

Nigel stared. "Ballet? You mean gauzy white dresses and rows of dying swans?" He scratched his head, leaving a faint smear of chocolate in the wavy brown hair.

"Well, I know I'm not the most observant chap around, but I really don't remember anything like that going on last night — must have been one of the times when the others were queueing. They sort of took it in turns, once we knew Clive would be back in time to come with us — to make sure enough programmes were stamped," as Miss Seeton looked puzzled again. And no wonder, he berated himself silently. Enough to puzzle anyone, the rambling way he'd come out with his explanation. You had to admit it, there was something about the air of Sweetbriars — or, to admit the absolute truth, about its owner — that could be alarmingly infectious when it came to telling people things they didn't already know. He took a deep breath, and began again.

"You can't just turn up at the Last Night of the Proms, you see, and expect to be let in, because it's tremendously popular, and even in the Royal Albert Hall there'd never be room for everyone who wanted to attend. So there's a sort of ballot system — I'm not entirely sure of the details — for people who want to do the thing in comfort, sitting down — but for Promenaders, so long as you have your programme stamped from however-many-it-is previous concerts, they'll let you in to stand in the pit. But of course, because you don't have numbered seats, it's first come, first served for the best places, which is why some people queue on the pavement for days beforehand — except that most of us YF lot are much too busy, as you so rightly said." Nigel rubbed his spine once more. "Some crazy types think it's *fun* to sleep outside for a night or two, just to soak up the atmosphere! In fact, I believe some of our less busy members did, even though between us there were more than enough ticket stubs to squeeze an extra person in — Clive's been abroad for a year, you see. He arrived back last week" — a pucker faintly etched itself on Nigel's normally unfurrowed brow — "just in time to join the rest of the party for the Last Night, once he was over the jet lag."

"And what a delightful welcome home it must have been," said Miss Seeton, with an approving smile. "To be able, through your great kindness, to accompany so many of his friends on so pleasant an excursion. I believe, from something dear Lady Colveden said, that he was the young man with the Union, er, Flag painted on his face? From the brief glimpses I had of him, I should say it had been most carefully done."

Nigel nodded, sighing. "He sweet-talked Heather into helping him — said after a year in New Zealand he really wanted to fly the flag, but he couldn't remember what it looked like." He frowned again. "I volunteered to lend him a mirror and my old Boy Scout manual. He ignored me . . ."

Miss Seeton was used to the sufferings of Nigel in love, and knew that silent sympathy and a change of subject would be her best way to help him now. "You were telling me," she prompted, "about the ballet?"

And by the time they had unscrambled the difference between *points* and *pointes*, Nigel was almost his normal cheerful self once more.

Chapter 15

Almost, but not quite. Mr. Colveden finally departed homewards with a brave smile and repeated expressions of thanks for the loan of Miss Seeton's umbrella; but such repetition only reminded him again that, though he had indeed attended the Last Night of the Proms — and for most of the evening had been pressed encouragingly close to Heather in the crowd — he had only the fond opinions of his parents and friends that he had presented so splendid a spectacle on the television screens of the nation. One day, he said, wistfully echoing his mother's lament, someone would invent some method of photographing television broadcasts in the home, so that people could see what they looked like afterwards . . .

As Miss Seeton returned to her interrupted weeding, she found herself musing on her young friend's words. Why, she wondered, had somebody *not* invented an apparatus of the kind he described? The benefits would surely be enormous. One could photograph, for example, natural history programmes — if *photograph* was the correct terminology — which were all too often broadcast after children's normal bedtime; and could then take them to school next day — the programmes, not the children, who would naturally be there already — unless, of course, the next day should be Saturday, or Sunday — and screen them, in much the same way that Mr. Jessyp occasionally brought out the old school projector to show some of the — it had to be confessed, rather dull and scratchy now — old educational films which the children seemed so to enjoy. Which was very probably, Miss Seeton told herself with a smile, because the watching of a film was not so obtrusive a teaching method as an ordinary lesson, though certainly as worthwhile, one would have thought. Because watching a film — or a copy of a television broadcast — was bound to encourage one's pupils to look, and to see, and to remember . . .

"Art programmes, too," murmured Miss Seeton, fired by this vision of fifty eager pairs of eyes focussed on the wonders of Rembrandt, of Michaelangelo, of Leonardo; larger, perhaps, than life, so that every detail of their genius could be pointed out by one whose talent — Miss Seeton tried not to be envious, but she could not help sighing — was of a sadly lower degree. "Impertinence," scolded Miss Seeton, as she shook earth from an uprooted tuft of grass. Even daring to think of herself in such elevated company . . .

But to show to — to share with — one's pupils — to plant perhaps the very smallest seed of enthusiasm and appreciation, which one day might grow into a truly enviable gift — that, acknowledged Miss Seeton, made her task of teaching the young so rewarding. One lived forever in hopes that it would fall to one's own small lot to recognise true and budding genius, to encourage it to blossom . . .

"Genius," said Miss Seeton, addressing the rosebush about whose roots she had been grubbing as she pondered; and was somewhat surprised when the bush seemed to answer back.

"Genius? Much good it's done him if he is, dear — or anyone else, for that matter!"

Miss Seeton, glancing over her shoulder, recognised Martha Bloomer as she approached from the direction of the gate in the side wall, and rose from her knees with a smile of welcome. "Now, let me guess," she greeted her trusty servitor, ignoring the strangeness of Mrs. Bloomer's salutation. "Cabbage? They're still in excellent shape, I would think. Or carrots — or peas, perhaps — or even broad beans," more tentatively, as Martha, who had at first seemed to nod, now began shaking her head, as if the last thing in the world she planned to do was pick a single plant from the vegetable plot so lovingly tended by her husband. Miss Seeton studied her friend's appearance as she drew nearer. Martha was pink of face, and slightly breathless; her eyes were bright; her apron was twisted halfway round her waist, as if she'd started to undo the knot and then thought better of it.

"Martha, dear," said Miss Seeton. "Something seems to have upset you. Is there anything I can do to help?"

"Upset? Me? Whatever gave you cause to say that?" Mrs. Bloomer tossed her head, and tried to sound as breezy as she always did; but too late. Observing the knowing eyes of her employer upon her, she heaved a deep, shuddering sigh, and seemed to shrivel where she stood. "Well, in normal times I'd not want to bother you . . . but with everything the way it is I'm that confused I don't know if I'm coming or going, I really don't, dear. I mean — for such a thing to have happened, and the family always so respectable — and when they said poor Beryl was in hysterics, I can't honestly say I was surprised, because I'm sure I'd be hysterical, too, if it was me, and my only son took away by the police for murdering that poor girl, not to mention the other one last year — and Stan . . ." Martha broke off, fumbled in her apron pocket, sniffed, and took out a handkerchief to rub briskly at her eyes.

"Stan?" Miss Seeton, who had already uttered one little cry of dismay on hearing the word *murder*, now sounded truly horrified. "Stan has been — been murdered? Oh, Martha, no! Or" — as Martha lowered her handkerchief to stare — "or do you mean rather — surely not — that Stan has been *arrested*? But — but that is dreadful! There must be some mistake!"

Martha, after a moment's frozen silence, suddenly burst out laughing. "Mistake? I'll say there is, dear." Apart from the quiver in her voice, she sounded much more like her old self. "And it's you that's made it, bless you — cheered me up no end, you have — and don't I wish I could get you to have a word or two with poor Beryl," she added, while Miss Seeton smiled faintly, relieved that things were evidently not as bad as they had at first sounded. Then she frowned, as she tried to recall just what Martha had originally said. She felt sure there had been some mention of murder, and an arrest . . .

"And so there was, dear," Martha told her, "only with me in such a state I don't wonder you're a bit muddled. It's poor Beryl's boy Barry they've arrested — well, taken off to Ashford to help with enquiries, they said, but it all comes to the same thing, doesn't it? And Stan, when I told him who it was when I put the phone down, he said he wasn't a bit surprised, what with me saying all these years he'd end up in Queer Street — Barry, I mean. Not that I'd ever tell Beryl so to her face, understand, just how sorry I was she'd kept having such a time with him and his pop star nonsense — only so's she could let off steam in private, with no bones broken arguing with him, because when all's said and done he's her son, isn't he? Blood being thicker than water any day . . . poor Beryl." The gloom had returned to Martha's tone as she remembered. "I was so upset, hearing about it on the phone — and then Stan — I let the cabbage boil away right to nothing, so I thought I'd best slip over and pull another head and have myself a breath of fresh air at the same time — killing two birds with one stone, as you might say — except now I wish I hadn't said it," and she fumbled for her handkerchief again. "Two people killed — and Beryl's boy suspected! It doesn't bear thinking of, it really doesn't — but what am I doing," putting the handkerchief briskly away, "worrying you with my nonsense? It was only — with you knowing the police like you do, I wondered . . ."

"A trouble shared," said Miss Seeton slowly, "can indeed be a trouble halved, Martha dear — but, apart from lending a sympathetic ear to your family troubles, which of course I am only too happy to do, I fear I can conceive of little, if anything, that I might do to assist. I could hardly, for instance, act as a character witness on your young cousin's behalf, since I have never met him. And, although after so many years I believe I may claim, if not close friendship, then certainly a professional relationship — if it is not immodest of me to say so — with Superintendent Brinton, he would not, I fancy, take at all kindly to the interference in his affairs of one who is a mere amateur in matters of, well, of criminal investigation. Which is not to say," said Miss Seeton hastily, "that I necessarily believe your cousin to be a criminal — the police, after all, are only human, and mistakes can be made — besides which there is also, if my understanding is correct, the fact that he has not, or so it would appear, been arrested. I myself," and Miss Seeton blushed with discreet pride, "might, after all, have been said on occasion to be helping the police with their enquiries — and I would hope," firmly, "that nobody would ever suppose me to be under any cloud of suspicion as I did so. It is no more than one's plain civic duty, is it not? To help, I mean. And, though your cousin may be still a comparatively young man with a . . . a somewhat bohemian attitude towards his responsibilities . . ." Miss Seeton looked back on some of the bohemian types she had known in her own young days. With a smile, she patted Martha kindly on the arm. "The police, Martha dear, are obliged to ask questions, if they are to solve any of their cases. Your cousin, I feel sure, need have no great cause for anxiety."

It must be nice, thought Martha as she returned Miss Seeton's smile, to have as few worries about life as dear Miss Emily seemed to have. She was always so kind — never more so than at times like this, though heaven alone knew she hoped

there'd never be another time like this —
but it didn't seem fair to take too much advantage of her kindness. Some people, reflected Mrs. Bloomer, just never could see
the dark side of anything — and it would
be downright wicked to break it to them
that life wasn't all sweetness and light, the
way they thought. Martha smiled again at
her employer, and said she could well be
right about there being nothing to worry
the family over after all, and she'd get
along now and pick her cabbage and be off
home to cook it before Stan died of starvation, if that was all right by Miss Emily . . .

"Quite all right, Martha dear. And I am
so glad," Miss Seeton said, "that I was able
to be of some help . . ."

Only after Martha had gone did Miss
Seeton start to ask herself just how much
help she'd really been. One had been so
preoccupied with the weeding, and so startled by the news of Stan's arrest — which,
though it turned out to be untrue, had
been most disturbing for some minutes af-
terward . . . and, though one recalled that
Martha had smiled and waved as she
slipped out through the garden gate — the
click of the key in the lock had sounded almost cheerful — there had perhaps still
(mused Miss Seeton, tidying away her

trowel and fork) been something of an air of . . . disappointment in dear Martha's mood. Nothing so strong, one hoped, as accusation, or criticism that one might not have done all that one could — yet one might, she supposed, perhaps have done rather more — although really it was hard to know what . . . Or was she (she wondered, as she began to prepare for her luncheon picnic beneath the apple tree) confusing Martha's understandable agitation with dear Nigel's regret at not having been able to watch himself — and his borrowed umbrella — on television? Not to mention (Miss Seeton smiled, and shook her head) the emotional coils one understood to envelop dear Nigel, and his friend Clive, and that pretty girl — something of a flowery name. Erica? No, Heather — who had been standing next to him . . .

Until her own mental confusion might be resolved, Miss Seeton knew she could have no enjoyment in her picnic, or her garden — indeed, in anything, while her restless fingers remained unstilled. One could hardly trust oneself to slice tomatoes, to cut bread, or to carry a loaded tray in safety; and certainly not to wield secateurs or shears. One might deplore one's regrettable tendency to be ruled — sometimes there was really no other word for it — by one's desires (Miss Seeton, even in the privacy of her home, blushed) — but the fact of the matter did seem to be that when one's fingers tried so pointedly — dear Nigel! — to dance, one was spared much useless agonising if one simply let them carry on as they wished until the irritation — if that was the word — had worked its way out of one's system.

Miss Seeton, bowing to the inevitable, sighed; and slipped a beaded muslin cover over her half-prepared meal before hurrying from the kitchen to the cupboard in which she kept most of her sketching gear. Pencils, eraser, charcoal, and paper — even while reaching for her equipment, she felt the tingle in her hands as an almost electric shock, followed by a surge of relief as she collected everything together and set it out on the sitting-room table under the window. Now barely conscious of what she did, Miss Seeton seized one of her pencils and began to draw . . .

Stan, Martha, Nigel Colveden, and his parents, Sir Stanford Rivers, Dame Lavinia Sheering tumbled together from the graphite tip as Miss Seeton worked. Stan, with his comfortable, slow smile and his hands bearing a wicker basket full of gleaming fruit . . . Martha, clad in everyday dress while incongruously adorned with jewellery — necklace, earrings, brooch and bracelets, a heavy tiara — no, a crown — on her head . . . Sir George, standing at the salute beneath the Union Flag waved by his wife . . . Nigel, carrying an umbrella decorated with horseshoes and sprigs of white heather, looking as if he were about to turn cartwheels in his exuberance . . . Sir Stanford Rivers, frivolous as he could surely never be in real life, his flowing white locks crowned by the flowing, feathered headdress of a Red Indian chief, his body contorted with the tension of coaxing music from tuneless hordes . . . Lavinia Sheering, in the splendid Britannia costume with which she had delighted the Promenaders . . .

Dame Lavinia. Good gracious. Miss Seeton blinked, and stared. The postures in which she had drawn some of these children of her imagination were certainly varied. There was dear Stan, looking much as he ever did — and Martha, who seemed awkward and unhappy in her extraordinary finery — it came as no surprise, of course, that Sir George, a military man, should salute his country's standard with ramrod stiffness, or that his wife should so gracefully pose with the flagstaff in her hand; but that Nigel should even attempt to turn cartwheels while carrying an umbrella — and one knew that dear Nigel was a resourceful young man — seemed, well, odd — and Sir Stanford, one felt sure, would never, even in private, indulge in such energetic antics, such flamboyant fancy dress. Whereas the fancy dress worn by Dame Lavinia was perfectly in keeping — and yet . . .

"India, of course," said Miss Seeton, as light dawned. "She must be, as I am, a practitioner of yoga . . ."

For why else would the stately soprano be standing, with such undoubted poise, upon her head?

Chapter 16

"But surely not," murmured Miss Seeton, as she continued to stare at her drawing, "in a helmet? So very uncomfortable, as well as being most precarious when trying to keep one's balance . . ." For, despite her topsy-turvy pose, Dame Lavinia still carried, as she had during her television appearance, the trident and shield of Britannia.

"Upside down," mused Miss Seeton. She frowned, stiffened, and stared more closely at the figure of Sir George Colveden — or rather, at that of his wife: and in particular at the flag she waved above his head, while below and to her right, in the shadow of the flag, their son prepared to engage in his gymnastics. "Does not the flag, too, appear to be upside down? I believe it does," as her eye noted that the white border to the diagonal cross was narrow, rather than wide, on the side near the staff. "Yes, of course. Girl Guide signals — and that story of the Admiral's which dear Sir George told us last night . . ."

The general atmosphere of reminiscence

had continued at Rytham Hall long after the television had been switched off. Miss Seeton had contributed one or two more thirty-year-old episodes from her wartime teaching days; Lady Colveden had appropriated from her spouse (and, in deference to their guest, censored) a few of his more repeatable anecdotes; and Sir George, nettled, had countered by narrating some of Admiral Leighton's more humorous experiences, gleaned during the Battle of Britain Day get-together. One which had particularly amused Miss Seeton, who recalled from her schooldays the difficulties in which enthusiastic Guides could find themselves, had concerned an exchange of signals between two ships. The eye of the senior ship's captain (Miss Seeton, whose own eye was not slow, smiled again with approval as she remembered) had been as quick as the wits of the junior . . .

"How long do you expect to be after leaving harbour?"

"Three hundred and ten feet, as usual."

According to the Admiral, there had followed a brooding pause. Then: "Your Union Jack is upside down." (And here Sir George explained to his appreciative audience that such a display of the national flag is a recognised signal of distress.)

A wounded pause. Then: "This is how it was received from Naval Stores, Portsmouth."

A triumphantly brief pause. "Some people would drink sulphuric acid, if it came in a gin bottle."

("Which reminds me," concluded Admiral Leighton, after everyone had finished chuckling. "Another drink, anybody?" But Sir George saw no need to elaborate on this . . .)

Acid, of course, mused Miss Seeton, was used to etch metal. Possibly a reference to the patterns on Britannia's shield — but farfetched, she felt, as a connection. Yoga was much more probable — the Indian attire of Sir Stanford — cowboys and Indians . . . school days . . .

"Of course!" cried Miss Seeton, happy at last that the puzzle was solved. "My new method of teaching the children to see. That must be why . . ."

And she held out the sketch at arms' length for one last look, before putting it safely away with hands that neither tingled nor twitched any longer.

As the little convoy of cars had drawn up at the entrance to the Cana Hop Garden, it appeared that Brinton and his associates were about to do no more than repeat the same tired routine for the umpteenth time, achieving nothing . . .

But appearances can be very deceptive.

"Pull in here a minute," instructed the superintendent, when the neatly lettered wooden signboard came into view. "Wave her over — I want a quick word before we go in."

Foxon sounded his horn, and flipped on his indicator. Her reporter's curiosity aroused, Mel drew in behind the police car as it slowed, and hurried to undo her seat belt.

"Thought I'd better explain, Miss Forby," said Brinton, as she poked her head in at the passenger window and demanded an explanation. "He's a bit of a character, the bloke who owns this place — Hezekiah Aythorpe. Hasn't owned it all that long, for one thing. And for another, he's one of the Holdfast Brethren —"

"You're kidding! That hellfire and damnation crowd over in Brettenden?" Mel had written a carefully disguised Piece on this unusual religious sect several months ago. "They're all rabid teetotallers, surely — and you don't grow hops to make non-alcoholic beer, do you! What on earth's a guy like him doing with a place like this?"

Without waiting to be invited, Mel opened the rear door and slipped gracefully into the car: if Briton's explanation turned out to be as involved as she suspected it might, she was bothered if she'd hang around outside bending down with a crick in her neck while she listened. Brinton, with a nod of absent welcome, carried on with his tale.

"Hezekiah lived in Brettenden all his life — he's seventy-eight now — until a couple of years back, when his second cousin Jabez Buntingford died and left him this lot." Brinton jerked a lugubrious thumb in the direction of the wooden sign. "Old Man Buntingford fancied himself as a bit of a wag. This used to be Frogbit Farm, you know, before Hezekiah changed the name. Jabez had some daft joke about frogs hopping, and rabbits hopping, and that's what the farmer did, too." Brinton snorted as he said this, and failed to notice Mel's delighted giggle. "Still, you can't run a bloke in for having a warped sense of humour — though Hezekiah would have liked to, I dare say, for getting him in bad with the rest of the Brethren by leaving him the farm. Left a tidy sum for everyone to have a party after the funeral, too, which didn't go down at all well in certain quarters. Some scorching sermons preached that week, there were. Fire and brimstone . . ."

He paused in some surprise as not only Mel, but Foxon, exploded in stifled mirth. Superintendent Brinton was apparently unaware of the nickname which his hasty temper had won him. ". . . and regular breach-of-the-peace stuff, some of 'em," he continued, glaring sideways at Foxon and trying, at the same time, to scowl over his shoulder at Mel. "Anyway, that's neither here nor there — I just thought I'd warn you Hezekiah needs careful handling, Miss Forby. I'd like you to keep as much out of the way as you can. Temptations of the flesh," he said rapidly, turning pink round the ears and the back of the neck. "Er — oh, yes, and none of your candid camera shots, either. The Brethren call photographs graven images. He'd probably just chuck you bodily off the property if you tried to speak to him, but you poke a lens in his direction and he'll go bananas."

Mel's journalistic instinct outweighed her feminist indignation. How, she enquired, since the principles of the Holdfast Brethren were so firm, had Hezekiah Aythorpe contrived to square his religious conscience with the shocking nature of his inheritance?

"Money," said Brinton, "talks. All the other Brethren pay the normal ten per cent tithe — but Hezekiah coughs up twenty-five, so I've heard. And they very kindly let him keep the rest . . . Jabez must be laughing fit to bust inside his coffin, the old cynic."

Mel was still digesting this remarkable history as they drove up the rutted, weed-free track towards the main area of activity at the Cana Hop Garden, formerly Frogbit Farm. It was a bustling, well-ordered place, with row upon row of hop cages hanging heavy green curtains to the ground, row upon row of bare wires beneath now-empty frames. There were long benches surrounded by chattering, busy-fingered hordes, and trailers driving from bare wires to those benches laden with high-piled vines whose bounty, stripped and borne off in wicker baskets, would come at last to the horsehair nets and sulphur fumes of the oast-house drying floor.

The approach of unknown vehicles made the workers pause momentarily in their labours, though nobody did much more than glance fleetingly up before returning their attention to the vines. Hop gardens pay on a piecework rate. Even the head men of each gang merely registered the presence of strangers, then carried on as before: it was nothing, their expressions suggested, to do with them if there were visitors. Let the big boss sort it out!

Hezekiah Aythorpe was indeed a big man, despite his many years. He loomed suddenly out of a green-gold leafy archway as the three newcomers climbed from their cars, and replied to Brinton's greeting with a grunt and a scowl.

"Police business? Today is the Sabbath, Mr. Brinton, and Bible-bound to be kept holy. Six days shalt thou labour, and do all thy work — that is God's law, Mr. Brinton, and you being sworn to uphold the lesser law of man should set an example to other miserable sinners, not prove yourself and your colleagues to be the worst transgressors of all."

Brinton glared pointedly in the direction of the trundling trucks, the hop cutters with their long poles, and the crowded benches. "Plenty of work going on hereabouts right now, it seems to me, Mr. Aythorpe. If it's good enough for the likes of you and yours, it'll do just as well for me."

"Hired labour," said Hezekiah swiftly. "Outsiders, who know no better — unlike those who have spent their whole lives within the saving influence of the Brethren, yet seem heedless to their cause. Woe to the unbelievers!" It was unclear whether he meant by this the outside labourers, or the local heathen. "Not a soul," he went on, "who labours here in your sight comes from these parts, Mr. Brinton — if souls, indeed, they have." His tone suggested considerable doubt on this point, despite those evangelising attempts which the creed of the Brethren required of its members.

"Suits me fine," countered Brinton, "because it's the outside workers we want to talk to. I'm not too bothered about the locals, at present."

The whirr of Mr. Aythorpe's brain was almost audible. "That's as may be — but you'll be wanting to take them off their work, I suppose, to ask your questions? That'll put me all behind — and *they* won't thank you, either. Paid by the bushel, so they are. If you waste their time —"

"It shouldn't take long," Brinton assured him, remembering how quickly his questions had been answered in the other farms they'd visited that day. "Besides, I'd have thought you'd be pleased they'd be, er, furthering the interests of justice. Helping the law . . ."

Hezekiah favoured him with one last scowl, enjoined him to take no longer than necessary, and grudgingly agreed that he might as well get on with it. He only hoped the superintendent wouldn't change his mind and want to waste yet more time tomorrow, when the local workers returned on duty . . .

"Most probably not," said Brinton. "Though if I have to, I will. But let's see what this lot can tell us first, shall we?"

They were summoned from their various tasks one gang at a time, in much the same way as had happened on the other farms. The same questions were posed, and the same answers given. Were they all known to one another? They were. Did they work together, or at least within sight of one another, every day? They did. What about after work: where did they go? They were too tired to go anywhere, and stayed in and around their huts until it was time for bed. Had there been any change in their routine during the previous week? There had not . . .

It was not until the fourth group were being questioned that any deviation from the norm could be noticed. While Brinton introduced himself as a superintendent of police, he observed a woman in her late fif-

236

ties give an obvious start, which she tried to suppress; and one or two curious, knowing glances were darted in her direction. The woman, her face already flushed with the sun, turned still more red.

Brinton affected to ignore her reactions. "So, now, I'd like you to tell me whether there's any of you that doesn't know the others quite so well as the rest. Or are you all friends together?"

"A sight too well, some of us," a voice was heard to mutter; and the red-faced woman's eyes slid sideways towards a tall, thick-browed young man with large hands, who was staring at a girl who tossed her head and carefully ignored him. Everyone else, after a moment or two, agreed that none of them was a stranger to any of his, or her, colleagues.

"Family, friends, and neighbours?" asked Brinton; it was the usual hopping arrangement. A general chorus confirmed it, though the beetling young man was heard to mutter again, and the girl — a pert brunette — once more tossed her head. The older woman had better control of her emotions and her eyes, and pointedly looked the superintendent straight in the face. Brinton made another mental note, even as he enquired:

237

"Work together mostly, do you?"

"Near enough all the time," they chorused; and went on to agree that teamwork was the way to get things done.

"The same team every day, of course," said Brinton. "So how about last week — any different?"

Again that curious, indefinable feeling that those he was questioning knew more than they wished to tell, that the two women and the young man were the most closely involved in whatever . . . conspiracy? No, that was too strong a word . . . in whatever evasive tactics the entire group clearly thought necessary. Brinton knew that he must find out what those tactics were — and just why they had been thought necessary. A few more questions — a better feel for what was going on — and then —

And then everything changed. The woman, still with her eyes fastened in over-innocence upon his face, stiffened — the girl's eyes gleamed — the angry young man scowled — at the sound of a motor vehicle's bouncing approach up the long, rutted drive. With a collective movement that was barely more than a thrill, the group signalled to Brinton that here came someone who must be asked the most searching questions of all.

The motor — a large, ramshackle, and aged pickup of a make Brinton did not at once recognise — rattled to a halt just before reaching that part of the drive where the visiting vehicles blocked its way. A tall, well-built young man with wavy brown hair and a smudge of oil on his face climbed out, and waved to the figure of Hezekiah Aythorpe where that large, ramshackle, and aged personage lurked in the shadow of an untrimmed hop bine.

"Got the spares okay — fix the tractor now, shall I?"

Then something about the stillness of the faces turned towards him made him falter in his stride. Brinton looked quickly to the woman: from being flushed and frozen, she was now grey and trembling. He glanced at Foxon, nodded, and advanced, holding out his identification.

"Morning, sir. I'm a police officer. I wonder if you'd mind answering a few quest—"

"Bloody hell!" The young man's eyes darted from side to side, then back, as if judging the distance to the pickup. He took a deep breath, and rocked on the balls of his feet, swinging his arms.

"Barry!" cried the woman, as his whole

body tensed. "Oh no — Barry . . ."

Her cry seemed to anger, rather than calm, him. "Dropped me in it again, haven't you!" he shouted, spinning round without waiting for a reply. But Foxon was before him, cutting off his line of retreat, standing in front of the aged pickup with his arms folded and an official glare, class one, on his face. Barry hesitated.

"Now, look," said Foxon, stern but soothing. "There's no need for any of this — the superintendent just wants to ask you a few questions, and then —"

"Questions be damned!" roared Barry. "I'm bloody sick of questions — poking and prying and never any peace! Why the hell can't you lot leave me alone?" And, with a scorching oath, he clenched his fists and charged.

Foxon, unfolding his arms, moved with surprising speed to intercept him. Barry swerved — Foxon followed. Barry dodged — Foxon darted — snatched — caught him by the sleeve. Barry swung his arm in a vigorous arc, and narrowly missed the detective's nose — Foxon, shaken loose, drew himself to his full height, flexed his muscles, and hurled himself in a rugby tackle about his quarry's knees as Barry once more prepared to run.

Arms and legs flailed, fists flew. Brinton wondered about rushing in as reinforcement, then decided he was a quarter of a century too late for that sort of thing. But Foxon had never shirked a fight, even single-handed, in a good cause; and Barry's nerve had begun to fail. By the time people had started to dust down both the combatants — Foxon with his tie under his ear, and two buttons torn from his jacket; Barry breathing heavily, his sweatshirt crumpled, his hair over his eyes — there could be no doubt as to the winner.

Nor could there be any doubt that, though his original loquacity had given way to a stubborn silence, Barry Panfield was under arrest.

Chapter 17

By Monday morning, the only thing which was keeping the blood pressure of Superintendent Brinton under control was the thought of what his wife would say if he ended up in hospital. Old Brimstone wasn't exactly scared of his wife, but . . .

"If only the silly juggins would agree to a solicitor," he growled, for the umpteenth time. "I've never seen anyone to beat that lad for stonewalling — though you, Foxon, have your moments. Dumb insolence," he enlarged, as his sidekick looked at him in some surprise. Foxon grinned.

"And you can just stop pulling such horrible faces, laddie! Between you and this Barry character, I'll be white as a sheet before the day's out, if not worse," and he clutched at his hair, groaning quietly to himself.

Foxon was all seriousness now. "If he's acting so dumb we only know his surname from what his mother told us, poor woman, then we've no real hope of finding out whether he's got a proper alibi for the night of the murder, have we? Unless we try a touch of the rubber hose and truncheons, sir — well, yes, only kidding," as Brinton turned purple. "But we can't hang on to him for ever, sir — what about good old Habeas Corpus? I'm surprised our friend Aythorpe hasn't turned up with a brief in tow, screaming to have his hired hand sprung so's he can carry on hopping, aren't you? Knowing how the Brethren like to hold fast to the letter of the law, I mean, sir."

"Shuttup, Foxon," said Brinton, with a sigh. "*Must* you be so damned cheerful, this early in the morning? And don't tell me it's past ten — it feels one hell of a lot earlier from where *I'm* standing!"

There was a thoughtful pause. Foxon, tentatively, broke it. "I've been thinking, sir." Brinton glared, and began to mutter. Foxon hurried on:

"No, sir, no kidding. Look — the main reason we're interested in Barry Panfield is because he won't say where he was the other night, isn't it? Not to mention he fits the description — though as you said yourself, sir, that's not saying much. And of course, he did take a swipe at me, for no obvious reason," he added, absently fingering the zigzag kipper tie which had replaced that wrenched out of shape during the previous day's struggle. Brinton, who did not share his subordinate's outlandish taste in dress, groaned again, but made no comment.

"Well, sir, perhaps we should try a . . . a process of elimination," ventured Foxon, after a pause. "I mean — granted he looks like the bloke we think we're after — wouldn't it help no end if we could be a bit more sure? We could start chasing his hopping gang for more information — bring his mother in and ask her what she's hiding —"

"We *know* what she's hiding, laddie. All the trouble her precious son's got up to in the Smoke, over the years, and the way his details are filed away nice and tidy on the computer. Just because all we know about's the petty stuff, it doesn't mean he hasn't been getting up to a helluva lot more we don't know about yet, does it?"

Foxon murmured vaguely about dogs and bad names; Brinton ignored him. The young man frowned. "If we could bring one or two of those witnesses in for an identity parade, sir . . . well, it's not as if we'd be much worse off, is it?"

Brinton, on the point of groaning again, caught himself up and stared, instead. Foxon radiated silent optimism in his chief's direction, and waited.

"We'll have to get it out of the way pretty smartish," said Brinton, at last. "Before that reporter female finds out what we're doing — I'm surprised she isn't camped out on the doorstep already."

"She'll be off laying one of her false trails, sir, if I know Mel Forby," said Foxon. "Or writing articles about Why Cockneys Turn to Crime. And you know what they say — while the cat's away . . ."

"Right, laddie." Brinton had made up his mind. "I want you on that telephone this minute, rounding up those three witnesses — or as many of 'em as you can find, anyway," he amended, recalling that it was, after all, Monday morning. "I'll send Buckland out to collect a bunch of likely decoys — shouldn't be that hard. With luck, we'll have the whole thing over in half an hour — once you stop daydreaming round the place and buckle down to some honest work, for a change. Get on with it, Foxon!"

And the superintendent's final roar showed a gratified Foxon that Old Brimstone was once more back on form.

PC Buckland was accordingly ordered into the streets of Ashford for the purposes of strictly legal procurement; and found it harder than he might have expected to acquire half a dozen men in their middle twenties with thick, wavy brown hair and broad shoulders. Persons of such an age and physique are generally supposed to be in regular, full-time employment: such employment rarely requires their presence out of doors at ten thirty on a Monday morning. PC Buckland made advances to a postman (who rejected them), three drivers of delivery trucks, a shop assistant on his way to the bank, an office worker in his coffee break, and a plumber — this last leaping into his double-parked van and speeding away before the uniformed constable could explain he had no intention of booking him. PC Buckland scratched his head, and sighed.

Then he brightened. Coming out of a side street with a package in his hand, walking with a confident step and a head held high, came a young man on whose thick, wavy brown hair the sunlight gleamed, across whose sturdy shoulders a casual jacket had been flung. PC Buckland strode forward.

"Excuse me, sir — why, it's Mr. Colveden from Plummergen, isn't it?"

"That's right," said Nigel. "Anything wrong?"

"Oh no, Mr. Colveden. It's just I was wondering if you'd mind helping us out for a few minutes, if you could spare the time. A matter of an identity parade, see, and Mr. Brinton's told me to find six or seven blokes that look, well, a bit like you, so's our man gets a fair chance. Would you be able to step along to the station now, sir?"

Nigel nodded. "I'm in no tearing hurry now my father's back on the farm strength — and I've never been in an identity parade before. It'll be interesting."

"I'm most grateful, Mr. Colveden." PC Buckland fell in glumly beside Nigel, and they headed for the police station. "You'd think your kind, begging your pardon, sir, 'd be two a penny, but they're all at work, of course, this time of day. The others went on ahead. So long's they've not got fed up with waiting, I think we'll have enough, with you. And," he added, "if Mr. Brinton's still not happy, there's always Foxon, now he's cut his hair."

"Good heavens, has he? Hard to imagine him without it touching his collar." Nigel chuckled. "Don't tell me, though, that he's gone over to pin-striped suits as well. My faith in human nature would be completely shattered."

Buckland grinned. "He hasn't. Old

Brimstone — er, the super — still bawls him out every morning for making such a spectacle of himself, but you know Foxon, sir. Water off a duck's back, with him . . ."

On reaching the station, they found that would-be Detective Sergeant Foxon of the no-longer-flowing locks had indeed been added to the little group chosen for the identity parade. When he had observed the appearance of Buckland's first selection, Superintendent Brinton sighed heavily, warned Foxon to keep out of sight just in case, and detailed Desk Sergeant Mutford to accept delivery, so to speak, of the witnesses previously summoned by telephone. Mutford, one of the staunchest of the Holdfast Brethren, duly plied his captive audience with weak tea (too strong a brew being sinfully stimulating), thin biscuits, and a lengthy sermon on Doing One's Duty from which the recipients could hardly wait to be released.

The arrival of Nigel at last released them. Chatting cheerfully amongst themselves, the half dozen decoys shuffled into line. Nigel, complimenting Foxon on his new look, ended up beside his friend, who remarked that the pair of them together must be a sight for sore eyes, and he'd bear it in mind next time he had a night on the town; to which his neighbour, who drove a laundry van, said he'd never met a house-wife who was quite that desperate, and only wished he could. All joking stopped, however, as the door to the yard opened to admit Superintendent Brinton, PC Buck-land, and a scowling, silent Barry Panfield.

"You can choose to stand wherever you like, lad," Brinton told his captive almost kindly. "End of the line, middle — you just please yourself. But I don't want a peep out of you, mind, if anyone identifies you. All right?"

Barry, glaring sideways, shrugged, hesi-tated, then walked slowly across the yard to join the rest. He seemed to pay no par-ticular attention to any of them; he almost drifted into place, hardly noticing those on either side of him. There came the clearing of a few nervous throats as everyone real-ised who he was, then a complete silence, broken only by the voice of the superinten-dent.

"I'd like to thank you all again for sparing the time to come along to help us this morning, gentlemen. This won't take long, I hope. In a moment, we'll bring out the first of three people who are going to walk up and down along the line and look at you all carefully. Perhaps they'll recognise one of you, perhaps they won't — but, if they do, all they'll do is put a hand on your shoulder. They won't say anything to you — and I'd ask you not to say anything to them, either. Any questions?"

There were only a few, and soon dealt with. Brinton nodded to Buckland, who disappeared indoors, while the young men began to fidget and cough. One even managed a laugh, but stifled the outburst speedily. There was silence.

And then the door opened. A middle-aged man, wearing a trilby hat of a noxious green, marched out beside PC Buckland, his ramrod shoulders back, his jaw set. Barely waiting for Brinton to give the signal, he strutted across to the line of young men, and stood for a moment in front of them, raking the row from right to left, from left to right, with a keen and eager eye.

As his glance passed PC Foxon, he seemed to quiver, and they heard him utter an exclamation, "Just take your time, sir," warned Brinton at once. "Have a good, long look before you commit yourself, won't you?"

Green Trilby squared his shoulders still more, and swung round to the far end of the line, striding across to peer into the face of the first man before, with a shake of his head, passing on to his neighbour. He peered, paused, and passed on again — and again . . . and came to where Nigel Colveden stood, next to DC Foxon.

His examination of those remaining — who included Barry — was perfunctory. Having reached the end of the line, he spun round, headed straight back to Nigel, and clapped his had triumphantly on the young man's shoulder. He turned to face Brinton, and gave a quick, decided nod.

"Thank you very much, sir," said the superintendent, as Nigel stifled the startled protest he'd been about to make. "You've been a great help. If you wouldn't mind going out through the far door, so as not to bump into the other witnesses . . ."

"Two a penny, as Buckland said," remarked Nigel, more shaken than he cared to admit. "Let's hope the next person doesn't fix on me as well, or I'll start to think I actually did it — whatever it was," he added, a note of interrogation in his voice. But Foxon, for all his long acquaintance with Nigel, was giving nothing away.

"You can stand next to someone else, if you'd rather," was all he said. "Perhaps I bring you bad luck! But you'd be surprised how many times this sort of thing happens," in consoling accents. "Witnesses can be notoriously unreliable — that's why we prefer hard evidence, if we can get it. And when we can't — well, we have to start somewhere. But don't worry about it," in a whisper, as the second witness emerged under the care of PC Buckland. "You're innocent until proved guilty, remember!" And then Brinton's glare silenced the entire line.

Though Barry hadn't bothered to change position, one or two of the others had. The young woman in the flower-sprigged dress moved with less certainty than Green Trilby down the expectant line, and stared at Nigel no harder than she did at anyone else. He found himself sighing in relief as she passed him . . .

And then froze as, having reached the last man, Flowered Frock paused in thought, turned, and walked all the way back along the line as far as the point where he stood — and laid a tentative hand on his sleeve. Beside him, Foxon choked as Nigel gasped. Flowered Frock grew bolder, and ventured to give Mr. Colveden's arm a little shake.

"Thank you very much, miss — er, madam," as Buckland muttered that Flowered Frock had left a pushchaired infant under the care of WPc Maggie Laver, grumbling that at such short notice she couldn't be expected to pay for a baby-sitter, could she? "Thank you, madam," said Brinton, ushering the witness out with the same warning he'd given Green Trilby about bumping into the others . . .

Nigel was more than half-expecting the plump, elderly widow who now arrived to stake the third claim on him: and his expectation was fulfilled. With almost as much certainty as that of Green Trilby, this final witness paid absolutely no attention beyond the average to Barry Panfield, but seemed to home in on Mr. Colveden as if he were an especially delicious cream cake. "I'm sure of it," she said, forgetting Brinton's warning in her excitement. "This is the man I saw talking to that poor girl!"

And so, once Barry had been escorted back to the interview room, and the rest of the parade had been dismissed by Brinton with further thanks, Nigel Colveden was asked if he wouldn't mind staying behind, for a while, just to answer a few questions.

Chapter 18

Though their first efforts at self-sufficiency in oil had been so dramatically thwarted, Miss Nuttel and Mrs. Blaine, after a suitable period for recuperation, were minded to try again. After all — as Mrs. Blaine sulkily pointed out — they might as well find *something* to do with their spare time, since it seemed nobody was showing any interest whatsoever in their adventures.

Thwarted also in their ambitions to appear in the national press, both Nuts were in an irritable mood by Monday morning. Mrs. Blaine had spent most of the weekend alternately washing and setting her hair, or peeking through the net curtains to see if the expected press and broadcasting hordes were in sight — which they never were. Monday's breakfast was cooked and served with a very bad grace, for Mrs. Blaine was barely on speaking terms with Miss Nuttel — as is often the case with persons immured in close proximity for any length of time.

Miss Nuttel had used her period of self-imposed seclusion in the thoughtful re-

reading of *Food for Free* and various other of her small collection of practical literature intended to assist those pursuing an independent lifestyle. She had gleaned several new ideas, and was fired with a fresh enthusiasm for her original project which, eventually, she persuaded Mrs. Blaine to share.

"Been thinking, though," said Miss Nuttel, as Mrs. Blaine gave her hair one final, ill-tempered pat, then came to sit by her friend away from the window. "Going to be hard work, mincing so many. Said all along it was the one thing bothering me —"

"Yes, but not much," retorted Mrs. Blaine. "Because we both know who would have ended up doing most of the mincing, don't we? I know you *said* we'd share it, but —"

"But there's no need," broke in Miss Nuttel, "if we buy a proper mill. Not easy to find, mind you. Might have to adapt something, instead. A kitchen blender —"

"No!" cried Mrs. Blaine at once. "*Not* my blender, Eric — think how too ruinous for the blades! Not to mention," she added, raising a plaintive hand to her brow, "the frightful *noise* it would make. You know how I suffer with my head." And her expression contrived to make Miss Nuttel feel guilty that she had ever made so selfish a suggestion.

"Well," said Miss Nuttel, when Mrs. Blaine had permitted some colour to return at last to her plump cheeks. "Adapt something else, if we can't buy a proper mill — continental, you see. Not too many around these parts — worth looking in junk shops, though. Not that far from the Channel, are we?"

"Oh, Eric, how clever of you!" Mrs. Blaine was now all smiles. "There are any number of strange things I *know* you could adapt — cream separators, and those old-fashioned bookbinding presses — I think I remember noticing one in a window in . . . Ashford, I believe, last time we were there. Do let's go and see! And the day out will do us both so much good, won't it? A change of scene . . ."

And, an olive branch having been thus offered and accepted, the Nuts began to plan their trip to Ashford.

There is no direct public transport link from Plummergen to Ashford. To reach the area's largest shopping centre, one changes buses in Brettenden; and, unless it is market day, or one's requirements are so nice that Brettenden cannot fulfil them, it is a journey not frequently undertaken — and seldom on a mere whim.

For which reason, when those Plummergenites who were on Monday morning's bus realised the Nuts were among their number, it caused no little interest that on arrival in Brettenden, rather than heading out of the bus station with the rest, Miss Nuttel and Mrs. Blaine moved to the next platform but one, and boarded the bus for Ashford.

Speculation as to the purpose of the Nuts in travelling so soon again to Ashford was immediately rife. Still bearing a grudge over the failure of their experiences to make headline news, they had deftly turned the subject when questions were posed about their activity during the past few days, and about their future plans. Barry Panfield, had he taken lessons from Miss Nuttel and Mrs. Blaine, would have been their star pupil in the art of stonewalling. The Nuts had been generally ignored, and were now ignoring in their turn. With little, therefore, on which to base a theory, it took a while before the general opinion was reached that the Nuts must mean to revisit the scene of their earlier crime — with intent (the most vocal insisted) to gloat, since the police seemed to be having no more success than they'd had last year in finding the killer of the Blonde in the Bag.

It was loudly lamented that nobody had been able to think up in time a good excuse to jump on the Ashford bus in pursuit; and when everyone had completed their shopping, and was waiting at the Plummergen platform for the arrival of the return bus, tongues wagged frantically in speculating as to what else the Nuts might have been doing . . .

The Ashford bus at last arrived, decanting its passengers: amongst whom were numbered Miss Nuttel and Mrs. Blaine. And the manner in which, after glancing once at each other in an electric silence, they took their places at the end of the Plummergen queue, made it clear that the Nuts had News to impart — News which, since they had returned in safety to impart it, meant either that the police hadn't yet found enough evidence to arrest them, or (disappointingly more probable) that they might not, after all, have done anything to warrant being arrested in the first place.

To Mrs. Blaine was given the honour of firing the opening salvo. Her cheeks flushed, her eyes bright, as she settled herself against a pillar, she uttered a little moan. "Standing so long, in all this heat, after such a terrible shock, Eric — I only hope I can hold out until the bus comes." She passed a hand over her brow, and shuddered. "I feel too, too weak . . ."

"Hardly surprising," returned Miss Nuttel, as Mrs. Blaine snapped open her handbag and fumbled inside for her pocket handkerchief. "Gave me quite a turn, too."

"But you know my nerves have never been as strong as yours, Eric." Mrs. Blaine dabbed daintily at her eyes, then began frantically fanning herself, emitting further little moans as she did so.

Miss Nuttel thumped her encouragingly on the shoulder. "Try not to think about it," she advised. "Could be some perfectly rational explanation. Perhaps. A mistake . . ."

"A mistake?" Mrs. Blaine's blackcurrant eyes glittered. "An explanation? I doubt if I could bear being given *any* explanation for the police arresting him *in broad daylight* — it's bound to be something almost too dreadful to repeat, and I'd have nightmares for weeks, I'm sure, if I knew what it was. I mean, you don't start arresting people like that unless you're absolutely certain they've committed something a good deal more serious than a . . . a motoring offence!"

Mrs. Blaine, fluttering her handkerchief

again, appeared oblivious to the press of eavesdropping Plummergen which edged ever closer as the earlier promise of scandal began to be fulfilled. Miss Nuttel, seemingly concerned for nothing but her poor friend's mental sufferings, patted her again on the shoulder, then applied a tactical, tension-building break in the narration by enquiring whether Bunny would like her to go in search of a glass of water.

Mrs. Blaine, smiling bravely, rejected this offer with a sigh and a quivering lip. "Too much to bear, Eric, if you missed the bus with trying to help me, and I had to travel home *utterly alone*." She was still firmly oblivious to the close-crowding queue. "I wouldn't have a minute's peace, I know I wouldn't, until you were safely home!"

"But if they *have* arrested him, Bunny, nothing to worry about any longer, is there? No matter what he's done. Not going to give him the chance to do it again, are they?"

Mrs. Blaine gulped. "Oh, Eric, I wish I could believe you. But really, there's nothing to say they won't let him go again — on bail, or remand, or whatever it is. Remember, his father's a magistrate. You know how these people always stick together. The law . . ." And the spirit of a vast Establishment conspiracy was invoked with one all-encompassing wave of Mrs. Blaine's versatile handkerchief.

The gasps which greeted this monstrous slander were highly gratifying, though both Nuts still affected to be unaware of their audience. Miss Nuttel shook her head.

"His mother I feel most sorry for, Bunny. A Justice of the Peace — they're hardened to anything, of course. Training. But Lady Colveden . . ."

The gratifying gasps erupted into a universal thrill, as Plummergen gave delighted tongue at last. Did Miss Nuttel and Mrs. Blaine — *could* they — mean that Nigel Colveden, of all people, had been arrested? Miss Nuttel and Mrs. Blaine, dismayed at being the bearers of such grim tidings, sorrowfully — and loudly — admitted that they did. Eric (went on Mrs. Blaine) might try to make excuses for what they'd seen with their own eyes — too charitable of her — but charity was sometimes only another word for being soft-hearted.

"Which is only a way of saying afraid to do one's duty — to speak the truth," said Mrs. Blaine bravely, "and shame the devil. And it must be a too devilish crime for them to send a uniformed policeman right up to him in full view of everyone to drag him off to the police station like that!"

"In handcuffs?" came the eager query.

Dearly as they would have loved to be able to confirm this additional ignominy, the Nuts had to confess that the squire of Plummergen's son had been allowed to walk without restraint in the company of the police constable who apprehended him: although — as Mrs. Blaine pointed out — the man had doubtless warned his prisoner that should he try to make a break for it, he would be pursued without fear or favour through the Ashford streets, with all the subsequent . . . awkwardness this would entail.

"Poor Lady Colveden," chorused Plummergen, echoing and enlarging on Miss Nuttel's lament. "Never live it down, the shame — ought to know better, the likes of him!"

"But what," someone wanted to know, "d'you reckon they arrested him *for?* Must've thought he'd got away with it, whatever it is, to go wandering through Ashford so bold."

"That's the aristocracy for you," said someone else; and everyone agreed it was. One or two strangers, drawn to the crowd by all the commotion, opined (there is a flourishing Socialist element in Bretten-den) that the sooner such class distinctions were done away with, the better.

Mrs. Blaine shuddered. *"Droit de seigneur,"* she moaned, with quite as much glee as ever Emmy Putts had uttered those words. "It's too obvious what they think he's done. That poor girl from Murreystone, of course — oh, dear!" And Mrs. Blaine trembled at the memory of last week's woodland excursion. Once more Miss Nuttel, herself much moved by the recollection, patted her friend on the shoulder. A sympathetic murmur surrounded the Nuts as they struggled to contain themselves.

"Too, too dreadful," sighed Mrs. Blaine, blinking back horrified tears and licking lips that should, she felt, have been even more pale. "And the other poor creature last September as well, I shouldn't wonder. They develop a taste for that sort of thing, don't they? *Serial killers.*"

"Had a fair number of girlfriends over the years, young Nigel Colveden," someone remarked. "Funny how none of 'em ever lasts, as you might say. And now we know why."

"Find out what he's really like," theorised someone else happily, "and get away in time — the lucky ones, that is."

"Depraved tastes." Mrs. Blaine, the centre of attention, was starting to feel that the gallons of shampoo and setting lotion she had applied over the past few days hadn't, after all, been wasted. "The *worst* of it is, of course, they'll try to hush everything up. And I shall be *very* surprised if they fail, with Sir George having the police in his pocket — and the *excessive influence* you can't deny *certain local elements* exercise over the press. Just look at all the peculiar things Miss Seeton has done since she's lived in Plummergen, for example. But do the papers ever say so?"

Everyone roundly agreed that Miss Seeton's name appeared suspiciously seldom in the national — or even the local — press, and that Mrs. Blaine had the right of it. Influence, clearly, was being brought to bear on Miss Seeton's behalf — Scotland Yard was mentioned by several people — and would doubtless be used for the benefit of Nigel Colveden, too.

"Shouldn't wonder," said Miss Nuttel, "if she hadn't come down on purpose. Odd she's turned up just when she'll be most useful, isn't it? That reporter woman," she enlarged, as not everyone realised at once who this useful female might be.

"Oh, Eric, you're so right!" Mrs. Blaine made a face of disapproval. "*Corruption,* that's what it is, nothing less! It's *only too convenient* for them to have her staying right on the spot, ready to suppress any stories that might leak out of whatever *dreadful things* he does next — Miss Seeton as well, I've no doubt. They'll work out a cover-up between them, and he'll be free to carry out more *unspeakable* crimes — oh, Eric! Thank goodness you're coming back with me on the bus. The *worry* of it all — if I'd had to wait at home alone because you missed it —"

"No need to worry, Bunny," said Miss Nuttel, squaring her shoulders. "Shan't miss it now . . ."

And Bunny heaved a deep sigh of relief as the Plummergen bus appeared at the far end of the bay, rattling cheerfully along the platform. Its noise and blue-grey smoke dispersed the listening crowd: those who had their own buses to catch moved reluctantly away; and, striving nobly to conquer her fears, Norah Blaine allowed herself to be escorted up the rubber-covered steps by Erica Nuttel, elbows on overtime. As the other Plummergenites perforce fell back to let them pass, the Nuts staked their claim on the front seat as compensation for the dreadful experience they had both undergone; and, throughout the six-mile journey home, they loudly reminded each other, over and over again, that if they had not witnessed it with their own eyes, they would never have believed it.

Chapter 19

When his third witness had so firmly identified Nigel as the young man thought to have
been one of the last people to see Myrtle
Felsted alive, Superintendent Brinton knew
he could do nothing else but question this
unlikely suspect with as much resolution as
he would have applied to anyone else —
with, indeed, more, lest charges of favour-
itism should at any time in the future be lev-
elled against him. Brinton did not have
definite knowledge of what was already
being said; but, had he been asked to predict
the general attitude of Miss Nuttel, Mrs.
Blaine, and others of their kind, he could
have done so almost word for word.

In the end, the superintendent allowed
Nigel to leave the station without pressing
charges, although he took care to leave his
options open. Brinton was not a happy
man as the door of the interview room
closed behind his suspect's back; the
lengthy talk with young Mr. Colveden had
not been as straightforward as he would
have wished.

Foxon had been taking notes. He looked

at his chief in some dismay. "I just can't —
won't believe it, sir. Not Nigel Colveden!
There's got to be some explanation — he's
a decent sort, is Nigel. You know he is!
Not one of your average Chopper thugs
with no brains and a broken home — his
father's a magistrate, for Pete's sake. Sir."

"You're not telling me anything I don't
already know, laddie. Think I didn't go
through it all myself a hundred times or
more, while we were talking? But you
shouldn't need me to remind you what can
happen, in cases like this." Brinton sighed.
"Nearly everyone who's done somebody in
has a host of friends and relations pop out
of the woodwork bleating that he's a nice
boy, and they can't believe it of him, and
there must be some mistake . . . It's human
nature, Foxon. People don't like to think
their nearest and dearest are capable of
killing — and especially when it's something as cold-blooded as this joker. The
heat of the moment I can just about —
well, not *excuse,* but I might stretch a point
and admit I *understand* how it can happen.
A pub fights gets out of hand, a lad throws
a punch without realising his own strength,
a bloke bumps his napper on the way down
and dies from a cracked skull — that's your
normal murder, Foxon. It doesn't surprise

me sometimes when a jury goes sympathetic and lets 'em plead manslaughter, instead — not that it helps the poor devil who's dead, or his family, but if there's any consolation they know it wasn't some lunatic lying in wait, and the bloke who's gone down for it probably feels as sorry as they do . . .

"But this Blonde Bagman's a different kettle of fish altogether, Foxon — and I don't care who he is, I want to feel his collar and get him out of circulation before he does it again. He might not wait another year — he could be getting a taste for it, and crazy killers on my patch is something I won't put up with. If he turns out to be young Colveden, we just have to say it's tough on the family he's turned out bad, but that everyone else'll be glad we managed to grab him in time — including us. Trouble is," and Brinton rubbed a massive hand wearily across his face, "I like the lad, as well. If he'd been able to come up with a decent alibi, I'd have been as pleased as anyone . . ."

Foxon, who in normal circumstances would not have hesitated to remind Brinton that alibis can be faked, found himself unable to make even the most feeble joke to cheer his gloomy superior.

The office was filled with a brooding, exhausted silence. They had questioned Nigel for what seemed an eternity, though common sense and the clock told them it wasn't; but the questioning had been rigorous, and the two detectives knew there would be more to come.

"Because," said Brinton, with a sigh, "we'd be falling down on the job if we didn't start checking up very closely on what young Colveden's been getting up to over the past week or so, and exactly where. Odds are that Chummie *is* the lad seen chatting to Myrtle at the bus stop. Everyone who saw 'em thinks it looked as if they already knew each other, so if we can find out he had a chance to meet her . . . I hate to say it, but Nigel's the most promising lead we've got so far — the lad may look the picture of innocence, but —"

Foxon uttered a choking cry. "Picture, sir!" Brinton shot him a hostile glance. Foxon ignored it. "Couldn't we, sir? Ask her, I mean. You were probably thinking of it in your subconscious anyway, sir, and —"

"No." The way Brinton uttered that single syllable suppressed Foxon in a way he'd rarely been suppressed before. The look in his superior's eyes startled him.

There was a long pause. Foxon hardly

dared to breathe. Brinton wrenched his thoughts back from whatever worrying byway they'd been wandering in, and favoured his young colleague with a thoughtful stare.

"Well, you may be right after all, laddie. About two heads being better than one, I mean — but," as Foxon opened a tentative mouth to speak, "I can't agree with you about whose head the other ought to be. I said at the start of all this I didn't want Miss Seeton involved — and, if it comes down to someone from her own village being a suspect, I want it even less. Just imagine if Chummie *is* Colveden, and she helps us nail him. How's the poor old biddy going to feel about facing his parents and the rest of the village once word gets round? Because it would — and pretty damned fast, as well you know. At her age, she can do without that sort of bother." Brinton sighed. "I'll take half of your advice, though — the sensible half. You'd like me to consult someone who knows what makes young Nigel tick? Get me the Yard on the blower, will you — and if the Oracle's not there, I don't want to talk to anybody else."

"Not even Bob Ranger, sir?" enquired Foxon, picking up the receiver to ask for an outside line.

Brinton shook his head. "For at least two good reasons, laddie. One, in working hours it's pretty much a case of where the Oracle goes, Ranger goes with him, so if one's not there, the other won't be, either. And two, Ranger's more of an age with young Colveden, like you. Your precious Miss Seeton would know what I mean when I say I'd like a different perspective . . ."

The different perspective had to wait. Scotland Yard informed Detective Constable Foxon of Ashford that Chief Superintendent Delphick and Detective Sergeant Ranger were working on a drugs investigation, weren't in the office, and wouldn't be back in the office until later. Later that same day, yes; as to how much later, no, it wasn't possible to say. Would anyone else do in their absence? In that case, would DC Foxon care to leave a message? Very well, Mr. Delphick would be asked to ring Superintendent Brinton at Ashford just as soon as —

The disembodied voice broke off. "Superintendent Brinton," it said again, with a chuckle. "Ashford. That's in Kent, isn't it? Something to do with, er, umbrellas?"

"Mr. Brinton wants it made clear to the chief superintendent," said Foxon firmly, "that this has got nothing to do with Miss Seeton. Nothing at all, understand?"

But Foxon found it hard to sound convincing when he didn't believe it himself; and the gleeful voice from Scotland Yard obviously didn't believe him, either.

A lesser man might have sat and counted the minutes before Delphick phoned him back; Brinton had no intention of wasting them. With the timetable of Nigel's recent activities — as far as the young man had been able to recall them — in front of him, the superintendent detailed as many officers as he could spare to undertake some discreet checking. He told the desk to put through no calls unless they had a direct bearing on the Blonde in the Bag case. By half past six, after a series of inconclusive reports, he was on his third packet of peppermints; and when the telephone at last tinkled on its cradle, he snatched it up long before it had time to emit a proper ring.

"Hello? Oracle!" Brinton clutched at his hair. "Where have you been, for heaven's sake?"

"Out," replied Delphick, who could tell his friend didn't much care where or why he'd gone, but needed to let off steam. "How are things with you, Chris? What's Miss Seeton been getting up to now?"

Brinton closed anguished eyes as Foxon, listening on the extension, snickered. "She hasn't been getting up to anything. Didn't they *tell* you I said she's out of it?"

"They did." There was amusement in Delphick's voice. "I found it hard to credit, however, knowing her usual . . . shall we say proclivities, when there is major crime in the vicinity? Not to mention minor crime, on occasion — though I take it" — he became serious at once — "you don't wish to chat about petty theft, or our old friends the Choppers going off the rails. The newspapers have given me sufficient warning, over the past day or so, that you're still preoccupied at present with one particular major case — or sack, I suppose one could say. Or bag."

Brinton sighed. "The Blonde in the Bag, Oracle, guessed it in one. And a regular nasty one it is, too."

"The details I've gleaned from the papers have certainly lent to that supposition. Do I take it that it's the sheer unpleasantness of the whole affair which prompts you to keep Miss Seeton out of it? It's a kind thought, if you're thinking of her nerves, but Miss Seeton's nerves are —"

"Oh, I admit it was, to begin with. I didn't fancy the blame for giving the poor

274

old trout nightmares and a nervous break-down, looking for lunatic knifemen under the stairs and in the cupboards because I asked her to take a gander at the scene-of-crime snaps — but that isn't the half of it, now. Because now . . . well, we've got a suspect in the frame."

"You sound," said Delphick, as Brinton fell silent, "rather less than overjoyed at this circumscription. Might one enquire as to the reason for such gloom?"

Brinton took a deep breath. "The sus-pect . . ." He would never have believed it could be so difficult to say. "Well — re-membering that he *is* only a suspect, Or-acle — he . . . he comes from Plummer-gen."

"In which case, I should have thought you could nail him easily without needing to trouble Miss Seeton, even though I would say her nerves were more than equal to —"

"It's a friend of hers, Oracle!"

There was a startled silence. Brinton took another deep breath. "It's young Nigel Colveden — yes, I know," as both Delphick and Bob, listening in at his supe-rior's request, exclaimed. "A friend of yours, too — of Foxon's, dammit. You could even say of mine, come to that. But the more I look into it, the blacker things seem against the lad . . ."

Having broken the bad tidings, he was now better able to tell the tale in full. He told of the three witnesses, and their positive identification of one who'd only been roped into the identity parade by chance. He told of the hurried enquiries into Nigel's almost nonexistent alibi . . .

"Says he can't really prove what he was doing most of the time last week, especially not the night of the murder. They're pretty busy on the farm right now. Easy for him to slip away if he wanted — everyone'd just think he was somewhere else if they didn't see him around for a while. The trouble is, he's a good farmer, Oracle. He could easily put on a burst of speed to catch up on the time he'd missed before anyone noticed he'd skived off those couple of hours. His father was sitting on the bench all week to replace someone whose lumbago's giving 'em gyp — the men'd never dream of doubting the boss's son, so long as the work was seen to be done in the end — and as for this rubbish about his car breaking down on Thursday night . . ."

"The night of the murder." Delphick's tone was calm, his words unhurried. He, like Brinton, found it almost impossible to see Nigel Colveden as a killer; but step by steady step was, he knew, the only way to clear any sort of path to the truth through the tangles of circumstantial evidence. "What does he say he was doing?"

"Fixing his car," said Brinton.

"Oh, dear." Delphick knew as well as Brinton the value of mechanical problems as an alibi — unless —

"Did he call on either of the motoring organisations to help him?"

"He didn't, more's the pity. He says after so many years he knows that MG inside out, and if he hadn't dropped his torch, he'd have done it in half the time. But he did, and he didn't — and he says he doesn't remember that anyone passed him on the road, either. It was a pretty out-of-the-way spot. He couldn't even find it on an Ordnance Survey map when I asked him, not for certain, though he knows there was a bit of a slope because he had to push-start the car after he'd sorted out the dynamo brushes. All he can say is that he never got as far as Wisborough Green, which is where he was headed — something to do with the lawn mower race the Young Farmers are running on Saturday. It's pretty well in the middle of nowhere, over in Sussex. Nigel says that by the time he'd sorted out the car, he was filthy with oil, and thoroughly fed up, so he turned right round and went home, and rang the bloke he was supposed to meet from the Hall to apologise, and to fix another day."

"You've checked with the Sussex boys in blue in case they spotted him, of course."

Brinton was too preoccupied to take offence at what might have been a slur on his professional abilities. "Had a word with Harry Furneux at Hastings. No joy, unfortunately. Well, in view of what Nigel said it was always going to be a long shot — and Harry's crowd were all having fun and games Bedgebury way, right on the county border. A load of youngsters who sound like second cousins to our Choppers blocked off some of the back roads and started racing their bangers and bikes round the place like lunatics, and Harry's lads had the devil's own job chasing 'em. They missed a few of the blighters in the dark — but they wouldn't have missed a broken-down MG if it had been anywhere near, which if he was heading for Wisborough Green, it wouldn't. Assuming he's telling the truth about where he thinks he was in the first place, that is."

"Chris, I know as well as you the perils of letting personal prejudice come into it, but suppose we give Nigel the benefit of the doubt, for the moment. What about when he finally completed his repairs and reached home? There's little point in talking to the man he was going to see, of course — if Nigel *is* guilty, he could have telephoned from anywhere to set up his alibi. But are his parents able to confirm what time he arrived?"

"He got home before them. Sir George was sick-visiting the lumbago bloke, to tell him how many cases they'd cleared, or whatever. Lady Colveden was at some meeting about the Christmas pantomime, and it got a bit heated, or so she apparently told everyone next day, so she was late getting back. Young Nigel says he didn't bother waiting for either of them: he had a hot bath, fixed himself a nightcap, and went to bed. He was asleep before his parents got in — he says," he added, reluctantly.

"And at his age," mused Delphick, "they wouldn't bother checking to see if he was safely tucked up, of course. This could be difficult, Chris."

"Difficult? That's the understatement of the year, Oracle. His father's a magistrate. The family's respected. The lad's never been in any bother, even as a youngster, and on paper he seems the most unlikely person . . . but you know what *that's* worth, in real life. He's a bright bloke. He's as capable of working out an alibi as anyone, and better than most, I'd have said. Myrtle was picked up from the bus stop around half past five — well, we've already established he could skip from the farm and nobody would notice. As for seeing this man Gavin, what better alibi could there be, if you look at it from Nigel's point of view? The sun sets," he added, as Delphick drew breath to expostulate, "quarter or half past six, this time of year, remember. Nobody with any sense expects a working farmer to visit them until it's dark — and, as he never even got there . . ."

Delphick was silent for some time. Bob, slowly recovering from the shock of knowing that someone he'd partnered in a cricket match was a murder suspect, ventured — London was, after all, several miles out of missile range — to ask why Mr. Brinton had so strong a wish not to consult — he begged Mr. Brinton's pardon — Miss Seeton about this unhappy turn of events. Foxon smothered a chuckle, but Brinton, for once, neither groaned nor cursed.

"Your dear adopted Aunt Em, Sergeant Ranger, is, despite her unholy ability to chuck herself in and out of adventures and come out unscathed, an elderly woman. Even before this thing with Nigel Colveden, I didn't want to upset her by involving her in something quite so nasty — and now, well, I still think we're better off not involving her. Never mind how awkward it could be for her in the village if he's guilty, just imagine taking her as a . . . as a character witness, if that's what you call her drawing nonsense. It *may* be instinctive, or remote control, whatever you want to call it — but catch her subconscious letting her spill the beans about someone she's fond of, even if he did it fifty times over!"

Brinton did not see the gesture with which Delphick silenced a protesting Bob, though he heard the sergeant's sharp intake of breath. It was Delphick's voice which now spoke in his ear.

"I dislike contradicting you, Chris, but I think you're wrong, in this instance — oh, I don't mean about suspecting Nigel, because with what you've got I'd suspect him myself. There's more than enough circumstantial evidence to make him a likely candidate for further investigation, implausible a killer though he seems — but as for Miss

Seeton, I really must disagree with you. Her overriding quality, remember, is her conscience. Her strong sense of duty would never allow her to . . . to perform any kind of whitewash, even if she wanted, which I'm convinced she wouldn't. And neither would her subconscious, which is where her undeniably useful gift seems to spring from. You could do a great deal worse than have a quiet word with her about all this — no need to go into too many details, if you're bothered about upsetting her, though I honestly don't see that as a problem. It's my opinion Miss Seeton hasn't a . . . a nerve, or a spark of imagination, whatever you want to call it, in her whole body — certainly not of the kind to give her nightmares. What she *does* have, however, is a remarkable ability to see right to the heart of the matter — and, when things are as confused as they seem to be for you just now, that can't be a bad idea, surely. Why not give it a try?"

Brinton took a lot of persuading. Delphick was unable to pull rank, for Scotland Yard has no authority over other forces unless brought in officially to a particular case, which had not happened here. But the Oracle argued long and with conviction. In the end, Brinton agreed to sleep

282

on the matter and see how he felt the following day. He need not, Delphick pointed out to his friend, mention to Miss Seeton the name of Nigel Colveden; he need not dwell on the more gruesome aspects of the deaths of the two young women. All he would need to do would be show her, for example, the witness statements, the (edited) reports from those police officers who had tried to trace Nigel's movements at the relevant times, and the photograph, passed to the police by her parents, of Myrtle Poppy Juniper Felsted.

"And then," advised Delphick, "sit back — and wait."

Chapter 20

The shock of Brinton's disclosures had entirely driven from the mind of Chief Superintendent Delphick the presence in Plummergen of Fleet Street ace Amelita Forby. A comparable amnesia had also affected the Ashford constabulary, and for similar reasons.

There must have been some strange quality in the air of southern England that September evening, for Mel, likewise, was afflicted by the same condition — although in her case the cause was far more acceptable. And, as the young reporter spent Monday night in first quarrelling, and then becoming reconciled, with Thrudd Banner, instead of calling upon Miss Seeton as she'd originally arranged, it was not until Tuesday morning that the telephone rang, with a most insistent ring, on Superintendent Brinton's desk.

Brinton, having — as promised — slept on Delphick's proposal, had been on the point of allowing himself to weaken. Foxon, he was about to say, should accompany him on the drive to Plummergen . . .

"Brinton," he barked into the receiver. "I thought I'd made it clear I wasn't to be bothered unless — what? *Who?*" At his desk, Foxon jerked to attention at the note in Old Brimstone's voice. "Well, stop wasting time, and put him through, can't you? . . . Potter? Yes, speaking." He motioned to Foxon to pick up the extension. "What is it?"

The cautious tones of Plummergen's village bobby sounded in four listening ears. "It's about Miss Seeton, sir. Your standing orders —"

"Yes, yes. Take all that as read, Potter — just tell me the worst. What's the woman been up to now?"

"I'm ringing from Sweetbriars, sir. I've Martha Bloomer with me, and Miss Forby from the *Daily Negative*, staying at the *George*, not to mention Mr. Banner, of World Wide Press, who's, er, staying there, too." Potter cleared his throat before continuing: "Old friends of Miss Seeton's, as you know, sir. Not ones to make a fuss, you'll agree —"

"I'll agree to anything you want, if you'll only get on with it, man!"

"Well, sir, as to Miss Seeton, it seems like she might be . . . missing." Brinton and Foxon exclaimed, and Potter hurried on: "Mr. Jessyp, he'd been expecting her at school again today, only when she never turned up, he phoned to ask if she was ill, and Martha was here, and no idea she hadn't. Course, she could just have had an absentminded sort of fit and popped into Brettenden on the bus, only nobody remembers seeing her at the stop, and she's not took her bike, Martha says. And she's not left a note — and there's yesterday's supper in the larder and the washing-up from her afternoon tea not put away — and her bed looking like it's never been slept in. Though with her being such a tidy little soul," he added in judicial accents, "that's not to say she didn't make it soon as she got up, instead of leaving it to air for a bit the way she usually does, so Martha s—"

Potter's recital was cut short by an exasperated chorus of voices: three in Plummergen at one end of the telephone, two in Ashford at the other. Brinton's voice, being not only the loudest but having, to the ear of PC Potter, a greater authority, prevailed.

"You mean she could have been missing all night? Why in heaven's name didn't someone say something earlier?"

"Nobody knew about it earlier, sir." Potter sounded pained. He'd rung Ashford the very instant he'd satisfied himself that the three agitated persons demanding his immediate presence in Miss Seeton's cottage weren't imagining things: what more did Mr. Brinton expect him to do? Short of putting her under permanent police guard . . . "Miss Forby, she'd meant to visit Miss Seeton yesterday after school and a bite to eat, only she never did, and when she remembered this morning, she popped across to explain, and there was Martha — Mrs. Bloomer, sir, it being one of her days to oblige at Sweetbriars — and *she* a bit later than usual arriving, on account of all the bother about her cousin, because her son —"

"Spare me the family history, Potter! You're trying to tell me Mrs. Bloomer's too *bothered* to remember whether Miss Seeton said anything about anything, is that it?"

Martha's voice could be heard in the background, saying that it wasn't like Miss Emily not to let her know when she was called away unexpected, especially when she was meant to be teaching, and if anything had happened, she'd never forgive herself, because what was a cousin, when all was said and done, with a mother and family to care for him, and poor Miss Emily with nobody but her and Stan?

"No note, no message, no sign she was in the house after . . . early evening, at a guess." Brinton barely waited for Potter to confer with the unseen trio and confirm the guess before he hurried on. "I suppose it's too much to ask if she's ever had her burglar alarm fixed after that lightning hit the house? . . . Yes, well, I'm not really surprised. Any signs of a struggle? No," giving Potter no time to reply, "you'd have said, if there was. So what," he demanded, "was she wearing — does anyone know?"

"Mrs. Bloomer's had a quick check, sir. Seems her hat's gone, and her umbrella — not her best, though," as Brinton could be heard to mutter. "A light jacket, and her handbag, but her binoculars are still here, so she's not gone bird-watching, and her shopping basket's in the cupboard under the stairs, besides which she hasn't been seen in The Street all day. If she *has* been kidnapped," said Potter, "she was tricked into going, that's for certain. Whoever he was, it doesn't seem like he had to force her —"

"If he existed at all." Brinton scowled at the telephone, then sighed. Who was he fooling? The kidnapper must almost certainly exist. He — Potter — everyone sharing that electric conversation — knew

Miss Seeton of old, as they also knew Plummergen. If it was out of character for Emily Dorothea Seeton to wander from home without mentioning her plans to one or other of her friends (with particular reference to the Bloomers and, in the current circumstances, Headmaster Martin Jessyp), it was equally out of character for the whole village not to notice whatever she did around the place — when she *was* around — and to be able to report fully on same when asked. But Potter had said nothing about any such reports — and he was a good man. He'd have checked . . .

"I suppose nobody," said Brinton, with little hope, "has seen anything. No possible leads?"

"Afraid not, sir. That is," as a female voice could be heard putting some energetic point of view, "Miss Forby's of the opinion we should be looking at her sketchbook, sir, as she's not took it with her — Miss Seeton, I mean, not Miss Forby. She thinks it might give us a clue about where she's been taken, if she has — Miss Forby, I mean. And, er, Miss Seeton, sir. Er — sorry, sir."

Potter would be more than sorry, reflected Brinton, once he was within proper shouting distance — what the hell did the man think he was playing at? Blast Foxon! What did *he* find so amusing, sniggering like that when heaven-knew-what was going on heaven-knew-where, and nobody with the wits to think straight about it? Miss Seeton didn't even need to be nearby when the trouble started — just being in her cottage was enough to send an ordinary hardworking copper off his head burbling complete nonsense.

Nonsense? Perhaps not *complete* nonsense . . .

"Foxon, get the car. Potter, dig out that sketchbook — but first, get a *detailed* description from Mrs. Bloomer of what Miss Seeton's wearing. We'll relay it to all cars the minute we reach you — and don't let anyone go anywhere until we do! Reach you, I mean — oh!" He ground anguished teeth for his own burbling — Miss Seeton's influence was stronger than ever — but perhaps, just perhaps, it might mean, as it had done on previous occasions, that the case was about to break. And there was only one case right now that interested Superintendent Chris Brinton.

"Foxon, bring the — oh." Useless to instruct Foxon to bring the duplicate Blonde in the Bag files with him — he'd already left the office, and was probably sitting in the panda now, with the engine running. He'd know as well as his chief there'd be little time to waste now that things were hotting up. "I'll bring 'em myself — and we'll be with you in ten minutes, Potter. Don't go away!"

The problem was, brooded Brinton, as Foxon sent the panda racing out of Ashford along the B2070, that he'd never been very good at making sense of Miss Seeton's weird drawings. That sort of thing, he generally left to the Oracle — and Scotland Yard was forty miles away. There was the Forby female, of course: he couldn't deny she'd been helpful in the past; and there was the telephone — always supposing the Oracle hadn't gone off hunting dope dealers again. He ought really to have checked before rushing out of the station . . .

A short radio call; a nail-biting wait. "Not there," groaned Brinton, as the panda lurched sharp right at the Hamstreet crossroads and headed for Brettenden. "Step on it, Foxon! Seems we're on our own, laddie. The sooner we get going, the better!"

They sped through Kenardington, through the leafy greenness of Great Heron Wood, past the ancient dignity of

ruined Clarion's Hall, and into Plummergen Heath, where for the first time
Foxon dropped within the speed limit.
"Don't want to set 'em all by the ears as
we drive down The Street, sir," he explained, as he heard Brinton's teeth
grinding beside him. "You know what
they're like around here . . ."

Brinton grunted, but said nothing,
scowling as they passed the post office,
glaring at the startled figure of Miss Nuttel
as she closed the front gate of Lilikot behind the plump form of Mrs. Blaine. Five
hundred people in this village, and they
had to be spotted by the two who talked
more than the rest of 'em put together!

"Too late to do anything about it," he
muttered, as the panda slowed and prepared to swing round in a wide curve to
stop outside Sweetbriars. Foxon, intent on
his driving, caught his passenger's final
words, and was shocked.

"Don't say that, sir! It's never too late for
MissEss. She's had a few hairy moments in
the past, remember, and she and her brolly
have always bounced back again. Born
lucky, I'd say Miss Seeton was."

"Let's hope," Brinton grimly remarked,
as he undid his seat belt, "her luck hasn't
just run out, laddie . . ."

An anxious little group clustered about the open door of Miss Seeton's cottage on hearing the panda car's arrival. Brinton was barely halfway up the short front path before the four of them — PC Potter, Martha Bloomer, Mel Forby, and Thrudd Banner — all started talking at once. Brinton shot a fierce look towards the only one of the quartet over whom he had any nominal authority.

"Got the description, Potter? Then give it to Foxon, and he'll pass it on to radio control."

"Got her sketchbook, too, sir," Potter told him, as Foxon hurried back down the path to alert headquarters. "And Miss Forby seems to think —"

"Miss Forby," broke in Mel's exasperated voice, "*knows* — and darn well, too, Potter! Come inside, Mr. Brinton," as the superintendent hesitated.

"Yes, do come in, Mr. Brinton," said Martha, with great firmness: hadn't she known Miss Seeton years longer than any newspaper reporter? Wasn't it far more *her* place than Miss Forby's to welcome visitors to Sweetbriars? Mrs. Bloomer was not, she hoped, jealous of her employer's friendship with Mel and Thrudd — of course she wasn't! "Come in, and quick as

293

you can — the sooner you start hunting for Miss Emily, the happier I'll be." Much — even the arrest of her cousin Beryl's son — could be forgiven the man on whom Martha Bloomer had pinned her hopes of Miss Seeton's rescue from whatever danger she might be in.

"The happier we'll *all* be." Mel gave Martha a consoling pat on the shoulder. "In the sitting room, Mr. Brinton — on the table. Her sketchbook — there are a couple of pictures I — we — think might be worth taking a look at."

The siting room was comfortably cosy for one or two: for six — Brinton, Mel, Thrudd, Martha, Potter, and Foxon, who'd come panting back up the path after sending out his message — it was crowded beyond belief. The superintendent took a deep breath, and ran a finger round his collar as he forged his way towards the table. Not his place to ask for a window to be opened: not really his place to ask half of 'em to wait outside. One, perhaps . . .

"Foxon, what the devil are you doing here? Hop on back to the car in case anyone radios in they've seen her. Now, Miss Forby — let's have a look . . ."

"It's those cartoons of hers that matter," said Mel, as Brinton began to leaf back through the most recent sketches in the waiting book. "Don't bother with trash like that — a complete waste of time, for our purposes," as a dainty landscape in pen-and-ink wash came to light.

Martha drew in her breath to expostulate — she'd thought Miss Emily's little picture very pretty — but Mel, as Brinton turned a frowning face towards the young reporter, grinned wickedly.

"Haven't you cracked the code after all these years, Mr. Brinton? She takes pains over it — it's pointless. Dump the detailed stuff — any fool could do it," with a fond wink in the direction of Thrudd, looming thoughtfully in a corner of the room composing paragraphs in his head. "We had an idea *that* might mean something, though . . ."

That was a swiftly executed sketch which bore all the hallmarks of what Mel was wont to call a Seeton Special. With the Taj Mahal and its long reflecting lake in the background, with turbanned figures about him at a respectful distance, a man posed in eighteenth-century costume, complete with wig — yet with a twentieth-century face that was unmistakeable.

"The Duke of Windsor — what the devil's *he* got to do with anything?"

"You can see why the others are wearing turbans — it's their national costume, for heaven's sake — but there must be a reason for *his* fancy dress," said Mel, bright-eyed.

Martha tossed her head. "Always going on tours of the Empire, he was — the Prince of Wales. The Delhi Durbar, and shaking hands with people till he got so tired he had to put his arm in a sling — or was that his dad?"

Thrudd, staring in his turn at the picture, said that he had an idea the Durbar had been for George the Fifth, not his son, but that he didn't see how either of them came into this at all. And, much as it annoyed him to say so, he had to agree with Mel. Why the costume? When Edward wasn't even wearing a crown . . .

"That's in one of the other pictures," said Mel, barely containing herself. "Go on turning back, Mr. Brinton!"

Brinton reached the composite picture in which Miss Seeton had doodled so many animated — instantly recogniseable — figures. Stan Bloomer, the basket of fruit in his hands — Martha, bejewelled, with a crown on her head — Sir George at attention, his wife — Nigel with the decorated umbrella . . .

Brinton said nothing as he stared at the face of his latest murder suspect and long-time acquaintance, looking up from the paper with a merry, open smile . . .

Sir Stanford Rivers in his strange attire . . .

"The other sort of Indian, this time." Brinton stabbed a finger firmly towards the conductor's feathered headdress. "Don't I know this chap's face? Wait — let me . . . the Last Night of the Proms, of course. Well, I know they go in for fun and games, but I don't ever remember . . . and just look at the Britannia woman! How can anyone be expected to sing when they're standing on their head?"

Not for the first time, Brinton found himself wondering whether Miss Seeton might not be starting to show her age, although with the eyes of so many of her friends fixed upon him he would never have dared say so. He sighed, and turned another page.

"Now this chap," he said at once, "there's no doubt *he's* singing, is there? Or whatever passes for singing, with his sort." He revised his opinion of Miss Seeton's mental abilities: nothing old-fashioned about this particular picture — or pose. "Must be more than a bit uncomfortable for him, twisted around like that — but you can almost hear the noise he's making, can't you?"

With bold, flowing, swift strokes of her pencil, Miss Seeton had drawn a long-haired, leather-clad, buckle-belted, hipster-jeaned male of strutting, sexual aspect, with a microphone close to his open mouth, and the flex snaked suggestively about one thigh, trailing off into an inde-terminate distance where three vague fig-ures played on drums and guitars. A fourth figure, unnaturally tall, was striding away from the group; proving, as Brinton peered in some amazement, to be on stilts.

He grunted, and turned another page, and blinked. That same leather-clad young man, now crouched on a motorbike, was shown racing furiously against a second young man clearly pushing, of all things, a lawn mower — a young man who bore a distinct resemblance to Nigel Colve-den . . .

"That's some imagination she's got," muttered Brinton.

His words were the signal for everybody to start talking all at once, and for a while there was bedlam in the little sitting room. Then Mel, being closer than the rest, won.

"It *isn't* imagination — well, not all of it.

Go on," to Martha. "Tell him! And I bet whatever you like," to Brinton, "it's all tied up with your Blonde in the Bag . . ."

Chapter 21

"It's — I think," Martha amended, "it's my cousin Beryl's boy, Barry. I was telling Miss Emily, you see, how he'll worry his mother to death, poor soul, with all his nonsense about wanting to be a pop singer instead of sticking to an honest job. Come down here every September for the hopping, the whole family — that'll be where she got the stilts from, I suppose, me telling her how it was when I was a girl, and Beryl and Barry and the rest of it."

"Turning his back on his old career, obviously." Mel's decisive finger indicated the striding form, whose speed was suggested by a series of blurred hatchings. "He can't wait to get away, can he?" She giggled. "Barry Bloomer and the Underclothes, or something — sorry, Martha," as Mrs. Bloomer gave her an awful look. "Barry Bloomer and the Flowerbeds, or the Bordermen, then —"

"He's not a Bloomer, thank goodness, as Mr. Brinton knows full well." Martha redirected her look, in modified form, to the superintendent. "His name's Panfield, like his poor mum, and —"

"Barry Panfield!" Brinton turned purple. "Are you trying to tell me this bloke's the lad who had a go at young Foxon in the hop garden? The one we took in for questioning and he's stayed dumb the whole time?"

"Yes," said Martha, unusually succinct, while Mel, who'd spotted the resemblance almost at once, smirked.

Brinton stared: first at Martha, then again at Miss Seeton's supposed likeness of his silent suspect. "Yes, I recognise him now — it was the hair and the get-up that fooled me. Odd. For all the daft capers he's cutting, he doesn't *look* like a bad lad. . . ."

"He's not," said Martha promptly. "Not *bad,* just worrisome, out half the night mixing with heaven-knows-who —" She remembered that Brinton was *Superintendent* Brinton, and shut up. Beryl's anxieties about drugs were best kept quiet if Barry was to come out of this business safely.

Mel, who had sufficient tact not to let Martha know she had been there when Barry was arrested, said: "Wouldn't you think Miss S. is saying he didn't do it, Mr. Brinton? Whatever," belatedly, for Martha's benefit, "you think it was. He may look like a crazy, mixed-up kid — but show me a pop singer who doesn't. And if that's

301

the case, then he's just a . . . a high-spirited type with big ideas — and there's no law about having ambition, is there?"

Brinton grunted. Mel continued, in her most coaxing voice: "And I don't reckon, according to this, that Nigel Colveden's guilty as charged, either — oh, yes," as Brinton exclaimed, "the news is all over town this morning. Seems a couple of the Plummergen . . . ladies . . . happened to be right on the spot yesterday when one of your boys in blue carted poor Nigel off to the Ashford nick. Think you could keep a story like that from getting out — even," pointedly, "if you didn't leak it to the press yourself?"

Brinton restrained himself with difficulty. "He hasn't been arrested, Miss Forby. I hope you and your colleagues aren't going to say otherwise, because the Colvedens have a lot of influence, you know. Slander's a serious matter."

"And so's libel, which is what publishing it in the press would be," Mel informed him cheerfully. "Keep your hair on, Superintendent. People say a lot of rude things about Fleet Street, but we know how to use our discretion. Whatever you think Nigel's done, it's a mistake, pure and simple — even before I saw what Miss S. had drawn

I'd have taken my oath on it —"

"Three different people identified him!" cried Brinton, goaded into indiscretion and thoroughly bemused by it all. "What the hell d'you expect me to do except haul him in for questioning when every single witness said they'd seen him?"

"An identity parade." Mel's brain was whirring. "Guess you grabbed him to make up the numbers, right?"

Brinton nodded. Mel, recalling Barry Panfield's appearance, nodded too. "Makes sense," she murmured, while Martha cried that it certainly didn't make sense to her, and never a wrong word would she hear of Nigel Colveden, that she'd watched grow from a baby and one of the nicest lads around, and she only wished there were more like him.

"Like Barry?" Mel suddenly beamed. "You bet, Martha! See here, Mr. Brinton, it *is* all a mistake, as I said. And I can tell you how you came to make it, what's more. I only wish," she added, as Brinton exclaimed again, "I could tell you where Miss S. has gone, and who with . . ."

"Never mind that!" Brinton was unconscious of any incongruity in the inference that he preferred to clear a murder suspect — who hadn't even been arrested — than to search for a possible kidnap victim. "What makes you say it was all a mistake about young Colveden?"

"Easy." Mel nudged him out of the way as she turned the pages of Miss Seeton's sketchbook. "Well, easy*ish,* if I'm right — look! The Last Night of the Proms, you said. But how did you know that's what it was meant to be?"

"Oh, that was easy," Brinton told her, before realising what he'd said. Mel's eyes glittered as he grinned a shamefaced grin. "That's the bloke," said Brinton, with a nod for Sir Stanford Rivers, "who was conducting, and the woman who sang 'Rule Britannia' — I knew them almost straight away, for all she was upside down. We watch the Last Night every year, me and my wife."

"Plus about half the population of this country," Mel told him in tones of triumph. "Including me, in my lonely room at the *George,*" with a quick wink for Thrudd. "Except that I watched in the Residents' Lounge while I was chatting to Doris — but that's the point," as Brinton moved his hand in an impatient gesture. "*Everyone* watched it — and especially people from around here, because of the Young Farmers getting up a party and telling all their friends to watch in case they were on — which Nigel," in even greater triumph, "was. There were two or three close-ups of him waving Miss S.'s umbrella — she told me she'd lent it to him when I saw her Sunday evening — and *he* hadn't got flags painted all over his face like the boy standing behind him, or a hat pulled over his eyes like the other young lad they kept showing. Nigel was instantly recogniseable. Identifiable," she concluded, with emphasis. "As you might say."

Brinton let out a long, low sigh. "And as three otherwise honest witnesses might say, too, the chumps. Miss Forby, you — you're a marvel, girl. Banner, you're a lucky man! They'd have been idiots if they *hadn't* identified him, with the Last Night only two days before, and the murder two days before that . . ."

Relief gave way to anxiety. Nigel had been cleared — he knew Mel must be right — of suspicion of murder, but *could* suspicion be lifted with such certainty from Barry Panfield? If it could — if Mel was right about both young men, using Miss Seeton's sketches to prove her point — then the killer of the two Blondes in the Bag was still at large . . .

And so was the kidnapper. "Miss Seeton," said Brinton, pushing the unopened Blonde file away as he bent again to study the sketches. "We've got to find her, haven't we? As soon as possible," turning to Mel, whose instincts he was inclined to trust.

Mel nodded, the gleam fading from her beautiful eyes. "If Miss S. is on her usual form, she had one of her — you'd laugh if I said premonitions, but — well, a kind of *feeling* for what was going to happen before it did. And she'll have drawn it out of her system in these sketches, if we can only make sense of them. Trouble is, Mr. Brinton, I'm a stranger in these parts. Guess the clues are for you locals to sort out now."

Reluctantly, she stepped back, drawing Thrudd (who had long ago stopped hovering and closed in on his lady) back to allow Potter and Martha Bloomer to move towards the table on which lay Miss Seeton's sketching pad, still open at the Last Night of the Proms cartoon. Martha, grateful to Mel though still uncertain, stared at the clearly limned forms of herself and her husband, and spoke the first words that came into her head.

"Me with a crown and all that jewellery,

and Stan in his overalls carrying them blackberries, or whatever they are — a right pair we look, and no mistake, though I don't think she was wanting to make fun of us, somehow. More like remind herself of something — which I don't really see how she can, me never having been much of a one for precious stones, though of course Stan's a marvel with his fruit and veg, for all she's drawn brambles as we'd rather find in the hedgerows than taking up space in the garden —" She broke off, remembering, and cast a woeful look about the sitting room before stifling an emotional sniff. "Oh, dear, poor Miss Emily — where on earth can she have gone?"

Mel uttered a little yelp. Her *The Natives Had a Name For It* series of articles on dialect words and country customs had been a great success in the *Daily Negative*; a faint flicker in her subconscious was fanned into flame with every word Martha spoke. Mel blushed as people stared, but held her head high. The flames were starting to crackle . . .

"Jewellery and blackberries — precious stones and brambles — well, fruit, anyway. But could you swear to it these are blackberries, Martha? Might they be grapes, or cherries — or raspberries?"

"They're a sight too dark for raspberries, I'd say — and *black* grapes they might be, but never green ones — and as to cherries, well, they might and they might not. I mean, in the basket and all, with the shadow, it's hard to tell."

Mel's eyes gleamed. "Might they be . . . mulberries, for instance? Little and round and dark like that?"

Again Martha studied the basket shown in her husband's hands. She looked at PC Potter, fellow countryman, a fascinated observer of the scene. "I suppose they might, since you insist, though I'd have thought there were more important things than worrying about berries, whatever they're called —"

"Oh no there aren't!" Mel whirled to face Brinton, her eyes bright. "Superintendent, do you know what another word for the mulberry is? For the blackberry as well, in some areas, come to that. Have you any idea?"

Brinton shrugged, and shook his head. PC Potter cleared his throat. "Beg pardon, sir, but if Miss Forby's thinking of *murrey*, I believe I've heard the term used —"

"And precious *stones!*" supplied Mel at once. "Murrey, stone — she's got to be there, simply got to! How she knew beforehand I don't know, but —"

"But that poor girl came from Murrey-stone, Miss Forby," Brinton reminded her, sighing: for a moment there, he'd almost thought she'd cracked it. "Myrtle Poppy Juniper Felsted — that's who Miss Seeton'll have been thinking about while she was drawing this. Juniper plants have berries as well, don't they? And myrtle and poppy are more plants — although why she thought the girl was at the Last Night of the Proms when she was already dead — but that doesn't alter the main point. I'm sorry, I don't think this is much of a lead, after all."

"So far, it's the only lead we have." Mel was starting to lose her temper. "Unless you can think of anything else, Mr. Brinton, I can't see we'd lose much by — well, by going to have a look round Murreystone for, well, clues . . ."

Even as she spoke, her confidence faltered, and she began to see how hopeless the whole thing was. Miss Seeton's strange drawings needed more inspiration to interpret them than Amelita Forby felt right now she possessed. But Potter was clearing his throat again, more forcefully this time.

"Excuse me, sir, but I think I might be, well, getting the hang of all this." He waved a wary hand over Miss Seeton's sketches. "And you couldn't be expected to know, sir — about how Old Man Barnston in Murreystone died a few weeks back, and he'd got no son, and the farm's been took over by the Chelmers as farm next door, so the farmhouse is empty yet while they make their minds up what to do with it, his nephew and two nieces. Crown House Farm, it's called, sir, with being on top of the hill . . ."

Mel could have kissed him. "Crown House Farm in Murreystone, Superintendent — that's where you'll find Miss S., or I'm a Dutchman!"

Her confidence was catching. Brinton nodded. "Could be — yes, I believe it's worth checking. One of the outbuildings, most likely. Potter, you come in your car, I'll go with Foxon. Three of us ought to be enough — I don't want to wait for reinforcements from Ashford, just in case. Is there a way we can reach the place without being spotted?"

"Four of us," said Thrudd, speaking for almost the first time.

Mel mustn't be the only one of their partnership to play a starring role — besides, he had a soft spot for Miss Seeton — and, most of all, there was the story . . .

"Five," flashed Mel, reading his mind, before Brinton could say anything. "It's a free country, Superintendent," as he glared at her, and opened his mouth to expostulate. "Guess if a lady and gent choose to take a drive in the good old country air, why, it'd be police harassment if anybody tells them there's places they can't go — and a pretty good story, too."

Brinton eyed her very sternly. His normally ruddy face turned red, then purple — and then, releasing his pent-up breath, he chuckled. "More blackmail, Miss Forby?"

"Right on, Mr. Brinton." Mel dug Thrudd sharply in the ribs. "Come on, Banner, we've work to do. And nobody tells Amelita Forby it's man's work, or I splash you male chauvinist pigs all over the front pages. Do we go in my car, or yours? The more the merrier," she enquired of Brinton, "or do we play it sneaky and quiet?"

He thought for only a few moments. "Potter, come with me — Banner, you and Miss Forby follow, and for heaven's sake try to stay out of sight unless you're needed. If word gets round there were civilians involved, I'll be in rather more trouble than I like to think about."

"Hang on, Mr. Brinton." Martha

Bloomer had listened with growing incredulity to the quick exchange. "There's me you seem to be forgetting, not to mention my Stan, if you give me time to run and fetch him — both of us so fond of poor Miss Emily as we are, and with more right than any of you, begging your pardon. We'll not be left behind when she's in trouble! She'll be glad of a friendly face when she's safely found . . ."

The look Brinton directed upon Miss Seeton's loyal servitor would have astounded Foxon, had he observed it. Kindliness was not normally a quality associated with Old Brimstone: but the superintendent's gaze was now very kindly indeed. "I'm sorry, Martha, but you'll be more use here," he said, as the others hurried from the room. "You're right, Miss Seeton will need you — but she'll need you once she's safely home again, with cups of tea and fruitcake and all the fussing you can give her."

And, as he followed his troops out of the cottage and down the paved front path, under his breath he repeated: "Once she's safely home again. *If* she is . . ."

Chapter 22

Clive Chelmer had never been an entirely comfortable member of the Brettenden and District Young Farmers. He joined in all their projects with just a little too much enthusiasm, and tried just a little too hard to be the life and soul of whatever parties they held, the charity events they organised, the excursions they made to various places of farming and countryside interest. Superficially, he was popular enough; deep down, he knew he wasn't. Many social misfits are untroubled by their status, accepting with reasonably good grace that such is the way of the world: Clive Chelmer was not one of these. He longed to mingle with his peers without having to make twice the effort they did, and it disturbed him to realise that this was no more than an impossible dream.

His parents were evidently unaware of their son's fish-out-of-water feelings towards his nominal friends, though they did sometimes wonder why the boy was almost always the one who made the telephone calls, never the one who was telephoned. They wondered why his girlfriends seldom seemed to last, and decided in the end it must be because he was too particular in his requirements. His father accused his mother of spoiling the lad, setting their son's prospective help-meet an impossible standard. It would do Clive good, said Hubert Chelmer, to get away from home for a while to find his feet.

"New Zealand," he pontificated, "is about as far from England as anyone in their right mind could want. And he'd pick up a few tips on sheep," he added, above the protests of his wife. "I didn't like the look of Old Man Barnston last time I saw him. I give him another couple of years at most — and you know none of the family's that keen to take over Crown House Farm when he goes. If I'm any judge, once they've inherited they'll sell off most of the land at a knockdown price, and tart up the buildings for some townies to live in and make pretend they're proper farmers. And if we can get our hands on those extra acres, we could expand the sheep side very nicely, thank you."

Brenda Chelmer, for all her apparent protests, needed less persuasion than Hubert had feared. With her perhaps excessive maternal instinct, Brenda was beginning to feel twinges of . . . nothing so strong as anxiety, but of doubt, indefinable though undeniable, over her only son. As Clive had grown older, she'd heard him grumble less and less about people until, this last year or so, he had never (to her knowledge) uttered a single word of complaint against anyone, not even the all-popular Nigel Colveden: and Brenda had to admit that as she was jealous of Lady Colveden, so it would come as no surprise if Clive had inherited an antipathy towards Lady Colveden's son. But Clive gave no sign — and such an attitude couldn't be natural! Surely it was inhuman not to feel like a good moan, once in a while? Yet Clive apparently never felt that way. Which either meant that she had given birth a quarter-century ago to a saint, which seemed most unlikely — or that he was bottling everything up inside him. Which seemed more than likely, if he was trying (as she began to suspect he might be) to boost his reputation for congeniality . . .

Likely — but, well, as she'd thought before . . . inhuman, to have such superb self-control. Inhuman . . . though not mad, of course! Hadn't Hubert said that New Zealand was as far away as anyone *in their right mind* could want? If her son were happy to go Down Under, then wouldn't his going be all the reassurance his mother needed that she'd been worrying about nothing?

"I think you're right, Hubert," said Brenda, and did not enlarge upon her reasons for agreeing with his proposal.

And so Clive Chelmer went to New Zealand's South Island to work on a sheep station. He had accepted the idea, after initial expressions of surprise, with equanimity: he'd tried so hard to be the best of good sports, and had grown a little tired of trying. The year's absence from everyone who knew him, among people he'd probably never see again, could only, he believed, be a benefit to him. It would be a welcome rest, a chance to relax and be himself where his true self wouldn't really matter . . .

It was in celebration of his imminent release from perpetual pretence that he committed the first Blonde in the Bag killing; it was as consolation for having returned from a year's freedom to the old, sad struggle to conform that he committed the second.

Myrtle Felsted had hardly recognised Clive, bronzed by twelve months in the antipodean sun, his shoulders broadened by harder work than any he'd ever done on his father's farm a mile out of Murrey-stone. Myrtle had been flattered when young Mr. Chelmer stopped for a chat, and insisted she should call him by his given name; she was still smarting from the latest fight with boyfriend Darren, and had been glad of Clive's company, of his offer to drive her home rather than let her wait for the bus. And when he'd suggested that the next day they could take the round-about route back to her lodgings, maybe stop for a drink, a meal, a change of scene, it had never entered her head that a son of one of the oldest families in the district could mean her any harm. It had never entered the head of Brenda Chelmer, even in her most pessimistic moments, that her son could be a double killer. On Monday, she went shopping in Brettenden; she parked her car near the bus station; she overheard excited chatter, and not unnaturally pricked up her ears as those chatterers on their way to the shops passed her by, and she heard them speak of Plummergen, and Nigel Colveden.

"You'll never guess," she told her husband and son later that afternoon as she took sandwiches and a flask out to the meadow, "what they're saying in Bretten-den."

"You're right, my dear." Hubert stirred sugar in his tea, and grimaced. "We won't guess, because we won't trouble to make the effort. It's unlikely to be of much importance, whatever it is — Brettenden's almost as bad as Plummergen for gossip. We'll stick to hard facts, thank you."

"But this *is* a fact," protested Brenda, one eye on Clive as he bit thoughtfully on a sandwich. "I wouldn't be telling you if it wasn't true, would I? That would be slander! But everyone was talking about it, so it must be true — that Nigel Colveden, of all people, has been arrested for killing that poor Felsted girl, and probably the other one last year as well! They say Sir George," she added, above the startled exclamations of her husband and son, "is going to pull every string he's got to get him off, though I suppose you can hardly blame him. Poor Meg Colveden!" Brenda did not sound in the least sorry for her ladyship, with whom she had never been on first-name terms. "She must be having a simply dreadful time, though they say there's a newspaper reporter already on the spot to help cover it all up, and that funny Miss Seeton of theirs" — everyone within a ten-mile radius of Plummergen had heard of Miss Seeton — "is going to help. I

318

expect she'll have a word with Scotland Yard — you know how they always do what she says."

Hubert blinked. "I'd have said her influence with the police has been much exaggerated, my dear. People do love making mountains out of molehills. If you ask me —"

"Molehills!" cried Brenda, in triumph. "Remember that business with the Best Kept Village Competition? I agree our people didn't exactly play fair, but everyone knows Miss Seeton was able to bring in the Yard to stop them cheating, instead of leaving it to the local police, the way anybody else would have had to. Doesn't that prove she'll wangle Nigel Colveden off the hook, and there'll be nothing anyone can do about it? You may laugh," as Hubert shook his head with a tolerant smile. "But I agree with the ones who say there's something almost uncanny in the way that woman pokes her nose into what doesn't concern her, and it's all sorted out to *certain people's* satisfaction."

"Don't you mean her umbrella, my dear?"

But Hubert's little joke fell on deaf ears, as Brenda's tongue wagged faster than ever. "Of course, Plummergen so often

gets hold of the wrong end of the stick" —
that old village rivalry was never entirely
forgotten — "but some of them say she's a
witch — though I don't believe that for a
minute — but I *do* believe she has, well,
power of a sort. Influence. If she hasn't,
why did the Queen invite her to a garden
party a couple of years ago? She's never invited anyone else from around here — except the Colvedens, that is." And Brenda,
after sighing, smirked as she recollected
the probable mood of poor Meg Colveden
at this moment . . .

Hubert was so busy pouring scorn on his
wife's opinions, and she was so busy up-
holding them, that neither of his parents
paid much attention to Clive's unnatural
calm. If they had, they would have attrib-
uted it either to shock at such revelations
about his Young Farmer friend, or to his
having not yet shaken off the habit of being
strong and silent, as the South Island
farmers were known to be. But they would
have been wrong. Clive said nothing because he was thinking too hard — thinking
how this news could be turned to his advantage . . .

When footsteps sounded on the path
round the side of her cottage, Miss Seeton
turned with a smile to greet the unex-

pected visitor. She had been wondering whether it would show too much self-indulgence if one went indoors for another cup of tea now, instead of waiting half an hour or so and having one with supper, for which one did not, perhaps, feel quite ready just yet, although dear Martha's raised pork pie and salad would be most welcome a little later. But Martha's pork pie recipe used a wide variety of spices, and Miss Seeton, having spent so much of the day indoors at school, had worked up a greater thirst than appetite since she'd come home and been making up for lost hours in the garden. This timely guest would serve as the perfect excuse, if any were needed, for indulging one's inclinations, and eating one's meals at a slightly unorthodox hour.

"Miss Seeton?" The young man with the thick, wavy brown hair and athletic build strode towards her across the lawn. "I hope you don't mind my dropping in on you like this, when we haven't met before. You don't know me, but —"

"Oh, but I do," said Miss Seeton, with a nod and another smile. "Know who you are, I mean. You're Clive — I do beg your pardon, but I don't know your other name — but you are a friend of dear Nigel

Colveden, are you not?"

Clive was horribly taken aback by such instant recognition. He, like his father, had been inclined to dismiss the rumours which reached Murreystone about Miss Seeton's peculiar powers; now, he wasn't so sure. But the old woman certainly seemed to be — sure, that she knew who he was — which meant he had to change his plans. All he'd ever meant to do (he told himself) had been find out what, if anything, she knew about . . . the Episodes, as he was accustomed to call the killings when thinking about them. He thought about them surprisingly seldom. Once the tension had been released, it took a long time for it to build up again.

But the old woman was sure she knew him — could therefore identify him when she told the police, as she was bound to do, that someone had been round asking questions about . . . about . . .

"Clive Chelmer," he said, shaking hands as he reached her, blotting out the rest of that uncomfortable sentence. "How do you do, Miss Seeton? Please forgive me for making so free with your name, but as a . . . a friend of Nigel's . . ."

He watched her closely, but saw no response other than pleasure at his mention of Mr. Colveden's name. Did she have no idea, then, of what had happened to her young acquaintance? Or had she indeed heard, but dismissed, the story, as daft an old woman as he'd supposed all along she must be, reports of her prowess as a detective no more than Plummergen nonsense? Except, of course, that there were the newspapers — it was no easier to fool them than it was to fool the police. Yet he'd succeeded at both, hadn't he? Flying off to New Zealand a week after the first . . . Episode . . . without anyone stopping him as he boarded the plane —

"Are you feeling a little unwell?" came Miss Seeton's kind enquiry, as she observed the strange expression on her visitor's face. "A touch of the sun, perhaps — you have, if I may say so, a rather flushed appearance. I was just about to make myself a cup of tea. Would you care to join me?"

Or — was she every bit as clever as people said? Making out she knew nothing — guessing his secret — hoping to trick him indoors and force a confession out of him. He was going to find her more difficult to pump than he'd expected. She was too much the twittering old woman to be real: everything they said about her was true — and pumping her wasn't going to be enough. Now that he'd met her, he knew. And he also knew she had to be . . . stopped, before she could tell anyone just what *she* knew . . .

He refused the invitation to accompany her into the cottage, making some excuse about fresh air being better for his head-ache. Miss Seeton was all clucking concern — overdone, he thought cynically — and he was pleased that in this, at least, he told no more than the truth. As soon as she'd said she knew who he was, he'd felt something like a dagger stab into the back of his skull, stab and twist and stab again, stab and cut and slash and tear, just like . . . just like . . .

"If you won't come in out of the sun," said Miss Seeton, in her firmest tones, "then I must insist you sit down under the apple tree — this garden faces west, you see, and keeps it until the very end of the afternoon — the sun, that is. I could fetch it out here, if you would prefer to be in the shade — the tea. It won't take me long to —"

"No! No, thank you," as Miss Seeton stared, then smiled as she realised how the poor boy's head must be troubling him, if his grimaces and jerky movements were a true indication of his feelings. One hesitated, of course, to interfere, but would it be an excessive impertinence to suggest that he saw a doctor? A migraine — Miss Seeton had never suffered such a thing in her life, but had in her student days known one or two victims whose paintings made their illness all too vivid — a migraine, she knew, could be very unpleasant. Dear Anne's father had been one of London's top neurologists before retiring to Plummergen — and was not migraine something to do with the structure of the brain?

"It might, you know," ventured Miss Seeton, as Clive, his face working, clenched his hands into fists, "be of considerable help to you if you spoke to him — Dr. Knight, that is. In the nursing home at the other end of the village," as he turned a puzzled face towards her.

She was trying to tell him she thought he was crazy, was she? That he ought to be locked away? She was wrong — they were all wrong. How could they even think it, when they had no proof? Hadn't he stopped the blood dripping on his car floor by wrapping . . . them . . . in plastic? Hadn't he left those sheep out in the open air where birds of prey could rend flesh from bones so that nobody could tell how they had died? If you couldn't prove it, it wasn't true . . . though there was always the risk they might fail to prove Nigel had done it, and then they'd say it wasn't true when it *was* — it was true that Nigel Colveden deserved whatever punishment came his way, for taking Clive's rightful place — for stealing the friends he ought to have had — for stealing away his girl . . .

"Heather," he said, with a groan. Miss Seeton frowned.

"Heather *honey,* certainly, but as to heather *tea* . . . you will forgive me for contradicting you, I hope, but I hardly think it likely. Tea, after all, is made from dried leaves, which heather does not have — of a sort suitable for drying, I mean. Leaves. And in the shade, if only you will come and sit down, the air is so much fresher —"

"Fresh air!" Clive clenched his fists even tighter, and took a deep breath. "Fresh air . . . Miss Seeton! How would you like to come for a little drive with me?"

Chapter 23

The plan of campaign was finalised in the road outside Miss Seeton's cottage, with Brinton uttering stern reminders that if news of so unorthodox a procedure ever leaked out, he would be in deep trouble. Mel and Thrudd assured him that, as free citizens in a democracy, it was their inarguable right to drive where they pleased on the Queen's highway; but rights, once won, to be maintained must be earned. To ignore a chance-met officer of police who asked for their assistance could be described as nothing less than dereliction of civic duty.

"Talking of highways," said Thrudd, "hadn't we better get going? If MissEss has been missing all night —"

"Miss S.," Mel informed him in a clear voice — she'd seen Martha, dismayed at being left behind, at Miss Seeton's open door — "is one redoubtable lady, Banner. What's all night to the likes of her? Why, with her yoga she could last a whole week, easily!"

"Let's hope it doesn't come to that," said Brinton, with a growl. "Everyone know what they're doing?"

Everyone did. There had been a slight change of plan, in that detailed knowledge of the Murreystone byways was essential to a successful assault on Crown House Farm. PC Potter, on whose beat Plummergen's rival village lay, went with Thrudd and Mel to give directions: time was too much of the essence — Mel's brave words notwithstanding — to waste it in repetition of instructions that might still be misunderstood or forgotten. Brinton and Foxon, local reinforcements, were in the other car. They were not the only ones to sigh for their customary colleague in adventure, big Bob Ranger of Scotland Yard. He and the Oracle — whose contribution to the Miss Seeton cases consisted more of an ability to interpret her sketches than to indulge in fisticuffs — were many miles away, however. Nobody said out loud that by the time Miss Seeton's oldest friends on the force were able to respond, it might be too late: but they did not need to. They all knew it, only too well.

The little cavalcade headed south from Sweetbriars, down the narrowed Street where it ran between high brick walls, over the Royal Military Canal to a sharp left-angled bend, on to Snargate, to Brenzett, to the crossroads. Both cars made for Ivy-church — where, with a quick flourish on the horn and a wave of her hand, Mel took the road towards Hamstreet, while Foxon drove on to the junction for Murreystone and waited there, just around the corner, for three anxious minutes. He then started the engine again, and drove on.

Brinton was grumbling to himself. "If Potter's missed the turning and gone straight on —"

"No earthly reason why he should, sir. He knows these roads better than anyone alive except the tramps and the poachers, I imagine — and he wouldn't want anything to happen to Miss Seeton any more than the rest of us do. I mean, she's from his own village, for a start."

"You're babbling, Foxon." Unusually, Brinton did not bark an order for his subordinate to shut up: the lad was nervous, understandably so. When Miss Seeton was involved, nobody knew what the outcome might be. No need to make him even more nervous, when he was driving . . .

"Sorry, sir. We're, er, almost there, I think — that's the sign for Pondicherry Lodge — the Chelmer place, Potter said, next door to Crown House." Even at so tense a moment, Foxon's sense of the ri-

diculous did not desert him. "Highfalutin'
names farmers in these parts choose, don't
they?"

Brinton grunted. "Delhi Durbar," he
muttered. "I only hope that Forby girl's got
it right. And where the hell is she? I should
never have let them talk me into it — I'd've
done better to radio for another car from
Ash— And about ruddy time, too!"

Mel's car appeared slowly around a distant bend in the road: the vehicular siege
of Crown House Farm was about to begin.
Brinton nodded to Foxon, who flashed his
headlights at Mel. She flashed hers in
reply, and slowed right down as he drove
the remaining few yards to the farm entrance, where he turned into the drive and
began to make his cautious way up the
short track to the house. Mel, following as
far as the gateway, pulled her car round,
reversed, and switched off the engine with
her front bumper touching the left-hand
post, her rear bumper touching the right.
Only a mobile scrapyard car crusher, or a
maniac colossus with a razor-edged
hatchet, could now go in or out of Crown
House Farm by that route.

"Quiet, you fools!" Brinton motioned
fiercely as Mel, Thrudd, and Potter caught
up with the early arrivals, who now lurked

behind a piece of rusting machinery whose purpose not even Mel — who'd researched several articles on *Implements Old and New: The Changing Face of Farming* — could guess at. The only thing that mattered now, though, was that it was sufficiently bulky to screen the sight of all five persons from anyone looking from the windows of Crown House Farm.

"Old Barnston's been dead a month or more," Potter had explained to the rescue party before it set out. "There's nobody living in the house, on account of how he left the whole caboodle in equal shares to his sister's kids, and they can't agree what to do with it. Mr. Chelmer next door's looking after the sheep while they make up their minds, but once the solicitor'd locked up and took the keys, they told me it'd be staying empty for a while, and would I keep an eye on it when I was doing my rounds. Only I don't do 'em regular, see, so as not to be . . . predictable if anyone fancies a spot of mischief."

Brinton glanced at Mel, a frown creasing his forehead. "And the locals'd know your routine for checking up on the place, Potter? That you haven't really got one, I mean?"

"That's right, sir, so they wouldn't be

surprised if I turned up in broad daylight, like now."

"They'd be surprised to see you in a car that's not your own," said Brinton, still brooding. "And then, anyone local ought to realise you could turn up any time of the day or night to look the place over. Would they really risk keeping her where chances are she'll be found before long?"

"How often," Mel enquired promptly of PC Potter, "do you head into the sticks on the Hacienda Patrol?"

He blinked, but answered almost at once. "Two, three times a week, maybe — to the farmhouse, I mean. I'm in Murrey-stone near enough every day, of course."

Mel turned to Brinton. "They'd risk it, for a couple of days — and she's only been missing overnight, for Pete's sake. If we don't hurry, he could take her some place else, and we'll lose the trail completely . . ."

And so they had followed the trail, and now crouched, all five of them, in a tense huddle behind the rusting cogs and gears and perished rubber belts of the unidentified farm machine, peering about them for any signs of life. There were birds overhead — rooks? crows? — and sparrows hopping for worms on the ground; a gentle breeze rustled the plastic sheet tacked loosely to the dilapidated roof of a long, low barn; leaves danced on a solitary tree beside the front door of the house. Nothing else moved . . . until Brinton did.

"Foxon and I will go round the back." He waved a quick, surreptitious arm towards the house. "Potter, you take the front. Banner, Miss Forby — that barn door catch looks as if it could be slipped easily — but for heaven's sake take care! I don't want your blood on my hands . . ."

"And we sure as hell don't want Miss S.'s blood on ours," retorted Mel, as she prepared to charge into action. Except that she knew she couldn't *charge* — stealth and cunning must be the order of the day, and she wondered whether she'd have the patience. Mel was fond of Miss Seeton, and more worried about the elderly spinster than she liked to admit.

Thrudd, who knew her every mood, gave her a quick hug. "She'll be fine, Forby. MissEss always bounces back — how many times have you said so yourself? And in print, what's more, so it must be true."

She flashed him a grateful grin, then began to creep as carefully as she could, head low, eyes alert, across to the barn. Thrudd followed, as quick and careful as his lady.

"Catch?" He jerked contemptuously at the ragged length of string which fastened the door through a rusty hasp. "If he put her in here, never mind hairpins, she could have used her umbrella to pick this excuse for a lock!"

Mel sniffed. "Chris Brinton doing the chivalry bit, of course. He must've guessed she wouldn't be here, and wanted us out of the way — still, may as well check inside, just in case. There's such a thing as double bluff, Banner. Don't let this" — with a tug which parted string from hasp in one movement — "fool you . . ."

And neither of them, as they stepped carefully into the dark coolness of the barn, liked to remind the other that he — whoever he was — might have been happy enough to leave Miss Seeton secured with so feeble a fastening because he knew she was in no fit state to undo it.

As PC Potter examined every inch of the front of the house, Foxon and Brinton were working their way in opposite directions around its sides, intending to meet at the back. No footprints, no bent blades of grass, no broken glass of a damaged window, no scuffs or chips of paint on sill or sash: with two detectives searching, nothing such could have stayed undiscovered.

They met at the back door. They exclaimed together.

"That's been forced!"

On the jamb, beside the lock, were gouges and scraping marks as if a slim, strong, supple instrument had been slipped past the metal flange and into the workings of the lock before the door was jemmied open. Open — then shut again. But shut behind whom?

And was he — were they — still there?

Brinton thought rapidly. "Banner and Forby are out the front — if he makes a break for it, they'll scare him even if they don't stop him. It's Miss Seeton I'm more bothered about. I'll bring Potter round to join us — we'll all go in together, but be ready to run like hell if he makes a bolt for it. I haven't seen a car, unless it's in the barn, but he can't get out to the road anyway unless he drives clean through the hedge . . ."

Foxon had his hand on the tarnished brass knob the instant his colleagues appeared around the corner. He turned, winced as the door creaked, turned again. The door creaked more loudly, then stopped as Foxon froze, listening. With a quick gesture, he beckoned.

"I reckon we can risk it, sir!"

He rose from the half-crouch he'd automatically adopted while opening the door, and balanced himself on the balls of his feet, ready to tackle whatever homicidal maniac might hurl himself out of the shadows on the approaching rescuers. Brinton jabbed a finger at Potter, pointed to the left — at Foxon, to the right — to his own chest, pointed upwards, and placed it finally against his lips, cautioning silence.

Only the buzzing of a puzzled fly, blown indoors by the breeze, disturbed the hush of the kitchen as the three men — trained police officers — moved away to quarter every inch of Crown House Farm. The kitchen's inner door, which stood open, led to a short passageway which turned into a narrow hall running the length of the lower floor. Doors opened on either side of passageway and hall; Brinton left his subordinates to open them and search, while he headed for the bottom of the stairs.

As he reached the newel post, he uttered a silent curse. Too late — and too noisy — to do anything about it now, but why had he let Foxon and Potter take the downstairs detail? Neither of them had as much bulk or as many years as he had. Every board would probably groan loud enough to wake the —

He shut off that uncomfortable thought,

and set his foot firmly on the first tread. It did not creak. Warily, he stepped up, sniffing. A strange smell, one he didn't recognise immediately, though he knew what it was, all right . . . Still no creak — no groan — no squeak. All he could hear was the stealthy movements of Potter and Foxon and the buzzing of that infernal fly, more rhythmic now — the thing must be zooming up and down the hall trying to find the way out. And it was growing louder, as he ascended — it was sounding less and less like a fly, and more like . . .

Like someone snoring.

Brinton, in common with all police officers, had not only taken a basic course in first aid, but had picked up a considerable smattering of medical jargon during his many years on the force. His thoughts ran riot. That smell — chloroform — stertorous breathing — *head injury* . . .

It did not occur to him that the snores might come from the kidnapper, soundly asleep while Miss Seeton lay captive, waiting for rescue. He forgot all caution, and thundered up the remaining few stairs, flinging open the nearest door and sweeping the room with a swift, side-to-side, all-seeing gaze. Nothing. The next room — nothing.

Foxon and Potter, hearing the commotion, rushed to join him as he opened the third door . . .

The three men stood and stared in horror at the bed, on which lay a rumpled bundle, wrapped in rags and bound with string — a bundle of human form, life-sized — a bundle from which those stertorous snores were all too clearly coming.

Chapter 24

The two cars drove back to Plummergen in a swift, tense silence. Even Foxon did not dare say anything to the brooding man by his side. Brinton, his jaw set, stared fixedly at the road ahead, counting the minutes until they reached Sweetbriars again.

Before the ignitions were switched off, the front door of Miss Seeton's cottage was flung open, and Martha Bloomer came running down the short paved path to greet them.

"Mr. Brinton! Mr. Brinton — Miss Emily —"

"Martha, we didn't find her." Brinton had wondered all the way back how best to break the news, deciding that the quickest words were the kindest. Martha stared, and seemed about to say something. Brinton, darting one of his most speaking looks towards Mel Forby, hurried on:

"I'm sorry, Mrs. Bloomer. All we found was one of the gentlemen of the road — Potter says he's a regular round these parts at this time of year. Name of Woodham, Walter Woodham. You know how these tramps take advantage — he'd heard the house was empty, and just broke in, meaning to stay there a few days — all bundled up in rags, stretched out on one of the beds, drunk as a lord on methylated spirits. I — we thought it might be Miss Seeton, but —"

"But of course it wasn't Miss Seeton! That's what I've been trying to tell you, Superintendent." Martha beamed as Brinton looked gloomier than ever. "She rang me, not half an hour since, from the hospital —"

"Hospital? You mean the Knights' nursing home? What's wrong? Is she all right? What did she say?"

Martha reeled back as the questions ripped like bullets from five anxious throats, and blinked twice before saying: "Not the nursing home, no — Brettenden General. But she's all right, she says, and I'm sure she'd never say she was when she wasn't, not even on account of not wishing to worry me — which is like Miss Emily, bless her, though she *did* just mention she was a bit hungry, with not having eaten proper since yesterday — but she was more worried about *him*, poor man, because concussion can be such a nasty thing —"

"Him? Concussion? Who?"

Once more, Martha stared. "Well now, I — I don't know, now you come to mention it. She didn't say. She just said the hospital wanted to give her a checkup before they sent her home, and she didn't like them having to go to the bother of an ambulance when she felt as fit as a fiddle, just a bit tired — which with being awake all night I'm not surprised if she was, poor dear, at her age, too — and would I ring Crabbe's Garage and ask Jack to pick her up in the taxi, because she couldn't remember the number. So I did, and his grandad told me Jack's out on a job but he'll tell him as soon as he gets back —"

"Oh no he won't!" Relief and exasperation mingled in Brinton's voice as he interrupted the flow. "If anyone collects Miss Seeton from Brettenden General, it'll be the police, not Jack Crabbe. *Our* nerves can cope with whatever she might get up to on the way home — his may never be the same again. Although why," he apostrophised the heavens, "should we be the only ones to suffer?"

"You're sure she was all right, Martha?" enquired Foxon, while Mel, recovering her spirits, was heard to murmur that it might be a hoax of some sort. Thrudd kicked her on the ankle, and she subsided as Brinton shot her another furious look.

"Nobody in their right minds, Miss Forby, is going to play a stupid trick like that for the sake of gaining half an hour or so's grace — not unless there's always been some sort of time element in the case, which there hasn't — in the short term," he added, remembering the calendar, and the September dates, and Harvest Moon madness which had resulted in two similar deaths a year apart. And hadn't he just now said *nobody in their right mind?* This Blonde in the Bag killer could never be considered sane . . .

While he'd been brooding, he'd missed most of the subsequent to-and-fro of talk while Martha explained as much as she could, and repeated what she'd already told them, and insisted Miss Seeton had said there was nothing to worry about. Brinton wished he could believe this, though for the life of him he couldn't see what could go wrong, once Miss Seeton was safely home . . . *Safely* being the operative word, of course. The sooner they got to Brettenden and District General Hospital, and collected their passenger from — from Casualty, or wherever she was, the better.

PC Potter could find no valid cause to

make the hospital trip, and announced, to his superior's approving nods, that he would stay in Plummergen and return to his normal duties. Mel and Thrudd, sensing that the story — whatever it might be — was about to break, nobly offered to fetch Miss Seeton in Mel's car, thus releasing a further two trained police officers for more pressing duties. Brinton, in belligerent mood, said that if they wanted to save him the bother, they could call in on their way up The Street and tell Very Young Crabbe his grandson's services would not, after all, be required. Mel smiled sweetly at Martha, and said that surely a telephone message would be just as good. Brinton said he supposed he couldn't stop her driving her car to Brettenden any more than he'd been able to stop her driving it to (with a scowl) Murreystone, but that heaven alone must help her if she was involved in a motoring offence, because the book he would be duty bound to throw at her was very heavy indeed. Mel again smiled sweetly, marched off to the car with her nose in the air, and then ruined the effect by having to turn back to ask Potter whereabouts in Brettenden she would find the General Hospital.

Once more two cars set off from outside

Sweetbriars, but this time headed north. Foxon, driving the first, remarked:

"Miss Seeton certainly seems to bounce back every time, doesn't she? Thank goodness!"

Brinton said nothing. And Foxon, in silence, drove on.

They found Miss Seeton drinking tea in the Casualty Department, and having (in her opinion) the worst experience of the entire adventure: except that she would hardly have seen it as in the least adventurous to have been abducted by a crazed serial killer and driven round the countryside in his car the entire night while he plucked up the courage to kill her, too. However, Miss Seeton, in her innocence, had no idea that this was what had happened; and she would, had anyone subsequently attempted to explain, never have believed them. Why (she would have wondered) could anyone possibly have wished to kill her? There must have been some mistake . . .

The strong, sugary nature of the tea brought her on Casualty Sister's orders was certainly a mistake. One was, of course, grateful for the kindness; it would be churlish to complain; but one looked forward to the arrival of kind Jack Crabbe and a speedy arrival at one's own dear cottage, with one's kettle ready filled and a caddy of one's favourite tea waiting in the larder.

"You're not drinking your tea, dear." The bright-faced young nurse — such a crisp, practical uniform — was hovering beside her, trying not to frown. The old duck, so Sister'd told her, had had a rough time last night, one way and another, and was still a bit upset about dialling nine-nine-nine, though if it hadn't been for her, he might have died. But she was no spring chicken, and they couldn't let her go, even though Doctor had given her the once-over, until they were sure she wouldn't keel over in a faint or something, and end up back in Brettenden General as an in-patient, not just passing through . . .

"Shall I bring you a fresh cup? This one's stewed. And how about a piece of toast, or something?"

But Miss Seeton had already undergone the Ordeal by Hospital Toast, and was not anxious to repeat it, though the nurse warned of low blood sugar and looked stern. *Leathery,* that was the word, mused Miss Seeton, as she smiled firmly and shook her head. The toast — so cold — not the nurse, of course, who reminded one of cherry blossom and fresh spring air. And only marmalade to spread on it, when one did (although not wishing to seem ungrateful) prefer jam — and forcing down most of one slice, for the sake of politeness, had taken the edge off her hunger. She would be happy enough to wait for anything else to eat until she was home again. If only Jack Crabbe would come. An ambulance — most embarrassing, as well as so unnecessary, when there were others far less fortunate than oneself . . .

Miss Seeton sighed, and gazed about her at some of those others. Bumps, cuts and bruises, broken bones and strained muscles, emergencies whisked away to the operating theatre: in her two hours — although it felt like longer — at Brettenden General, she had seen them all. Her fingers twitched on her lap as she began to draw mental sketches —

"Are you *sure* you feel all right?" The nurse couldn't remember offhand what dire medical condition was suggested by a severe attack of the fidgets, but Miss Seeton's strange behaviour made her wonder whether Doctor might have been a bit hasty in saying that the old lady was tired and a little shocked, nothing more. Perhaps Sister ought to take another look.

The nurse began to back away, stealthily, trying not to alert the patient —

"Oh!" There was a cry, a clatter, and a crash as she caught her foot on something which fell to the ground, followed, after a few arm-waving moments, by herself. Miss Seeton jumped to her feet.

"Oh, dear! Oh, no — not again! My umbrella . . . !"

She had forgotten her tea, which teetered in its cup on the low table at her other side, then tumbled to the floor in a sickly tannin downpour. Miss Seeton's cry of distress was echoed by that of the nurse, whose official grey stripes and dazzling white apron had suddenly been patterned with splodges of brown . . .

As the nurse, now dripping, struggled to her feet, while Miss Seeton babbled apologies and blotted desperately with a pocket handkerchief — and Sister hurried over in a crackle of starch to say, "Really, Nurse Jones!" — and those waiting patiently to see a doctor — any doctor — ignored the scene with true British phlegm . . . as all this was going on, above the commotion rose a weary, well-known voice.

"I might have known we'd find you here, Miss Seeton," said Detective Superintendent Brinton.

Nurse Jones scuttled away to change her clothes, Mel mopped the floor, Thrudd assisted Miss Seeton to retrieve her umbrella from where it had rolled under the soft red plastic bench, Foxon collected the shards of crockery. Casualty Sister, recognising police officers from Ashford, allowed the more senior of the pair to convince her that, blood sugar high or blood sugar low, Miss Seeton would suffer no lasting harm if she went home now: indeed, Brinton told Sister with a sigh, they had come for that express purpose, as they were, in a manner of speaking (he glanced over his shoulder as he spoke, but Sister had drawn him well out of earshot before starting to voice her complaints) probably as well qualified to cope with Miss Seeton as anyone.

"I'm not saying," said Sister quickly, "that she isn't a dear, because she is. And she's a marvel, considering what she's been through — *and* she as good as saved that young man's life by calling the ambulance, but . . ."

Another reference to the mystery man. Brinton, without regret, decided to ignore the chance thus offered to ask Casualty Sister what particular chaos Miss Seeton and her brolly had caused, apart from tipping trainee nurses head over heels, before rescue came; he would instead find out, at last, what on earth had been going on since Miss Seeton had disappeared the previous evening.

"This young man," he said. "What's wrong with him? And where is he?"

"Concussion, and a fractured skull — it seems he's one of the eggshell kind, poor boy — and he's in Intensive Care. He should thank his lucky stars, and your friend, that it's not the morgue. She saved his life, at a guess, although I'm not sure she quite understands. When we tried explaining to her, she seemed more bothered about having had to call the ambulance because she didn't know how to drive the car, and kept saying something about it all being the fault of her umbrella — shock, I suppose, which is why we didn't want her to go home just yet."

Brinton didn't believe for a moment that Miss Seeton was suffering from shock. The unknown young man, however, could very possibly be suffering from Miss Seeton . . . "So this, er . . ." Perhaps he shouldn't say *victim*. *Chummie?* Probably, but not proved yet. "This eggshell blighter," he said, with a sigh. "Not going anywhere in a hurry, I take it?"

"Good heavens, no. He's got wires and tubes and drips plugged into him left, right, and centre, and the last I knew he hadn't shown any signs of coming round. It could be two or three days before he even recovers consciousness, never mind leaving the I.C. unit and going to a normal ward."

A beatific smile lit Brinton's face, and his sigh this time was one of deep satisfaction. He turned, and beckoned. "Foxon — hop along with your boots and notebook, laddie, and keep an eye on the Intensive Care unit until I can send a uniformed replacement. And don't worry about the car," as Foxon began to raise objections. "I'm driving Miss Seeton home myself — it's the least I can do, I reckon!"

With Mel and Thrudd once more following, Brinton's car took the Plummergen road, with the superintendent driving and his passenger a most reluctant Miss Seeton. She had arranged for dear Jack Crabbe to collect her, she explained. She had no wish to put anyone to any trouble on her behalf . . .

"No trouble at all, Miss Seeton." Brinton turned the full power of his personality upon her. "It's no more than six miles to Plummergen anyway, so you wouldn't be taking me much out of my way — but the main reason I'd like to give you a lift home is what you might call an official one. Because I need to find out exactly what happened, you see."

Chapter 25

Miss Seeton, with a blush, fell silent. Her fingers ran up and down the now-battered handle of the umbrella across her knees, and she stifled a sigh. So very, very careless — and that poor young man in Intensive Care — and she had been so worried all along about dialling nine-nine-nine under false pretences — one had hoped the emergency might excuse it, but clearly the police did not see it the same way . . .

"The police — oh, dear! His car, Mr. Brinton. I know," Miss Seeton said, blushing again, "that lost, or rather mislaid, vehicles, although I suppose one should in this case say rather that it was abandoned — except that this makes it sound so deliberate, and I can assure you it was an accident . . . and traffic problems, too, would be of minor importance compared with your own work, Superintendent. But your saying that this was a— an *official* matter reminded me — and naturally I understand that it should be reported at the earliest possible moment. I can only apologise for my failure to do so earlier, but with my concern over his unfortunate injury, you see — although there may, I suppose, be some slight justification in that I do not myself drive, even if I am as sensitive as others, I hope, to the due and proper care with which the belongings of others should be treated . . . I am of the opinion, although I cannot be certain, that he had no time to lock it before we went for our walk. And after — well, afterwards, of course, he would have been unable to — and even they did not think of it — the ambulance men. And I am not entirely sure who should be officially advised of this. Is something so large as a motor car," enquired Miss Seeton, "regarded as litter?"

Brinton applied his brakes. He took a deep breath. "Let's get this straight, Miss Seeton. That chap in hospital — you went for a ride in his car? And when he . . . met with his accident, you abandoned the car to travel in the ambulance with him?"

"I thought, in the circumstances, it was the least I could do," she explained, unhappily. "If it had not been for my carelessness with my umbrella, poor young man . . . and then, you see, it was I who telephoned for them, and though I am by no means qualified except in the most rudimentary first aid — hysterical schoolgirls, and so forth — one could hardly leave him in such a condition without someone he knew to be with him as, well, *moral* support if not practical. As a . . . a friendly face, you see, except, of course, that this was the first time we had met. It was some years ago now — and one forgets, although a bump on the back of the head is a serious matter no matter what the gender, or indeed age, of the person concerned, which is why I had thought I could be excused for dialling nine-nine-nine . . .”

She floundered to a halt. Brinton said, very gently: “I’m sure you did the right thing, Miss Seeton, if what the hospital says is anything to go by. You probably saved his life by your prompt actions — but I still need to know what happened. Just how did this young man bump his head, Miss Seeton? And, er, how did your umbrella come into it?”

She blushed, and lowered her eyes. Her fingers danced on the folded fabric of the second-best umbrella, and he studied them for a few moments.

“Miss Seeton! You never upped and bashed him with your brolly, did you? That’s not like you!”

“Indeed it is not, Superintendent.” She sat upright and met his gaze squarely for the first time, in some indignation; then she saw the twinkle in his eyes, and responded with a faint twinkle of her own. Mr. Brinton, like dear Mr. Delphick, had a certain wry sense of humour which one had to be quick to appreciate fully. And, after a sleepless night and little to eat — Miss Seeton put up a ladylike hand to stifle a yawn — one's wits were rather more sluggish than one would have liked.

She relaxed, and sighed. "It was an accident, I assure you, Mr. Brinton — for which I hold myself almost entirely to blame, although he was in a . . . a certain state of mental perturbation, poor thing, which did not, perhaps, lend itself to observing as closely as one would have wished exactly how and where he placed his feet. It was nighttime, you see, after the moon had set, so it was dark. There are no street lamps, of course, on Shirley Moor, and —"

"*Moor!* What on earth were you doing wandering around in the middle of the night on Shirley Moor, Miss Seeton?"

"He said he needed to talk to someone." She blushed yet again. "A . . . a sympathetic listener, he said, and although I explained that I had been retired from teaching for several years now, and consequently understood far less of the problems of today's youth than someone younger would do, he was so insistent . . . indeed, one could have described his speech almost as incoherent. I wondered at first if he might not be . . . be intoxicated, even though he drove the car with what seemed to be considerable skill . . ."

She favoured Brinton with an appealing glance. "I know I am no expert, Superintendent, but I smelled nothing on his breath, and we didn't hit anything. It would, to my mind, be most regrettable if he were to be awarded a . . . a ticket, which I believe is the term."

Brinton felt hysteria bubbling up inside him. If his instinct was right, MissEss had spent the last twelve hours jaunting about the countryside with a double killer, and the only thing bothering her was whether he'd end up with an endorsement on his licence! An endorsement — when the bloke'd most likely been getting ready to drown her in Brettenden Sewer, or bash her on the head and leave her to die of exposure . . . Brinton wanted to bellow with laughter, to tear his hair. To keep his hands occupied, he started the engine and engaged first gear, glancing in the mirror to see if Mel Forby was still behind him. She was.

"We'll bear your testimony in mind, Miss Seeton — all of it. Shall I tell you what I think the rest will be? This ch— er, chap unburdened his soul and talked you ragged half the night, then said he wanted to stretch his legs and suggested you went with him, and somewhere along the line he tripped over your brolly and bumped his head on a tree root, or something."

"Good gracious, Superintendent. How did you know?"

"Call it a mixture of long acquaintance and lucky guesswork, Miss Seeton." He found himself chuckling. "And you spent the rest of the night trying to bring him round, then hunting for a phone — which can't have been easy, in a bleak place like that. And how did you manage to find him again when the ambulance came?"

Miss Seeton looked at him in some surprise. "My umbrella, of course. One may know little, Mr. Brinton, of emergency care for head injuries, but adequate shelter is always important. And on so very level an area it made an admirable landmark, as well, of course, as the car, which was — is — only a matter of half a mile or so distant."

Brinton's hand jerked on the steering wheel. Behind him came a reproachful hoot, and in the mirror he saw Mel shake her head. "Sorry, Miss Seeton. I'm trying to drive and to kick myself at the same time, and the two can't be done in safety. I ought to have remembered earlier the car's bound to be standing about waiting for someone to tow it away. And once we've checked out the number, we'll know who your mysterious one-night-stand acquaintance is . . ."

"Oh," said Miss Seeton, as they passed the sign welcoming visitors to Plummergen. A few minutes more, and she would be home! "Oh, but Mr. Brinton — I know who he is already. I would hardly be so rash, or so . . . so forward," with another blush, "as to accept an invitation to drive out in the company of a complete stranger. Most certainly not. Of course I knew him!"

Brinton held his breath, concentrating on negotiating the half-mile length of The Street without running into anyone or anything. It was not until they were sweeping round to pull up outside Sweetbriars that he dared to ask the all-important question.

"Who is he, Miss Seeton? Not . . . not Nigel Colveden?"

"Nigel? Oh no, Mr. Brinton. Nigel," said Miss Seeton, with a twinkle in her eye, "would never let anything — not even a bump on the head — persuade him to leave his motor in the middle of nowhere, now would he?"

She had seized the handle of the car door, but Brinton was too bewildered — and relieved — to think of reaching across as a gentleman should. He could bear the suspense no longer. "Then who is he, Miss Seeton, if he isn't Nigel?"

"I don't know," she admitted, her knees halted halfway round in their swing, the door open. "That is" — as an exasperated groan broke from Brinton's lips — "I don't know his *full* name — or rather, I have foolishly allowed it to slip my mind since he introduced himself when we first met. But his first name seemed enough, with an acquaintance in common, when he was so agitated, poor thing —"

"Miss Seeton!" Brinton gripped the steering wheel, his head bowed to touch his hands. He looked up, breathed in deeply, and steadied his voice to ask: "What is his name?"

Miss Seeton slipped nimbly from the car, bending to shut the door, conscious as ever of a gentlewoman's obligations. "I am most grateful to you for having brought me home, Mr. Brinton, when I know how busy you are. But if you can spare the time, would you — and dear Mel," as the second car, having parked on the paved square before the George and Dragon opposite, disgorged its passengers, "and Mr. Banner, naturally, care to come in for a cup of tea? His name," she added, as Brinton managed a wild-eyed nod of acceptance, "is — not Mr. Banner, that is, but Nigel's friend — is Clive . . ."

Mrs. Bloomer had boiled the kettle at the first sound of an engine, and tea was ready almost before Miss Seeton could blink. Martha allowed that she did really ought to have been up at the Hall, but she wasn't budging an inch until she'd heard from Miss Emily's own lips just what she'd been doing, and where she'd been doing it — and who with.

Brinton, struggling to sort out the facts for his imminent report, with Miss Seeton's permission — she was yawning all the more now, although the tea and toast and fruitcake were helping to revive her — favoured the little group seated at Miss Seeton's table with the story as he saw it, judiciously modified. Where he made grave errors of judgement or inference, Miss Seeton, with a ladylike cough, ventured to correct him. Mel Forby's eyes warned that she expected to be given the unexpurgated version as soon as the heroine of the hour was out of earshot. Martha observed the quick exchange of glances, and left the young reporter to help herself to a second cup. Miss Seeton stifled another yawn.

"But of course I would not have supposed that I should come to any harm," she said, surprised. "After so many years — though I am far from being *advanced*, particularly in the *mental* areas — but the book says most clearly that fasting can be of positive benefit to those who practice yoga." She buttered another slice of toast, and hoped she would be able to eat it before it grew cold. One understood, naturally, that one's friends deserved some explanation for one's having caused them, without meaning to, some evident concern — but surely dear Mr. Brinton's explanation had been enough?

It seemed not. The questions continued to come. Miss Seeton set down her toast, and raised her teacup instead. If one was going to speak at any length, a dry throat would cause more problems than an admittedly less-empty-than-it-had-been inside . . .

"I knew him for a friend of Nigel's as

soon as I saw him — the bones, you see, although the Union Jack — I mean Flag — was cleverly done, and altered his *superficial* appearance quite remarkably. But not the bones, of course — and I had heard dear Lady Colveden mention him by name when we saw him on television — one of Nigel's Young Farmers. So many ticket stubs, or programme stamps — Nigel was kind enough to explain when he borrowed my umbrella, but I fear the details have escaped me — so that everyone could attend, even though he has been in New Zealand for the past year. Down Under," said Miss Seeton, with a smile. "Culture shock — is that the term? To have everything so very different — the other way round from that to which one has been accustomed . . ."

Mel, remembering the sketch of Dame Lavinia Britannia on her head, spluttered. Brinton dared her to say anything to interrupt Miss Seeton's flow; Martha glared; Thrudd kicked her on the ankle. Miss Seeton ignored them all as she sipped more tea.

"He seemed so agitated when he arrived — and though I am far, in my opinion, from being the best person to offer advice, he was so insistent that I should go with him to lend a sympathetic ear — and then he talked, I must admit, what seemed to me a great deal of nonsense about knives, and the moon, and black plastic sacks — I confess I did wonder," and she appealed again to Brinton, "whether it might be *drugs* as opposed to drink. I don't, you see, know the symptoms, even though both are equally foolish — but I came to the conclusion that it could be nothing more than nerves, for when I chanced to remark that I had been a teacher he . . ."

She broke off, and murmured of confidences, and privacy, and professional discretion — even when one had retired . . .

Brinton nodded, but was firm. "Evidently you haven't lost the touch, Miss Seeton, if you managed to calm him down enough to talk to you like a sensible bloke — but you don't seem to realise that this *poor young man* you're so worried about is very likely a — yow!" Thrudd was becoming skilled at giving people surreptitious kicks on the ankle.

And, like Brinton, he was firm. "Miss Seeton — I'm sure I speak for all of us when I say we'd be most interested to know your . . . shall I say specialist views on your little adventure. If it's not too much trouble, would you mind showing us your sketchbook?"

Chapter 26

"I'll fetch it for you, shall I, dear?" Martha was on her feet in a flash, heading for the sitting room and the cupboard in which Miss Seeton kept most of her artist's paraphernalia. As she passed by Thrudd Banner, she favoured him with one of the most approving looks she'd ever given either of the two reporters: if that Miss Forby didn't seem to appreciate how clever Miss Emily was with her pencil, her . . . boyfriend certainly did! Perhaps he'd ask to put one of her pictures in the paper? She wouldn't much like it, of course — such a quiet little body as she was — but surely she'd be flattered to be asked . . .

Miss Seeton was apologising to Mel for not having been at home on Monday evening when the young reporter called as they'd agreed on Sunday night. She had been, she feared, rather preoccupied elsewhere, and —

"That's all right, honey," Mel was quick to break into Miss Seeton's train of thought. With luck, Little Miss Innocence wouldn't clue up to the fact that the crazed killer Mel had asked her to sketch, and the mixed-up young friend of Nigel Colveden who'd squired her around all last night, were one and the same. "Don't give it another thought," Mel told her, as firm as Brinton or Thrudd. "It's me who should be apologising to you, for not coming round yesterday when I said I would — but I was delayed," with a meaningful glance and a blush for Mr. Banner, who rolled his eyes and grinned as he reached for the portfolio and sketchbook Martha was carrying into the dining room.

"Mind if I take a look, MissEss?"

"Miss S. doesn't play favourites, Banner — you should know that by now." Mel winked at Miss Seeton as she pulled the sketchbook away from Thrudd, and more into the centre of the table, clearing toast rack, jam dish, and assorted crockery out of the way as she did so. "We'll *all* take a look, like you said. The pair of us will just have to go shares in the headlines!"

Miss Seeton, rather drowsy now, smiled fondly on her two young friends as they tried to outstare each other. Such a teasing, affectionate relationship, so pleasant to see — and both so good at their jobs, which made their apparent rivalry all the more amusing to those who knew them . . .

"Official evidence, Miss Forby," said

Brinton, feeling that it was high time he took a hand. "I think you're forgetting Miss Seeton's retainer from the Yard — *I'll* take a look at those first, I think."

Mel quirked an eyebrow at him. "Still sore because I couldn't do an Oracle for you? I did my best, Mr. Brinton, and nobody can do more than that. If you're desperate for the real interpretation, though, guess with the expert here you could save yourself — and us — a lot of time by asking her straight out."

She didn't wait for him to reply, but opened the sketchbook at Miss Seeton's drawing of the Taj Mahal reflected in the lake. "Interested in history, Miss S.? Why the turbans and the periwigs, or whatever they are?"

Miss Seeton blinked, shook her head, and dragged her thoughts back from her bedroom and comfortable mattress. It was absently that she glanced at the sketch and murmured:

"After Nigel came the other day and told me about him — and we were talking about the Abdication when he was on television — Clive, that is. Of India, although I am not entirely sure that the costume is . . . historically accurate." The final words were slurred, and she smothered a yawn.

Mel turned to the others in triumph.

"Clive of India! I remember him from history at school — though I can't for the life of me tell you why. Guess I'm more interested in up-to-date history, or something."

Brinton was staring at Miss Seeton, a curious mixture of respect and exasperation in his eyes. She'd shown them yet again who the killer was — but, yet again, she'd wrapped it up in so much kerfuffle they hadn't a hope in hell of working out what it all meant until afterwards. Unfair of him to take it out on Mel Forby for getting it wrong — with Miss Seeton, you had to talk — think — a whole new language. But better late than never, he supposed.

He smiled across the table. "We had our history knocked into us rather more in my day, Mel, than they did in yours," he said cheerfully. "Robert Clive — Baron Clive, they made him later, for services rendered — he was governor of India some time in the eighteenth century. Didn't do at all well when he first went out there, and tried to shoot himself two or three times, only the gun never went off. Thought there must be something wrong with it, but he couldn't see what — and then a friend of his came in. 'Oblige me, John, by firing this pistol out of the window.' " Brinton's voice took on the rhythm of school recitation. Even in her sleepy state, Miss Seeton smiled.

" 'Oblige me, John' — cool as a cucumber, when he'd been trying to blow his brains out not ten seconds earlier! I've never forgotten that." Brinton shook his head. "So this John fired it, and it went off, so Clive decided it was an omen, and he must be destined for great things — so he stuck to it, and he was. Amazing."

It was also amazing — except that, to those who knew and worked with Miss Seeton, after so long it oughtn't to be — how she'd muddled India and the Red Indians. Clive of India — and Clive Chelmer, friend of Nigel Colveden, as confirmed by Lady Colveden in a quick telephone call. Clive . . . who lived at Pondicherry Lodge, according to PC Potter. So what was a pond, if not a small lake? And if Pondicherry wasn't an Indian town, Brinton would eat one of Miss Seeton's remarkable hats . . .

"Not mulberries, Mel, but cherries, eh?" Brinton winked at the young reporter. "From cherry trees planted round a pond by the lad's grandfather, Potter said. Well, well — it was a pretty good guess, I must say."

Mel, after her initial surprise, was happy to accept the mellowing of Old Brimstone. "Hatchet buried, Mr. Brinton?" she enquired, with her most dazzling smile.

"For the present, anyway." Brinton hardly heard her: he had been flicking back through the pages of the sketchbook, and now gazed at the likeness of Barry Panfield as a pop singer. He frowned. "The silly young juggins! Whatever's he been up to he doesn't want us to know about?"

Martha peered over his shoulder, and sniffed. "Beryl's boy," she said, dismissively.

Brinton grinned. "So you said before. Tell me about him, will you?"

"His mother's my cousin Beryl. A great trial to her, he's always been, on account of his daft pop-singer notions and dressing in them horrible leather clothes and his motorbikes — not that he's a *bad* boy, mind, just taking a bit too long to grow up, if you ask me. Which is what I always say to Beryl when she will keep worrying about him. 'It's just a phase,' I tell her. 'He'll be settling down sooner or later.' Trouble is, it's getting later all the time, poor Beryl. Having you arrest him's most likely going to teach young Barry more of a lesson than he's had since his poor dad passed away — and I'm sure you wouldn't never have done it if you didn't think it was a good idea," she added, as Brinton began to turn purple.

He found his voice at last. "I haven't *arrested* your cousin's son, Mrs. Bloomer — he's just been brought in for questioning. And for trying to punch Foxon on the nose," he added. "But if he'd acted like a sensible lad when we asked him where he was the other night — or if he'd had the brains to talk to us since he's been in the nick — he'd be back at the hop garden this minute. But he's behaved like an idiot right from the start, and as the bloke we're looking for is . . . oh. The bloke," with a glance at Miss Seeton, who was nodding and blinking, "we *were* looking for, I mean. But we can't let him go until we know what the h— er, blazes he's been playing at." He found himself chuckling. "Foxon would never forgive me — young Barry packs a mean punch."

"Brawn as opposed to brain," murmured Mel, gazing wide-eyed at Thrudd. "Muscles, and black leather, and the hot smell of petrol — the power, the speed, the excitement —"

"Motorbikes!" Brinton slapped a sudden hand across his brow, and groaned. He snatched the sketchbook and turned back to Miss Seeton's drawing of Barry on his huge machine, the throbbing rush of exhaust streaming out behind as he raced against lawn-mowing Nigel. "He's a mechanical wizard — old Hezekiah had sent him for spare parts — I'll be damned if he wasn't in that all-night rally the Hastings boys had so much trouble sorting out! Harry Furneux said some of the blighters got away . . ."

Everyone except Miss Seeton stared at him as he clutched his hair, and groaned. "Those Choppers — they'll be the death of me yet, I know. Why the devil didn't I think of it before? Motorbikes . . ."

"Makes sense," Mel told him cheerfully. "Top marks for deduction, Mr. Brinton — seems you understand Miss S.'s pictures better than I ever could. And isn't it nice for Martha to know her cousin's not a — ahem!" as Miss Seeton's sleepy eyes drifted open. There was no need for Thrudd to kick his colleague this time. "To know," Mel swiftly amended, "that the worst he can expect is a fine and an endorsement!"

And Martha looked Amelita Forby straight in the face. "Yes," she said, with a smile. "Yes, Mel, it is."

Miss Seeton, having slept for most of the

day, was in the kitchen making herself a quiet cup of tea when there came a knock at the door.

"Nigel, how very nice to see you. What beautiful flowers." Her eyes twinkled. "Let me guess, now — you're on your way to visit your friend Heather?"

Beneath his tan, Nigel went pink. "Heather? Oh, these aren't for Heather, Miss Seeton — they're for you. With my thanks, and, er, all that. For helping to — well, for being the one to get me out of a rather uncomfortable hole."

Miss Seeton stared. Flowers — gardens — hole? Surely not the lawn at Rytham Hall! Had Nigel been practising for his race, and churned up the turf? But what had that to do with herself?

She twinkled at him again. "If you are trying out your apologies on me before offering them to dear Lady Colveden, then I should say that these beautiful flowers would appease the angriest of mothers. But you must promise not to do it again, Nigel. Is the honour of the Young Farmers really worth so great an expense?"

Nigel stared, realised she had no idea what he'd meant to say, and decided he couldn't face the effort of explanation after the stress of the past couple of days. He hadn't wanted to worry his parents about what he'd been sure was a genuine mistake on the part of Superintendent Brinton and those three witnesses: he'd felt sure things would soon sort themselves out — but it had been a lonely, anxious time. In a village, the very worst news is kept from those whom it most closely concerns, in an unspoken conspiracy for one to protect another so that should the worst happen elsewhere, others in turn will be protected. Nigel knew from their general attitude that neither of his parents had been allowed to learn what had happened to him; he realised that there was nobody with whom he cared to share the burden. Then had come this afternoon's personal visit from Brinton, heavy with apology, waving at him across the field he was in the middle of ploughing. Only after Brinton had gone did Nigel let himself relax, and feel able to talk about the affair. Sir George had huffed, saying that a trouble shared was a trouble halved, but Nigel had shown the right spirit in keeping it from the women. Lady Colveden, who'd turned briefly pale from shock, promptly turned pink with annoyance, and said it was a bit much to be treated like a hothouse flower after more than twenty-five years of marriage.

"Flowers," she said, inspired. "I'll pick the biggest bunch Miss Seeton's ever seen, and I don't care what it does to my borders. Martha says she's not to be disturbed, but you know how quickly she always bounces back — by teatime today, at a guess. You must take them down to her, Nigel, and say how very grateful we are . . ."

Miss Seeton was at last prevailed upon to accept the flowers, although still uncertain what she had done to deserve such generosity. Nigel, looking forward to tea on the lawn and a slice of Martha's fruitcake, was struck by a sudden inspiration.

"Look on them as bribery and corruption, Miss Seeton. Because I have the most enormous favour to ask you — about the Lawn Mower Race . . ."

The Young Farmers — especially Heather — had been greatly shocked to learn that one of their number was in custody on suspicion of being a double killer. News of Nigel's ordeal, and that of Barry Panfield, sent ripples of consternation throughout the immediate area. The reputation of the group was at stake: they must redeem themselves in the eyes of Kent. They must earn vast sums of money during the Lawn Mower Race — they would give Barry a wild card entry — they would cross Pondicherry Farm from their list of Possible Locations For Future Events . . .

"And we thought," said Nigel, sitting happily under the apple tree, "that it would be rather a splendid wheeze if you would agree to start the Grand Finale, Miss Seeton. We, er, wondered if, instead of waving a flag, you wouldn't mind opening your umbrella . . ."

The Lawn Mower Race raised one of the largest sums the chosen charity had ever received from so theoretically small an individual event.

Barry Panfield accepted his wild card, although he spent more time in the pits repairing faulty mowers than in racing the one he'd borrowed. Prevailed upon to enter at least the Grand Finale, he surprised and gratified one and all by coming a respectable second, dead-heat with Nigel Colveden.

And the winner? Nagged into entering for the sake of community spirit, scared of how it would be at home should he do badly — the winner was the Reverend Arthur Treeves.

About the Author

Hamilton Crane is the pseudonym of Sarah J(ill) Mason, who was born in England (Bishop's Stortford), went to university in Scotland (St. Andrews), and lived for a year in New Zealand (Rotorua) before returning to settle only twelve miles from where she started. She now lives about twenty miles outside London with a tame welding-engineer husband and two (reasonably) tame Schipperke dogs. She is a fully-paid-up member of the British Lawn Mower Racing Association. Under her real name, she writes the new mystery series starring Detective Superintendent Trewley and Detective Sergeant Stone of the Allingham police force.